LUCKY

By
Lesley Ann Eden

MAPLE
PUBLISHERS

LUCKY

Author: Lesley Ann Eden

Copyright © Lesley Ann Eden (2024)

The right of Lesley Ann Eden to be identified as author of this work has been asserted by the author in accordance with section 77 and 78 of the Copyright, Designs and Patents Act 1988.

First Published in 2024

ISBN 978-1-83538-220-2 (Paperback)
        978-1-83538-221-9 (Hardback)
        978-1-83538-222-6 (E-Book)

Cover design adapted from a painting by S.J.Jameson. Witches Stitch.

Book layout by:
        White Magic Studios
        www.whitemagicstudios.co.uk

Published by:
        Maple Publishers
        Fairbourne Drive, Atterbury,
        Milton Keynes,
        MK10 9RG, UK
        www.maplepublishers.com

Dedication

To Nigel for Freddie sitting and to my family and friends who make my world complete.

Contents

Dear Reader,

Thank you for your interest in 'Lucky' for it is not by chance that you are reading this letter, as your higher consciousness will guide you to oases of wisdom, to feed and quench your thirst for Universal Knowledge, assisting you on your spiritual journey.

'Lucky' is the first of seven books written in the new Sci-Soul genre and compliments the Eden Trilogy, where further information can be found regarding the author's amazing, true psionic experiences.

Luck is generally thought of as something happening 'by chance' e.g. good luck to win the lottery, good luck to be successful-but in truth, 'luck' is a vibration which can be accessed and used to great effect. It has been found that the more you internalise the 'lucky' vibration the more opportunities will open to you and you will begin to see the world differently.

The Universe speaks singly the language of 'vibrational frequency' and will only respond to your inner energy, which you outwardly display, whether it be positive or negative. The positive energy/vibration which the word 'Lucky' generates, is a high frequency code and in order to gain the best results from thinking lucky, you need to change your perception of 'LUCK'.

When you read, you subconsciously internalise information, messages and energy vibration which can affect you positively or negatively. In reading the 'Lucky' series, your brain will respond to higher spiritual laws which can help you gain a greater understanding of the Universal Law of existence, facilitating both physical and mental healing and a sense of well-being.

Luck is not random, haphazard or a hit-or-miss event-it is a cord of energy which can be wrapped around your being to be worn as protection from worldly negative influences and to enhance and enrich your quality of life.

Wearing 'luck' energy takes practice, but the results can be wonderful and truly amazing, so I'm not going to say-'good luck' in your endeavours to find all you need, but simply – "think lucky and you will be lucky!"

Lesley Ann Eden

LUCKY

"Those stars you're gazing at -they shine so bright 'cos they're dead!"

I turn searching old Albert's weary, wise eyes.

"Oh yeh, it's only in the darkness you can see 'em, 'cos they died millions of years ago. What you're looking at is the past."

"Where's the live stars then?" I enquire.

"Oh you can't see 'em, not yet; they're not dead!"

He laughs as he shuffles to the abandoned railway carriage, painfully hauling himself up the steps.

It's difficult to imagine that he was once an eminent scientist and now, like me, all he can do is marvel at the magnificent night sky and struggle to survive each day. I continue to search the bright galaxy. They will come. My whisperers will come. They promised.

The rest of the group sit silently around the night fire. Soon Jack will kill the flames and erase all trace of our gathering-just in case the blade guards sense our presence with their high tech luminous, electromagnetic weapons which stun, maim and exterminate dissidents. The robot killers are swift, efficient assassins and when our small band clustered together, just over a year ago, we agreed to abide by strict survival rules, as the blade guards show no mercy with rebels. We are lucky, all six of us, to have found this little outpost, our lost railway junction abandoned deep in the countryside, now reclaimed by forest brushwood and overgrown bracken. It must have been so pretty once upon a time with neat flower beds and welcoming café, where the tinkle of genteel tea cups and bright laughter on a sunny afternoon, were the order of the day when families took holidays together. Excited children waiting for their first glimpse of the sea would have bounced along this platform, waiting for the next train, while their mothers delightfully treated themselves to home-made cream scones and buns. That time is lost forever. I once knew a time like that. I knew my children's playful laughter. Now I am empty without them.

I sigh, as I watch Jack diligently perform his nightly task and feel a Motherly ache for his orphaned existence. He was barely eighteen when his family was killed in the final roundup leaving him to fend for himself in the dark chaos that ensued after the culling of 'useless eaters' – those people such as myself and others who refused to be imprisoned in the ultra, high tech Cityscapes, preferring to take our chances to survive as outcasts in the wilderness. Freedom comes at a cost and in this new world we pay dearly for our principles.

In the deep night's silence, Mauve and Ted wave a routine goodnight and retire to their little den in the once station waiting room. They are good people. Mauve had been a nurse during the first pandemic and her husband Ted, a plumber with his own business. Mauve tells strange tales during that time of how her hospital became a sterile desert when they enforced the closure of wards to cancer and critical heart patients and countless people died needlessly. Their deaths were reported as Covid related because the government accrued more money from the rise in pandemic mortality. I heard similar reports from my eldest daughter who was a midwife down south, but since the final roundup, I have no idea where she or any of my four children are living or even if they survived. It was a chaotic, frantic time when families were divided and herded off to different cityscapes, except for those of us who managed to flee to the countryside. At that time, I was living in the north in an idyllic parkland in a wooden lodge, and it was easy to escape to the dense moors where the population was sparse and the strict 'round-up' rules were not yet properly enforced.

On occasions when Mauve unburdens her soul, I listen with a heavy heart, for being psychic and having some psionic gifts, I see her fading. I have foreseen future events-even kept a diary of what was to be, where, when and how events would happen. My whisperers foretell all. They show me things. I know things others don't! They have been with me all my life and as a child I was bitterly punished for communicating with them. I did not understand that others could not see and hear in the same way as I and quickly learnt to live in two worlds at the same time.

Now we all exist from day to day, barely coping, trying not to remember our previous lives and the grave loss of our children. We wait with no end in sight for a miracle release, a return to some form of normality, but we all know, that will never happen. War is a terrible blight, which damages and disfigures all life. Everyone is splattered by the bile of greed which clings to innocent bystanders, while the victors wallow in vanquished, meaningless glory. After the second pandemic, war began breaking out like a malicious plague and no one, no government, no leader could prevent the devastating scars blistering across the world. The outcome was the New World Order, spoken about and threatened since President Bush Senior began to alert everyone to its inevitable materialisation. The New World Order and the creation of Cityscapes, with global currency and world law enforcement was on the horizon appearing in films and mass media, seeping into the sub-conscious mind of the masses.

I stare into space beyond the stars and I ache to go home. The longing is a constant grief-a hole in my being where darkness hides through caverns, cages of white bones, waiting for the eternal stillness to end the torture of not knowing, not being, not having, not living. I agreed to come to planet earth to help raise the higher conscious vibration of those seeking knowledge and through the magic of Performing Arts, especially for children, I devoted my life's work to giving children magical experiences to inspire them, but now the world has changed and I must bide my time to be guided. The enchanting cosmos beckons and to disappear into the myriads of crystal gems sparkling so brightly in a multiverse, beyond multiverses is my final goal.

The sky has lost its skyness. Now we have a cloudy dome lid created by continuous chemtrailing of the ionosphere and weather is modified and controlled from a central A.I. system. I turn away from the vast universe of promises and amble to my own abandoned carriage musing,' I am lucky to be alive; lucky to be part of a small cluster of survivors; lucky to have my own small space to sleep; lucky not to have the sickness. Inside my tiny tin box it is cold. I light a candle stub, such a precious commodity, but I want to gaze at my children's faces before I sleep. It's the only photo I have. Love hurts. I can't cry any more. My tears are dry. I need to hold onto the warmth of happy times-family times-times of great feasts and parties and dancing and closeness and love and loving. My old blanket is damp in the chilly night and I blow out what is left of the stub. Sleep does not devour me. Sleep is not my friend. My mind retraces the past. At the end of the first pandemic, a tidal wave of joy, releasing the world from war-like restraint exploded with love everywhere. There were photos of street parties, people jumping into fountains, families picnicking in parks, neighbours shaking hands and lovers kissing in shop doorways. Everyone was euphoric to be released and freed from home imprisonment. The summer was gifted to us by courtesy of the weather modification scientists and we rejoiced and were grateful. Returning to 'normality' that September was strange but wonderful with everyone braving and rebuilding the economy. Some doctors and scientists blamed the self-isolation and home imprisonment policy for the rapid return of the virus which had transmuted into other deadly viruses, claiming that if we had been subjected to the virus in the first place, our immune system would have coped better. The second round of the viral attack made people more fearful than before and they self-isolated almost automatically complying with all the world government's demands, losing a great deal of personal freedom. People became slaves in the system, slaves to the system, slaves for the system and no one fought back, well that is except a few of us. While many people lived in fear, laws were enforced banning anti-government meetings and freedom of speech was curtailed, little by little by the implementation of 'Politically Correct' behaviour and language imposed in all walks of society and educational establishments and in all forms of entertainment.

Recovery from the second pandemic never quite was; there was a weak attempt at' normality' but it was too late as a new social structure was in place and everyone acquiesced submissively. A certificate of movement was necessary for everything. It was issued only to those vaccinated and permitted people to travel abroad and to drive in their electric cars to buy things and to go to work and to access social media and be registered to attend social gatherings such as football matches and theatre performances. By the third pandemic, the virus transmuted into different strains and people who had been vaccinated and given boosters, still caught it ! Those rebelling against the system were threatened with House Execution, which at the time was a secret weapon where, quietly, skilfully a friendly executioner, a trained death practitioner performed the death penalty in home comfort, surrounded by family and loved ones. A few days before the assigned date for the execution, the prisoner would be drugged and fall into a peaceful coma before the final, lethal injection was administered. Death was instantaneous and clean. The body was disposed of quickly and effortlessly. I had known it, seen it all before. Many years previously, my whisperers had shown me the future and told me that when the time came I had to escape. When the government gave the final warning to all dissidents to comply with the rules-they called it the final roundup, I knew it was time to flee to the far regions of the country where there were no cityscapes. There was not much to leave behind. I had said my farewells long before when families were wrenched apart and split up and imprisoned in compounds to be prepared and brain-washed to live in the cityscapes.

As the first light streams in through the holes of my shredded curtains, I sneak a moment of normality, but as I open my eyes it vanishes. Time is lost. 'Being' is whatever I make it. Only the 'now' is. I could ask myself what is the point of this futile existence? All I have to do is hand myself in, give myself up. But I can't! When I was six years old I promised my people that I would try to live without using my gifts and stay grounded in human reality. Living in two worlds at the same time was too difficult and I had to totally immerse myself in earth-life, even though my earth family didn't understand me. I was like a cuckoo in the wrong nest. My earth Mother never fully accepted me, as I suspect she knew I didn't belong to her, as her own child died in the womb. She would tell me the story and watch my reaction as she described the look of horror on the nurse's face as her waters broke.

"It was black!" she scorned. "The nurses were so shocked!" She boasted, being in total ignorance of what it actually meant. She had no idea that babies often died when breathing in their own faeces. So her own child died in the womb and I was a 'walk-in' and took over that child's life. I remember my birth. I can recall my first lucid thought...'so this is humanity?' Even then as a tiny baby I didn't much care for the human condition. But I know the planet can be a wonderful place, so different from anywhere else in the universe and so I resolve to survive another day.

Early morning in the brave new world is quiet. There is no stirring of the dawn chorus as nature is yet to heal and become whole again. The 'sound of silence' does not exist because my whisperers tell me that 'silence' is 'sound vibration' and everything in this universe is an 'energy pulse', therefore we are all connected to each other and each to everything. As I rise from my ramshackle bed, I muse on the thought and sink into a deep receptive state to listen to the voice in my head:-

"life on Earth is a perpetual motion machine-a planet of continual movement in flux. Nothing ever remains static. Everything which humans have created, moves on earth in a linear fashion. Only humans need a 'time' structure to know themselves and to measure their existence, but in reality 'time' per se does not exist. Your past does not belong where you left it and your present is only fleeting and your future has already passed you by."

The voice fades as I walk out of the door. Jack is up at first light to make a little fire in the café grate where we boil a pan of water and make tea with the remaining café rations while Ted and Albert discuss the possibilities of another trip to get supplies. We ride the old pump trolley, once used to inspect the tracks, to make our way down to the abandoned village where the little corner shop still has untouched supplies and there are remaining houses to loot with all kinds of treasures for the taking, it's not really stealing, after all there's no one else around, only rotting bodies left forlorn in windows and encased in doorways and bodies of those who were struck by the radiation sickness which swiftly followed the third pandemic. Electromagnetic weapons and the enforcement of 5G communication frequency were installed in streets, schools and hospitals which fired rays of poisonous energy into the atmosphere. Radiation sickness, like the black-death, consumed many.

It's only the smell of rotting flesh which sours the air. Our home-made masks help to conceal the stench and protect against the decay in the atmosphere. You get used to it after a while, even decomposing faces staring into emptiness no longer register. We are lucky, that here in the countryside and being so far north, the electromagnetic weapon poles were never erected. For the time being, our tiny community has enough supplies to keep us alive. Gathered together, sipping our breakfast tea in subdued silence, subconsciously listening for intruders, Ted whispers:

"Think we should do another visit today?"

We use the term 'visit' because a 'raid' seems inappropriate to our purpose; we are merely making use of what others no longer need and we are lucky to be in a position to do so.

"Good idea!" replies Albert.

I nod and so do the others. "Albert and I will go this shift and who else...?

I quickly raise my hand and they agree. There's only room for three on the trolley especially returning with a stash of supplies, as it's difficult to pump the lever.

We set off as the sun peeps over the birch trees. The air is chilly and our home-crafted ponchos made from old blankets, keep out the cold wind. I smile to myself, thinking we three look like Mexican bandits. The sight of us stealing away like three stooges in an old-fashioned comedy strip, is amusing, but I know I must concentrate and focus on 'watching'. I watch the trees: I watch between the trees: I watch the dark hollows beside the trees and I hold the gun tightly. I have never had to shoot, but I am ready. Today I am nervous. Today something is different. Today as we near the village, the crows scatter. Do I hear the echo of voices through the trees? I am not sure if my ears are deceiving me? Albert and Ted hear it too and stop. They motion me to climb down and hide in the bushes while they go on ahead. I obey. I clutch the gun nervously and try to stop my hands from shaking. I feel sick. I can't see anything from my vantage point and I creep closer to the edge of the village where the road bends. I wait in the cold stillness. I wait afraid to move and then I hear two shots followed by laughter and an engine fires into action. It's a sound I haven't heard for a long time. I am afraid to move, rooted to the spot. Perhaps the men should have taken the gun? A truck speeds past heading towards our little outback station. Stealthily I move through the trees towards the store. I surprise myself how quickly I move. In the old life I had two hip replacements. In the new world my whisperers gifted me the secret age-regression process. It is working. My body, slowly is regaining its dancer's grace; maybe I will be able to dance again? The secret of age-regression, my whisperers explained;

"is to unlock the key code in your DNA and turn it on. This code is unique to every person and has to be sought through meditation. The brain is the engine to the body and the mind the navigator- together they work in harmony to create a total human being. What you think you are is what you become – 'as above, so below'. The human brain contains structures and shapes that have up to eleven different dimensions. The human heart also has computer-like cells similar to the brain with around thirty thousand neurites and has its own language and memory cells similar to the brain and if you learn how to harmonize the two organs in your body, you will have

tremendous power to heal yourself. You do not have to age. You do not have to grow old. Time has no meaning beyond earth. Time here can be bent and manipulated to speed up or slow down."

I understand what they postulate and know it to be true, because I have bent time and slowed it down, only when necessary to help my children. Age has no meaning beyond the beyond and I have forgotten my age, but I remember my surprise seventieth birthday party that my children so lovingly organised, inviting so many of my dancers and ex-pupils from all over the country. I was truly humbled. But now age is of no consequence. All that matters is that I can run. Nearing the main street, I brace myself fearing the worst and slow to a walking pace. My heart stops as I spy Ted lying face up with a hole through his fore-head. Blood is trickling over the pavement like dark treacle.

Albert is flat on his stomach, arms outstretched with a gaping hole in his neck. His head has fallen on one side and his mouth lies open in a silent scream. I retch on the spot. Three more shots echo across the fields. I can't return to our station outpost. I take a deep breath knowing that I must never give in, never give up and keep on going. My earth Father taught me well. He saved many men's lives during the second-world-war and was hailed a war hero after his battleship was torpedoed. He brought me up in a very strict, harsh regime explaining that when he held my head underwater, at the age of two, it was to teach me what it was like to drown. It was a warning to take deep water seriously. I didn't understand and can still feel the burning in my nose and throat when I remember and the times of being dragged out of bed in the dead of night and beaten for no reason was also part of the training. I forgave him and on his deathbed he said he was sorry for all the things he inflicted upon me.

"Keep on truckin'" I sing softly to myself, repeating the phrase over and over again grabbing a few tins of beans and cans of drink into a bag from the store. My heart is beating faster, pulsing, almost jumping through my chest-I must hurry in case they return, or worse still the outpost blade guards might respond to the shots and quickly advance here. Stepping over my friends' bodies I race along the road heading for the forest beyond the village. Hide, I must hide, take cover in the copse. I can survive. I pick up speed and make a dash through the hedge, jumping across a tiny brook and up the wooded incline, deciding to advance to the top of the hill where there is a better view of the surrounding farmland. From the top I can see the village in its sleepy valley knowing that when I feel brave enough, I must return to replenish my supplies before moving on. When it is safe I will forage.

There is a small hotel near the post office where I might find food and warm clothes. In the meantime I must wait. I perch on a boulder and gaze down at a tiny, mossy crack where a single daisy is waving in the breeze with its delicate, pure white petals turned towards the sun. A voice in my head, I know so well, speaks softly – "there where you least expect it – is life." A rush of gratitude and the realisation 'I cannot die' opens the floodgates and tears flow once more. Before I came to earth I was shown how humans have a body, which is their vehicle, their container in which to house their spirit identity, whereby they can experience life. Their inner energy is their true being and my spirit guide described the process of soul transference whereby the soul can enter another body, explaining-

"the Dalai Lama has had many re-incarnations and also the monarchy, but there exists more sinister applications of this where souls of the living are exchanged into other bodies. This will be explained to you at a later, more appropriate time. Suffice it to know that Soul migration or transference has always existed and the ancient Egyptians were very adept at this technique, as it helped to prolong their reign and keep the throne in the royal lineage. In the future, Soul transference from one body container to another will be commonplace."

But now I do not wish to think about such things as the sun is sinking and I must make my move into the village and not be afraid of what I might meet in the dark! Twilight in all its dying glory paints the horizon in magnificent swirls of purple, pink, orange and red.

Silhouetted against the sky is the imposing village church steeple. No bell tolls for the living or dead anymore. I race down the steep incline and arrive at the little bridge on the edge of the village. Cautiously I listen for movement. It's getting dark and I fear a return of the marauders. The hotel's modest forecourt is empty and the broken glass scattered around the entrance shows that the place has already been raided. With my gun at the ready I enter the foyer where the smell of damp, decay, rotting bodies and sewage spikes the air with an acrid pungency. Two half-eaten bodies lie slumped behind the check-in desk. Perhaps some hungry wild dogs feasted upon their corpses? In the dimming light I make my way to the bar where the shattered glass shelves hang by a thread. The kitchen likewise has been raided and only large bags of flour and a little rice remain. I hear rats scurrying into darkened corners as I hastily retreat into the hallway and climb the stairs. Maybe there's something left in the bedrooms-perhaps in the minibars? I carefully push open the first door which has been left on the latch and spy, lovingly placed in the centre of a double bed a child's toy panda. I rush to pick it up and hold it close. Pandas are my favourite animal. I travelled across China on a personal pilgrimage to learn how to be a panda keeper for a short while and it was a wonderful experience, but like in many of my expeditions to far off places, I encountered strange happenings. On the Yangtze river, I woke up one morning with unusual red marks on the bottom sheet of the bed where I had been lying on my back. They were little red indentations in unusual patterns as though I had been sleeping on a bed of nails. Similarly in Beijing, I found the same red marks on my pillow but I dismissed it as perhaps some make-up stains, but I knew it wasn't. On returning from China, I was very ill. It looked as though I was suffering from radiation burns but the doctor thought it was a nut allergy. My whisperers told me I would be ill on my return from China but the call of the panda close encounter was too great to miss! The illness lasted roughly a month but oddly I think that experience gave me some immunity to the Covid Virus.

Clutching the panda, I find the mini-bar and with great joy discover a packet of crisps, a bag of peanuts, two chocolate cookies, miniature gin and whiskey, a small bottle of red wine and a small bottle of white fizzy wine with a couple of cans of beer. What a find? I throw myself on the bed and begin tucking into an amazing feast. As the night descends, with a full stomach and floating head, I give in to the luxury of lying on a bed where sleep enfolds me in a cocoon of heavenly indulgence. From a deep, sweet slumber I wake harshly to the smashing and crashing of crockery and furniture with random gunshots ricocheting off the walls. Quickly I dive under the bed clutching the remains of my feast. My heart pounds, almost breaking through my chest as the cacophony draws close. The door flies open and like roaring wild tigers, youths pounce on the bed. If they catch me they will kill me, so lying still, as the gang freely jump up and down laughing hysterically like children in the playground, I concentrate on creating an invisible bubble around myself. It is not difficult with the understanding that the world around is energy and the human body is energy, therefore the faculty to magically blend the two can be achieved, just as the Cern Hadron Collider proved that everything is energy. The secrets of that base remain today and very few know the real purpose of the futuristic machine which has the capacity to access portholes from beyond. As I work my magic, I remember a time when I was called by a friend to exorcise a demon spirit from a young girl and in doing so, I placed myself inside a protective bubble. The next morning, waking up in my friend's house I forgot that all the corridors and all the rooms were alarmed and although she had shown me the code to turn them off, I forgot and freely wandered all over the house. Hearing me get up to make coffee she opened her bedroom door and the whole house shook with alarm bells. She was so shocked by what happened and although I tried to explain that I was still in a protective bubble, invisible to her alarms, she became afraid of me and it took many years to mend the friendship.

Suddenly I am shaken out of my memory as one of the gang shoots the dressing table mirror and glass shatters everywhere and another finds the panda that I have dropped in my haste to hide and tears it to pieces with a knife-the white stuffing falling on the floor next to my face under the bed. It is itchy and I feel a sneeze tickling my nose, but I manage to pinch my nose. An older accomplice appears in the doorway and the boys fall silent.

"You f..ing idiots! What do you think you're doing? We've got f... ing work to do!" a brash voice bellows.

The boys quickly jump to attention and race down the corridor. I wait silently, frozen to the spot while they trash the whole place until silence descends. I am afraid to move in case they lie in wait, but I know they have gone as stillness steals through the building. Suddenly an acrid smell wafts up the stairs and smoke drifts under the door. A terrible realisation dawns and I move swiftly down the stairs, stumbling over broken furniture. In the hallway sparks crackle and red flames curl forwards and I race through the kitchen to the cold air outside coughing and spluttering, glad to be alive having escaped the treacherous blaze.

Out in the early dawn air, the watery grey sky is turning pink in the east. I glance back at the billowing black smoke raging above the trees and prepare myself for a long walk ahead. I dare not tread the open road but must stay hidden by the forest edge in case the gang returns. The new day will bring me further to where I need to be and you are coming with me. I sense you. I know you. Together we are the 'now'. Your company gives me strength. Ahead I see the earth turning as clouds gather and dance. They hide many secrets, more than you will ever know and you trust me to tell you the truth, but now we must hurry as the rain is coming. I am weary. Over the hill and down by the loch we will rest. I hear your questions: perhaps one day they will be answered but in the now we must quicken the pace.

Out of breath I pause, having reached a good vantage point near the loch and spying a small boat tethered to a rickety landing, I decide to climb in. Finding the oars under the seat, I begin to row but I am clumsy and keep turning in circles until I finally get the hang of it. The water is calm and I manage to make headway veering towards the shore on the opposite side but I am slow, so by the time I reach the other side the sun is high and I am hungry and thirsty. It is quite difficult climbing out of the boat as it tips and rolls sideways every time I move, but somehow I manage to throw myself on land and the boat wobbles away out beyond where I can't retrieve it. So I abandon it and set off to investigate some small farm buildings ahead. Cautiously I climb over an old gate watching for signs of life and make my way down the cobbled driveway towards the barn. I pause by the door and listen closely with my ear pressed against the wooden slats. Something sharp stabs my back and a voice from behind cautions me not to move. My pockets and body are deftly searched.

"Turn around slowly!" the voice commands.

I obey and stare into the eyes of a large woman wearing a hat pulled down over her forehead and a large grey coat tied with string. Her black wellington boots stand firmly against my tiny feet as she gazes suspiciously into my face... searching for answers.

"What do you want?" she demands.

I splutter an almost incoherent reply, trying to convince her I want nothing but shelter for the night.

She shrugs and puts down the shot gun and rests it across her thick arms.

"You best come wi' me!" She snarls, leading the way.

Relieved I follow her through the barn and watch her clear away a stack of hay from a large wooden trap door. She stamps loudly beating out a rhythm on the wooden slats and from below a cheery face appears smiling, enquiring-

"Hey Mum, who's she?" he asks curiously.

"Never mind, now away wi ye!" She shoos him away like a bantam cock and he scurries into the dark carrying a large torch to light our way. Intrigued, I follow down a long passageway where we suddenly find ourselves in a large, warm sitting room complete with cosy candles and a large dining table, with old comfy chairs and a sofa. The family eye me with caution. The Grandfather puffs on an old pipe while the Grandmother stirs a stew on the make-shift grate. The young boy sits staring as does his sister and the large woman with the gun takes off her coat.

"Sit down" she requests. I meekly obey and remain silent. My gift enables me to enter into anyone's mind and see their past, present and future in a flash. I glean they are all good people caught in a time warp, living off the land like their forefathers, surviving the final roundup far away from the sterilised Cityscape. They are eager to know all about me and learn what has happened in the world outside and what my plans are for the future. Sitting at the table eating their delicious stew I regale them with all that I know and my stories entertain them for the rest of the night. The old man pours we three adults a dram from his coveted stock and we warm together as the fire dwindles. They make me a bed in the corner of the room when they all settle down in their allotted camp beds but the little girl Idris begins to cough. I recognise it and move swiftly to her bedside. She has a fever.

Her Mother sweeps me aside and wipes her brow with a cold rag. I watch as the fever takes hold and the poor child slips into a delirious coma as the Mother wrings the rag in panic, but I gently steer her away assuring her that all will be well. "Please let me try?" I whisper.

I was given the gift of healing. I did not want it. I ran away from it for a long time but when my children were in danger or in pain, I resorted to using it and my children took it for granted as it became part of their lives. I recall the time when my second daughter being, a rebellious teenager was messing around in her technology class and accidentally got a tiny piece of plastic in her eye. The school phoned me as they had ordered an ambulance but I managed to get there first with my eldest daughter, who watched as I miraculously healed her eye in a matter of a few minutes, whereby she was most indignant saying, "aw Mum, I'm gonna look stupid now when the ambulance comes as it's better!"

Fire in my hands-I call it as the healing energy rises up from my hands like fire and I pour it into the sick person with pure loving vibration, while the heat cleanses and heals as the sickness dies and fades. Idris responds and I thankfully watch the fever disappear. The family are so grateful and the Mother, with tearful face hugs and kisses me. So the night passes gently as I keep watch over the child and in the morning I am rewarded with a hearty breakfast. Real eggs from real hens are boiled and served with home-made bread and butter. I am lucky. It would be so easy to stay here and become part of their family, helping them with their daily chores but I am called elsewhere. Now I face another day, perhaps another challenge where my skills are needed? Saying goodbye is not easy and they hug me urging me to stay a little longer. They are kind and packed enough food and water to last me for a few days. I have no idea where I am going but I need to find my family. As I walk away with my backpack bouncing on my shoulders, I feel a welcoming presence-the presence I am beginning to know which hovers in my consciousness and shares parts of my journey. One day I will know you.

Perhaps you are me? Perhaps I am you? Together we have glimpsed through a crack in the universe the earth's diurnal round and we have walked together and witnessed the trials of daily existence.

Come with me a little way farther and I will show you one more time the magical twilight in my sphere, where the temple lights glisten and glide on waterlilies; where you smell the incense wafting through the arches where Anubis waits, for I have trembled in his presence and seen the power in his dark eyes.

I walk on and on until the light soaks like blotting paper in the deep velvet night and I look up into the night sky and see the stars – my home lies beyond in another galaxy and like old Albert said, they shine because they are dead. Know that in death we live. You and I are and always will be.

Remember to think lucky and you will be lucky. I am lucky to have known you and we will meet on another journey. Ah… I hear your question.

"What is your name?" you ask.

"My name is Lucky, for I am lucky!"

PURPLE

Days pass and I have travelled back from the Scottish border to the Yorkshire moors, sometimes walking, sometimes obtaining a lift from other rebel survivors and sometimes lazily lying in a bed of grass and hay on top of a farmer's truck. Some farm life lingers in the far regions of the desolate countryside, where sturdy folk continue age-long traditions and would sooner die than leave their land. Now, I am standing gazing across a purple sea where the heather quivers like a lilac ocean, undulating in the gentle afternoon breeze and the earth beneath my feet echoes with an empty thud on the narrow moorland path. I make my way to a small outcrop of rocks perched on a steep incline, camouflaging a secret cave, feeling the hand of nature still weaving its magic, unscathed by the militant onslaught invading the main cities and towns.

Sitting on the top of the cold rocks I wait for you, watching the lazy sun dip, feeling your presence, while across the valley the church clock still chimes a tender reminder of the old days, the old ways, a time when time was time and mattered. You are here and I sense your concern. It has been a while since first we met and you are uncertain of our meeting and yet you have come. You are curious to learn, but will not commit your reason and logic to fantasy; nor as yet, do you dare to freely enter the landscape of your imagination. Our first meeting was brief and I showed you a glimpse into the magical realms of universal law, and now you are here to delve deeper. One day you will understand that in the kingdom of fancy lies the reality of truth. But until then I will take you with me on another journey and you may make of it what you will.

The rock is unyielding to my touch. It keeps secrets below. I have waited long enough and now the icy air curls around my feet and it is time to join the seekers-those believers in the old ways. There are still many of us who will not bend to the new laws and continue to fight against the mechanical intruders. Survival is difficult but my whisperers guide me. I am lucky. Along the beaten path of warriors, tiny blueberry bushes still flourish, not tainted or poisoned by electro-magnetic pulses radiating from the cityscapes. The moorland cannot be conquered; it remains wild and untamed in all its rugged beauty. I remember my first glimpse of a purple prairie – an enormous wasteland expanding on and on: to me it was a magical vastness, only having known small farm fields separated by fences and hedges. Seven years old, I had not seen much of the world and through the old charabanc windows, with my face pressed against the glass, I was mesmerized by the undulating hills carpeted in violet, mauve and lavender rivulets rippling across the landscape. On the bus all was quiet. Our little village community sat awed by the brooding, moorland majesty. It was a time when working class families from small country villages, shared a bus to holiday for a week by the seaside.

Now there are no class divisions except for consumer grades; it's still the same, only with different tags. As we neared the coast a white veil crept over the hills and enveloped us in a mysterious mist. I remember the mist and fog of yesterday when we had natural weather. I remember the seasons in all their changing moods, until they merged into one controlled climate, and now the synthetic weather is modified under a grey, sealed lid. Rain, hail, snow and sunshine could be witnessed in a single day before the new order, but now all weather is modified for the cityscape dwellers. Fog and sea mists, once upon a time, were a natural phenomenon, quite beautiful when light, but dangerous when dense and I recall a time when the fog was perilous and an amazing miracle happened to me.

It was nearing Christmas and being the Vice Principal of a dance college, I was co-hosting a special ball and had to drive a long distance to the venue in Leeds. It was unfortunate that I had an extremely painful abscess under a tooth which prevented me from enjoying a sumptuous meal and festive dancing. After a while, I had to leave due to the escalating pain and to add to my angst, I had to drive home through dense fog. I didn't know the area very well and managed to manoeuvre my way onto a major road, which I thought would lead me back home, but the mist was so thick and my vision blurred and restricted to only a few paces in front of my car – even my fog lamps couldn't penetrate through the density, so I stopped the car. In the deafening oppressive silence, I was suffocating. Panicking, I got out of the car and immediately the damp air stung my nose and throat. I thought I had parked in a lay-by, but there was dried mud and grass under foot and to my horror, I realised I was stranded in a field. I had no idea how that had happened. My jaw ached and the pain intensified and I had been warned that if the abscess burst, I could be thrown into anaphylactic shock. Immersed in the icy-white stillness, I was drowning in a sea of fear and began shaking and trembling as I thought the abscess had burst as a bitter, sour taste flooded my mouth. I hurried back inside the car and slumped over the steering wheel, calling out to the Great Ones. I prayed for help with all my heart, placing my being into their care. Then, gently from the cosmos, a soft voice told me to start the engine. I stopped crying and obeyed. Somehow, I turned the car around and found myself at the entrance of an open farm gate. How on earth had I driven through that? Suddenly from my left a red light drove slowly past. I was so relieved to see another vehicle and I thought that if I followed it, I would arrive somewhere I might recognise. Anxiously, I kept close to the red light but couldn't see the car, but it was enough to get me away from the field. I followed up and down and around corners keeping the red light just in front at all times. Gradually the tiny roads widened and I saw the dim lights of a village. The mist had cleared, and thankfully I recognised the place. By this time the red light had rounded a corner and I followed expecting to see the vehicle under the street lamps, but strangely there was no sign of the car. I speeded up along the main street but it was deserted. It could not have vanished into thin air unless...? With humble gratitude I realised that my people had saved me once again and I managed to drive home safely, just in time, as the abscess fully burst pumping poison through my body. Later the next day, I recovered and marvelled at my escape from the fog. Miracles do happen if you ask with a pure heart and I am eternally grateful for my spirit protectors who rescued me that night in the terrifying fog.

Now in the dimming light, I can just make out the hidden cave doorway sealed to everyone, except the knowers, the healers and the messengers. The smooth dark rock harbours a few tufts of purple heather around the entrance, which are secret signs to the initiated, indicating the healing amethyst caves below. I take a last glimpse of the orange sunset as I enter under the lintel, and am reminded of the special magic of all plants, trees and flowers in the twilight haze, emitting a mystical vibration in which we can bathe and ingest the invisible, quivering energy. Entering the sacred amethyst palace, which is a sanctuary in the belly of the earth, a womb of love and light, friends gather with flaming torches and we descend the wet, slippery slope. We understand the magical knowledge of the law of colour vibration, knowing how to use the sacred energy, whose pure electric pulse affects all living cells.

Stepping farther into the darkness, the brilliant flames flash against the amethyst rock face and the power begins. Colour is power energy, the same energy as our inner being and the two forces working together spark a higher conscious response, which is fantastic beyond belief, especially when our inner being absorbs the direct power of a specific colour. We don purple hooded cloaks to blend in with the purple gemmed rock face and to absorb its power. All colours vibrate at varying frequencies and resonate specific electric pulses. Different colours affect our cell vitality and have the strength to alter our moods and emotions and can generate healing both mentally and physically. The vibration of colour interacts uniquely with everyone, either consciously or unconsciously and can work magic on our senses, enriching and heightening experiences. I recollect the case of a young teenage girl whose Mother was desperate to find a cure for her daughter who was on her death-bed. Lucy had been a champion swimmer and a gifted artist when she was suddenly struck down by a mysterious illness and no one knew the cause, even the doctors at the hospital had given up hope of her recovery. Her Mother heard about me from someone who I zapped (short, sharp shock of healing injected to the recipient) and she recommended her to seek my help. The mother, as a last resort brought her poor, weak, sickly daughter to me and I used my knowledge of colour power to re-energise her. Red for restoring her blood and passion for life; yellow to lift her spirit from deep depression, and orange, a mixture of the two, to encourage change of thought. I also regressed her back to her previous life. The date she remembered was 1876, where she was a young timid, sensitive girl who endured an arranged marriage to an elderly farmer because her family would benefit financially from the agreement. Poor Lucy had to withstand awful physical and mental abuse and in less than a year of being newly-wed, she was murdered by her cruel husband. The impact of such violence on a timid soul followed her into her next existence. Just before she fell ill, she met someone who triggered terrifying emotions from her past life, and the only way she could deal with it was to barricade herself inside her mind and close off the rest of the world. It took three long, intense sessions to affect her healing and from then on she achieved wonderful things including an M.A. in Art and later became the mother of two beautiful children.

The memory fills me with joy. Now as I descend the slippery slopes, my dull footsteps echo through the hollow earth and my cloak swishes through the damp air, as I surrender to the sovereignty of the moment. I am proud to be a worker of light in world service, trained in higher wisdom to bring to earth loving energy, sharing our special knowledge of colour to help and heal those in need. Knowledge of the varying frequencies emanating from different colours can strengthen and sharpen aspects of our inner self in a magical way, affecting cell regeneration.

We descend a myriad of passageways, some small with narrow trails edged with gaping chasms on either side and others empowered with cathedral-like architecture with gothic spires glinting in the torch light. The silence heightens as shadows dance and bounce off gigantic statues naturally carved through eons of existence. Eventually we reach the inner sanctum, the very bowels of the earth's crust and take our places in a semi-circle around a white, opaque, moon carved on the rocky floor. A soft, deep, resonant voice reminds us that we must ignite our intentions with the right kind of 'light'. We must only use the 'goodness' vibration in pure form, which responds to positive energy to send our healing energy out into the planet.

"Children of the universe unite in the power of purple vibration, emanating from the mingling of two colours. Blue for calm, peace and healing and that of passionate red – life-giving, powerful and intense. Blending the two, we create the highest healing colour purple," the voices in unison chant as the High Priestess mixes the colours on the amethyst altar. From beneath the white moon, purple smoke coils and curls in circles. Stringed music harmoniously rides lilac clouds and as the delicate mist clears, a panther appears. The magnificent creature with gleaming, wet fur and penetrating amethyst eyes, stands majestically before us. Its presence infuses the ceremony with traits of its animal instincts to help us conquer all that is evil and to endow its intuitive skills to penetrate the darkness with courage and valour.

Together in one voice we invoke love, peace and harmony to encompass the earth, fusing our love with all those on the planet who wish only light and healing to flourish. A high-pitched vibration resounds and a violet spark flashes at the panther's feet, flaring up around the creature in a furious purple inferno. One by one we step into the indigo flames. My body is washed in a cool breeze. It is refreshing and cleansing. It is cold fire with the intensity of red passion and the serenity of a calm blue sea. Together the two energies powerfully penetrate and heal. We direct our intentions out to the needy planet and an explosion of love reverberates along the earth's ley lines as we remain locked in the purple fire, until one by one we step back into our place. The panther disappears and the smoke recedes underneath the white moon. Our mission is complete and solemnly we return through the enchanting passageways.

I marvel at the natural power of colour which has been gifted to us and how each colour has a specific energy and purpose. I cannot imagine a colourless life. I briefly glimpsed the synthetic, unnatural colours of the new world and feel saddened that the artificial light, the fake plants and mock parks give nothing to people, only the alien hybrids and the various alien species, which are part of the new structure, benefit because they cannot live in the natural world's atmosphere.

Gradually chemtrails altered the air to accommodate the aliens' needs. My whisperers showed me a vision of future life where there are seven main genders co-mingling together. Looking back, I realise how we were all cleverly lead down a precarious path of gender confusion and disruption. The media mind-controlled mass deception in technological leisure activities, such as gaming, on-line gambling, quizzes and virtual reality sports, triggering confusion and identity disorientation, especially in the young and vulnerable, by making them question the validity of their sexuality. I recall how my teenage students became puzzled as to who they really were and where they belonged. Some of them wanted to be both genders and some wanted to be neutral, some even wanted to become 'furries' with animal tails attached to their clothing. Teaching became so different, remembering to use the correct code to address each student, taking into account all the different gender categories and memorising their personal name changes to numbers or unusual things or animals. Teachers were reprimanded if we didn't get it right, not to mention increased difficulties imposed by strict social distancing laws and how it affected the layout of classes and application of teaching methods. All that was a long time ago and lead the way for the planet to accept transhumans, robots, cyborgs and all manner of A.I. beings.

Now I hand back my cloak at the cave entrance. No words are exchanged as we telepathically communicate our goodbyes and I step into the dawn, dusky-pale shadows. The figures of the seers and seekers glide and blend into the horizon and disappear until next time. The cave is sealed. Its secrets are locked safely within, hidden from all that pass that way. I stroll towards the watery, white light of a new morning peeping through the trees and welcome the call of a new day.

Colour is slowly seeping back through black night patches and I am reminded that not only the magnificent array of natural colours have their place and purpose in healing and balancing our psyche, but also black and white colours have their own amazing qualities. Black for deep peace and soul renewal and white for ultimate cleansing and purity of spirit, a mixture of the two creating grey which has its own inner strength and power. But I cannot allow my thoughts to linger, as I must make my way to the main road ahead along the tracks to where the country's famous, early warning devices were stationed like giant golf balls perched on stands. The iconic balls were replaced by an advanced radar system resembling small pyramids which were not as impressive as the balls, then with the new, advanced technology, the base became obsolete and the country's early warning system grew reliant upon interstellar computers and drones in the ionosphere.

Arriving at the main road I watch for signs of life and prepare to dive into the bracken if the Blade guards appear with their electro-magnetic pulse blades, seeking anyone who refuses to live inside the cityscapes. I gaze alertly up and down the road and smile remembering the old Inn at the bottom of the hill, where a turf fire was kept burning constantly to keep away the devil, who was said to have scooped out the hills and valleys of the landscape with his hands. Many hill walkers and tourists paid a visit to the pub to see the fire that had been started in the 1800's. Now nothing remains of the past and we the' Outsiders' rely on a secret code of symbols and signs left in major places that can be read by all who have the knowledge. The code ensures information is relayed about recent events and the availability of lifts to certain places. There are 'certains' – that is a certain set timetable of transport is mostly available, but the mode of transport is subject to change, according to unforeseen dangers. It is a secret network that relies on trust and thus far has worked very well.

Waiting has become part of the new way of life and patience an accomplishment, which if you are to survive, is a necessary skill. Nothing is handed on a plate and everything gained is received with humble gratitude. Survivors are a unit and although there are a few outbands of murderers and thieves, on the whole the network feeds its people and secures their safety. Waiting, waiting, watching and waiting is all. Time is not what it used to be and no one can be held accountable to it anymore. Transport may be expected when the sun is high or thereabouts, or maybe later if there's a hitch in the plans. All anyone can be sure of is that transport will eventually arrive and vigilance is the key.

The air smells salty – how I long to stand on the seashore. By nightfall I hope to be in Robin Hood's Bay; a special place of seaside memories with my children. My stomach churns through lack of food and I suddenly panic hearing an engine chug in the distance. I am alert, ready to flee, but luckily, an old ambulance painted black, appears at the top of the hill and I watch it with relief coast down as fuel is sacrosanct. Petrol has long gone and the fuel used is made from a chemical process, much like pure alcohol. l make a sign and the ambulance stops. Climbing aboard, I am greeted with a warm, friendly welcome from a cluster of folk seated on cushions and blankets. Only the driver has a seat which is rickety, full of holes and jiggles up and down as we set off. A space is made for me near the door and I settle down holding onto a rail to steady myself. It's not far and not long to endure the uncomfortable ride with the smell of the fumes and unwashed bodies. I am grateful for the ride and have only a few beads to give the driver but anything is acceptable which can be bartered.

When we arrive at the tiny hamlet the sun is magnificently pausing over the horizon, oozing orange and gold rays across the grey sea. We all tumble out and leave the driver to park in a secret hide-out in the woods. I stretch my legs and inhale the fresh briny breeze and walk across the cobbled stones to the sea wall, then sliding down the wet stones to the damp sand below, I gaze across a steely brooding ocean, quietly magnificent in the calm of the twilight glow. My old, worn-out boots sink into the softness, releasing tiny rivulets of sea water from beneath the sand. I remember the old days when the beach strummed with the hum of happy folk and families with children and dogs running freely along the shore. I remember my own children with buckets and spades digging sand castles and my baby son falling into a rock pool and hauling him out with his little blonde curls covered in slimy green seaweed and donkey rides, strawberry ice-cream, toddlers splashing in the sea with sandy bottoms and laughter. Happy times all gone. People in the cityscapes no longer take breaks by the sea. Anywhere along the coast is out of bounds. The seas are polluted, not only with mountains of rubbish and sewage, but with toxic waste from nuclear plants spewing spillage into the oceans. No one would ever dream of swimming in the sea for fun nowadays and no one in the cityscapes would ever dare venture beyond the perimeters of their hi-tech prison.

The breeze curling across the icy sea pierces through my thick woollen shawl and I shiver as I walk back to the old inn by the sea wall. I wrap my shawl around my head like the fish wives in the old sepia photos, who tirelessly trod the beach searching for a few meagre cockles, waiting for their fishermen to come home. I glance ahead at the inn, solidly built as a sturdy fortress against the onslaught of the sea, remembering its wonderful fish and chips. How times have changed? Now in these dark days, desolate cafes are barred and shuttered and the once candy-striped bright shops have fallen into disrepair. Everywhere is stark and bleak. The little hamlet has long been abandoned with beautiful cottages left to rot and disintegrate. No street lights brighten the dreary evening and a solitary weather-cock creaks above a deserted butchers.

The inn of course is closed, but in the cellars beneath, life buzzes. I stamp on an old, wooden trap door in the courtyard and wait for someone to appear from a ramshackle shed by the side of the inn.

It's a great decoy, as no one would think it was the entrance to an underground, thriving community.

Inside the shed behind old plant pots and congeries of garden tools and broken boxes, a camouflaged door opens revealing steep steps leading into a deep underground tunnel, which meanders along ancient smugglers secret hideout caves and into a vast cavern where bright lights and a warm fire glows. An old generator provides electricity and ensures the basic needs of the community. Everyone, all fifteen of the core members work hard to maintain a reasonable existence and visitors are always welcome. There are no children or youngsters living in the commune, only middle-aged and older people who share their individual skills. Visitors who have something to barter, pay for their stay with whatever they can offer and people like myself who have nothing, offer labour-preparing food or undertaking menial chores. The system works well and everyone is happy with the arrangement. I take a seat by the fire sipping a flagon of home-brew from Danny, made from fermented potatoes and carrots. It has a strange taste. Danny was once a pharmacist and knows how to concoct a fine pungent liqueur and hands the six visitors a mug each to sample. The rest of the community gather around the fire to swap news and exchange views. Susan, a middle-aged, ex-police woman beckons us to an old wooden table where various bowls made from all kinds of utensils are laid out and we jovially take our places as a huge vat of fish and seaweed soup is placed before us and we help ourselves. I avoid the fish heads floating on the top of the greasy liquid but with wholesome, home-made bread it makes a filling meal. Fish is still caught and eaten by the community although they are aware of increased mercury levels in the sea from nuclear spillage, but are prepared to take their chances as it supplements their food supply.

When we have all eaten, the bowls are cleared away and Jack takes out his harmonica to serenade us with a sweet wistful melody. Sometimes the intense beauty of a moment pierces the past and I cannot bare to be reminded of what was, so I seek solace in the night air. Perhaps my people will come tonight? I search the sequinned galaxy watching for movement among the stars and wrap my thick shawl tightly around my shoulders. The tide is out leaving the ridged sand lit for miles by a full, silver moon weaving a shimmering pathway across the distant sea. Sitting on a rock I pull my knees up to my chest and curl inwards bracing against the icy wind, feeling privileged to be alive in the moment.

Suddenly, a luminescent-pink flash streaks across the horizon, followed by a massive, glowing magenta orb, rolling over the sea from right to left, like a snooker ball shot speedily and pocketed somewhere beyond. Thunder explodes and cracks the silence, but not in the sky; it roars and rumbles beneath me, shaking the rocks where I sit as the sand quivers and the black sea rises forwards like a massive tsunami racing ashore. Afraid, I run back to the seawall and turn to see the ocean parting in the middle as a gleaming, metallic saucer rises to the surface. Little by little, the gigantic silver craft rises majestically from the seabed filling the whole sky with a reflective aura. As it hovers above the harbour, a magnificent, futuristic city emerges, and I can make out dark, silhouetted figures pitted against bright oval windows moving around, engrossed in their duties. It is awesome in the extreme and I stand rooted to the spot in sheer amazement. No sound emanates from the craft; no wind generates disturbance of any kind. The ginormous city just hangs in the sky.

A spark of light suddenly shoots from the side of the vessel and flies above the shore like a warning flare. The orb miraculously transforms into a dazzling, floating bubble which melts into a small, translucent hovercraft, gliding smoothly onto the beach. As it lands, the sand lights up spotlighting the rocks and hillside and from within the vehicle, a golden sphere floats towards me pausing for a few moments before it bubbles and liquefies into molten gold, which flows down and smelts into the shape of a Greek god-like Adonis figure. I stare at the beautiful perfectly formed, golden statue with rippling athletic muscles and powerful shining physique. The golden figure steps forwards and I am awed and frightened at the same time. I am in the presence of a Greek, mythical god from another planet and under his gaze I am small, insignificant and unable to respond. As he steps forwards my fear abates as telepathically, I sense his kindness. He holds out his hands which bubble and dissolve, melting into the shape of a metallic goblet, into which he decants molten metal from his golden arms. He pours the liquid into a square mould where a glimmering key forms and then disappears.

He holds out the tiny metallic square for me to see and I hear the words, "remember the key is hidden inside". He leans forwards and carefully places it into the palm of my hand, where it tingles, pulsing electric charges up my arm and into my body with a surge of warm energy. It feels wonderful. Telepathically he tells me to keep it safe until I receive instructions. Automatically I nod in agreement and he steps back vanishing in a haze of metallic sparks, like golden rain splintering in the dark. Rooted to the spot, I watch the mothership fade into a hazy mist dissolving into the cosmos and I am left wondering if it really happened.

I clutch the tiny golden square in the palm of my hand – it is real and I walk back towards the inn pondering my mission. My whisperers had told me to go to the coast and I obeyed, thinking that my people might appear, but I had no idea I would witness an amazing, unbelievable event and be given an assignment. I search the night sky for signs of the visitors but there are none. All is calm. Back at the inn, a bed is ready for me in a corner of the main room, it is warm and comfortable, but I can't sleep as my head is full of incredible images and my mind keeps racing with unanswered questions. I sit up watching the fire crackle, clutching the golden square when, suddenly, the smooth surface alters forming a ridge around a stone. I sit up and examine it in the firelight. It is a purple stone – an amethyst. I remember the healing amethyst ceremony earlier that day and wonder if there is a connection? Purple being the highest healing colour-perhaps it has a connection with my assignment? The teleportation of the stone is not a surprise, as I have experienced many transferences of objects through time and space on numerous occasions and know that Beings from different planets have no difficulty in travelling through walls and transferring people through solid objects to other places – I understand this well from experience. Getting out of bed, pondering the stone's appearance, I remember an unusual teleportation incident of a special ring in the shape of a treble clef. In my early teaching days my students gave me a beautiful silver ring in the shape of a treble clef because I taught music. Unfortunately the design of the ring was dangerous, as the oval at the top of the clef kept catching in door handles and hooks. One day my finger was nearly torn from my hand as I caught the ring in a cupboard handle and I vowed not to wear it again and threw it in the bin in my London flat. One evening, twenty five years later, living alone in a town house in York, I was shaken by a terrific crash at the top of my stairs. My son, who was staying with me at the time, rushed out of his seat to investigate. A number of articles that had been hanging on the walls were thrown to the floor. I rushed to his side and was puzzled to see the mess and began picking up the bits when I saw an object in the corner of the wooden stairs. I picked it up and was stunned to find the treble clef ring that I had thrown away years ago in London. It was black and tarnished but as I held it in my hand it was restored to its former shiny silver surface. My son was amazed to witness its transformation. The house was built on an old leper colony and both my son and I experienced many paranormal happenings, but I believe the ring came back into my life, as a reminder of my music training and to encourage me to use my musical skills to better advantage. Years later after moving many times, somehow I lost the ring and forgot about it until my Granddaughter spied something on my mantelpiece and asked – "What's this Nanny?" To my surprise the ring had surfaced again from nowhere and I placed it back on my finger, upside down to avoid catching the loop in door handles and I wear it to this day.

Sleep evades me and I need to clear my head, so not wishing to disturb the others, I creep out into the courtyard and sit waiting for dawn to break across the sea. I take out my little torch to examine the square and am surprised to see a tiny round hole in the top, just big enough through which to thread a chain. I realize the square is meant to be a pendant and quickly search for the shoe-lace I keep safely in my coat pocket. I am lucky. It fits perfectly and I hang it around my neck securing it with a knot at the back. Almost immediately images appear in my mind and the words – "think gold" echo in my head. The meaning is familiar to me, having been taught by my people to live in my higher consciousness with goodness and love as the quintessential intention. Whatever I think, or do, I must do to the best of my ability and demand of myself only the highest standard of behaviour in order to receive only the best. 'Thinking gold' at all times is the optimum goal. The images fade as the sun peeps over a calm grey sea and I wonder what lies below the deep fathoms waiting to emerge into the light of day?

What will today bring? I have work to undertake to pay for my stay before I move on and this journey has been full of surprises-not what I intended. My golden key with my amethyst stone will lead me on a new journey and a mission. For this I am lucky – yes I am Lucky.

GOLDEN KEY

I have around my neck a little, square gold pendant which contains a secret key. Did I dream the night when the spaceship rose out of the sea and a bright orb shot out of the craft, dispatching a hovercraft to shore, where a golden, Adonis delivered a pendant containing a secret golden key? I have no idea what to make of the experience, or the purpose of the key, or what the whole mission entails? I need to wait and let it unfold as I walk along the calm seashore. Patience is a great virtue and something the first lock-down taught me.

The first lock-down was traumatic for everyone in so many different ways. Life patterns changed overnight. For me, one day I had tremendous responsibility for many children and adults in my own Performing Arts School and the next...the only obligation and commitment I had was singularly to myself and my pets. I missed the children and the social interaction and the creative environment and the great sense of unity. Day after day, I wished to return to some kind of normality, eager to re-establish my business, but I was lucky, to be imprisoned in a beautiful lodge in the woods-my home away from the urban jungle, although, after a time, even the loveliest gem can tarnish. One night when a storm was thrashing the trees in a sixty mile an hour squall and the rain lashing my decking and windows, I felt an oppressive darkness closing in, dragging timeless fears from the depths of my being. There was nowhere to hide and nowhere to run, with no one to share my despair. Just when the wind reached a fever-pitch screeching, I heard a voice speaking softly – White Cloud, my spiritual guide came to help me and being a Native, American Indian with powerful, natural wisdom from his tribe, the Blackfoot, he spoke with great authority and spiritual insight. He calmed my fears and dispelled my night terror. I trusted his council as we had a special connection from a past life and wishing to learn more about the Blackfoot Tribe, a few years previously I had made a pilgrimage to their reservation in Browning, Montana, spending time in a tepee and speaking to the Chief about his tribe's history.

In the bleakness of that evening, White Cloud spoke to me in his gentle, mighty manner and told me to be patient, showing me a vision of a prairie dust storm sweeping across his reservation, describing how his people would lock-down when a dust cloud rose on the horizon, hunkering together in their tepees, adding: *"when the storm attacks, be prepared to lie low for as long as it takes, for while the storm rages, ravaging all that can be torn apart or eaten alive outside, inside you are exposed to yourself; vulnerable to yourself; visible to your fears; weak to your fragile heart and there in your captivity you must choose patience as your friend. You must curl inwards and suffer the battle between you and yourself. Learn to listen without hearing. Learn to speak without speaking. Learn the 'I'; 'Me'; 'Myself' of who you are and find your inner warrior to fight the darkness. When silence deafens, you will know it is safe to rise and walk out into the open to begin clearing the wreckage of what has passed, to build afresh only what is necessary on new ground. Remember, only that which is necessary in the light of the new knowledge of yourself, is worth rebuilding."*

Walking by the sea shore wondering what to do, remembering his words of wisdom and understanding that being patient is sometimes hard – I knew he was right to advise rebuilding only what is important for the future and not to cling onto the wreckage of the past. Feeling the gentle wind ruffling my hair, his words echo in the breeze: *"do not worry what should be, or how it might have been, or what it will be...live now."*

The wind is rising and a storm threatens across the coastline. Waves are leaping and lashing like a caged tiger vaulting to the crack of a trainer's whip. A voice calls from the seawall... "do you want a lift to York?" I hadn't thought about it but suddenly yes I knew I did; I wanted it more than I could say, in fact it was just what I had been waiting for. It was right, it seems right. I hurry to secure my place with the driver and collect my things from the inn, thanking everyone profusely for their hospitality. I explain to the driver I have nothing to barter but he says it doesn't matter and that he has to make the trip anyway. Taking a last glance at the sea, savouring my awesome experience of the golden Adonis, I wonder if my mission awaits in York? I clutch the pendant around my neck, watching the ominous black clouds roll over the horizon, and am glad to flee the gale.

Sunshine ahead breaks through the early morning mist and an optimistic humour amongst the travellers brightens the day. Through the winding countryside, I spy the great moors, brooding and daunting in majestic isolation. Ahead, the famous North Yorkshire village, which was the backdrop for a popular tv series and home of a famous railway station for steam trains, nestles in a protective vale, but now the only remnants of the busy tourist spot are a few dilapidated houses and an abandoned pub. The church in all its quaint glory still stands and the little picturesque station lies abandoned and barred. The village holds a vivid memory for me-a vision of my own people from another planet. It was a time when a friend in the village, had a holiday house, which she let for short vacations to her family and friends. It was a very old, basic property without a television, or phone or modern facilities other than a wireless and it was an ideal retreat for all the family. Before our visit I had not been well and was bleeding heavily and during the course of our stay, the pain grew worse. Unbeknownst to me, I was carrying twins in my fallopian tube and was in grave danger.

One evening, on retiring early to bed, I managed to sleep for a while but as it grew dark, I became more uncomfortable with the pain. I turned to my right where, through the window, a huge silver white ball in the night sky floated towards me. I thought it was the moon. Hypnotically, it held my gaze and filled the bedroom with luminescent white light. On the opposite wall a door opened and two very tall, beautiful, glowing beings stood encased in glorious, radiant light, embodying all-embracing love. I had never experienced intense, powerful passion of pure emotion. I sat up and they held out their arms to receive two precious spirits from my body, as they were not meant for earth and could not survive here. I wanted to go with them but the beings gently persuaded me that it was not right and that I had to stay to complete my journey. The all-consuming sense of peace and divine tranquillity was overwhelming and I begged them to take me, but as I felt myself soothingly pushed back into my pillow, I fell into a deep sleep.

In the morning I awoke with a tremendous sense of celestial devotion and serenity. Recalling the experience, I looked towards the window where the moon had engulfed me in silver light, but there was no window, just a blank wall! I turned towards the door on the opposite side of the room where the beings had stood in a tunnel of light, but there was no door, only a blank wall. I couldn't believe what I had experienced. I tried to get out of bed but the pain was too much to bear and I was rushed to hospital where twins were removed from my fallopian tube. The doctors were amazed because both foetuses had grown to the size of small grapes, which they claimed was virtually impossible. I grieved for the loss of my twins but I know they returned home to our place of origin where one day we will be reunited. Miraculously, later, I was blessed with a beautiful daughter when I was told I was not able to have any more children.

Now we are driving through abandoned country villages, barren and lifeless, even the market towns are desolate ghost towns. The driver, Dave, with a swarthy face and hippy beard, wearing a heavy fisherman's jumper, chews on a stick and his thick, black army boots, kick the floor occasionally when he grinds through the gears. He has the look of a rakish pirate wearing a faded bandana over his long black curls and when he smiles his face lights up in child-like glee. Four of the others are playing cards in the back and two sit staring at their knees. Nearing the city, the great Minster still stands proudly dominating the skyline, set amongst piles of broken bricks and abandoned road signs.

Deserted pubs and derelict cafes have fallen into disrepair and piles of rubbish and rubble lie strewn across the once tidy pavements. As we hobble down a street that was once popular with tourists, lined with specialist shops and a famous fish and chip restaurant, I am saddened to see it reduced to debris like a disaster zone hit by a cyclone. Strangely many years ago, when I was driving down the same street, I involuntarily had a vision where all the buildings to my right disintegrated in slow motion and I yelled to my passenger: "it's going, it's going down!" She looked at me in amazement when I described the buildings disappearing as though submerged under water. Now the same street is the reality I previously witnessed.

We drive down the main street unhindered by the threat of the Blade guards, and I am wary in case we are targeted, but as Dave explains that after the third pandemic, most people adhere to the new rules and go peacefully of their own volition to live in the cityscapes so the guards concentrate on keeping law and order in the ever expanding districts and although the controllers are aware of a few dissidents still living in the outskirts, it is more important to them to maintain a high standard of policing the inner regions, than go chasing after a few strays.

Arriving into the city centre is sad. The great, historic city of York has fallen into a disaster zone; a desolate wasteland of emptiness. Here a lifetime of memories are shattered and burnt to ashes. I wipe away a renegade tear, refusing the indulgence of wallowing in the past and I stop myself meandering down a melancholic path. Dave asks where I wish to be dropped. Passing the Art Gallery, just opposite the Theatre Royal, which is still standing, seems a good place. The nightmare begins as I step down into the forsaken city. The fountains at the front of the Art Gallery have long dried up and lie buried under a mountain of refuse. The building is still intact but covered in a mass of anguished graffiti. I wonder if there are still paintings inside and suddenly have the urge to force my way in. Around the back of the building marauders have already ransacked and pilfered the site.

A hacked window hangs open swaying on its hinges and is large enough for me to clamber through. I land heavily on my feet on a dirty tiled floor in the soiled toilets where the stench is unbearable and I swiftly race out into a large open corridor with a high ceiling. A couple of paintings dangle precariously from the wall and are slashed and scratched with red paint and excrement. Emptiness echoes like a vacant school. I sit down in the main hall looking around at the mess, remembering the re-opening and refurbishment of the gallery, where my dancers performed my new choreography, especially created for the occasion. Such a long time ago-it seems like another lifetime since the whole world metamorphosed into an unrecognisable planet. I pause waiting for something – I do not know what or who?

I wander upstairs to see if there are any paintings left. To my dismay, upstairs in the community gallery, many squatters have left a trail of old, soiled bedding and empty tin cans, there's even evidence of open fires with black ash and bits of charred wood scattered on the stained floor. Some paintings remain but have been vandalised, and some paintings on the bare walls, have been creatively designed by young artists wishing to leave their mark. I turn and walk down a long open corridor and stop, shocked to spy peeping from behind a corner, a pair of beautiful long legs, in fact perfectly shaped shiny legs in tanned lycra stockings. A voice belonging to the legs commands me in an unrecognisable accent:

"Hurry up, I have been waiting for you. There is no time to waste!"

I quicken my pace to meet the owner of the legs who is perched on a high stool. I am speechless to gaze upon a stunningly, beautiful woman wearing a large black Ascot hat, trimmed with black net over her bright red hair. Her skin is flawless and white as marble. Her black, haute couture, tightly – fitting, two piece suit with low scooped neck reveals sumptuous breasts. Her penetrating bright green eyes are emotionless. I am envious of her black, patent-leather high heeled shoes. Standing tall she executes great authority and under her glare and watchful presence I feel insecure, insignificant and a lesser being dressed in rags.

"Have you brought it?"

I am confused and look puzzled, still unable to speak.

"The key, the key woman? Have you got it?"

It suddenly dawns on me that she means the pendant around my neck. I automatically touch it and she nods commanding – "Come with me!"

I obey immediately. In my uncertainty I feel your presence. You seem to arrive when my consciousness is fragmented and you find your way into my mind. You are like a monkey sitting on my shoulder, safe from the action. You watch from afar. Who are you? In the misty haze surrounding your presence you faintly reply but I cannot hear you and I must follow the stranger who walks like a superior female model, skilled at performing on the catwalk, placing her long exquisite legs in front like a stalking tigress. Having been a dancer all my life, I admire her physique and feel clumsy and ungainly in her wake. Her disdain of me is obvious, especially when she comments, "you are too close, please keep your distance!" I follow her carefully obeying her command down the long corridor which used to be so elegant, painted brilliant white with large Georgian windows, which are now cracked and dirty with the walls slashed in red graffiti and excrement. She stops by the silver lifts, long out of action and waits.

"I think...!" I begin to stammer.

"Don't think, it is not your place to do so!" she interjects sharply.

"I was merely going to point out that the lifts are not working!" I add shyly.

She flashes something with her hand, but the action is too swift for me to see properly and the lift slides open to her command and she steps in and I prepare to follow.

"No wait!" She holds out her arm to prevent my entrance into the small space; "Wait for the next one!"

Perplexed, I stand back and obey her order and wait until the elevator door slides open and I step in feeling it sail past the elementary first and second floors flying on and on somewhere out of the building and up into the atmosphere. I am told it takes eight minutes to reach Mars from earth or a little less to the moon. Perhaps I have entered a portal to another planet or a time band heading to the future? I imagine I am in a silver box, like a telephone booth speeding out in space, like a tardis spinning out to the stars. A slight swishing sound indicates our arrival, followed by a pause before the door glides open. I expect to see something spectacular but instead it is dark like an old railway station at night, smelling of diesel oil and engine fumes. She, the beautiful one, waits and commands me to step onto a small wooden ramp. I obey. Suddenly a capsule speeds up to the ramp and she alights like a royal princess, neatly placing her long legs to one side and beckons me to enter where I sit on a small seat opposite her. I am sure the sight of me, disgusts her, as I feel in her eyes, I am a lesser being. I try to open conversation but she ignores me as though she has internally switched off her connection. Outside the silver capsule it is black and I cannot see anything, I only sense we are moving at tremendous speed, faster than light, faster than sound. Then, as the vehicle slows, she turns on her communication code and addresses me;

"We will arrive in forty secundos" I presume she means seconds and she is correct. I count forty seconds precisely and the door opens. Her majesty with her fawn long legs, alights first and turns her back on me. I didn't notice before but at the back of her suit jacket is a cape fixed to her shoulders and it flaps slightly in the breeze, occasionally revealing a long silver zip. Standing under a spotlight in the pitch-blackness, I sense I am being watched and feel uncomfortable not knowing where we are heading. I watch her talking to her wrist, communicating with someone, then she nods commanding me to follow-I presume at a distance, so I hold back and proceed a few paces behind her. We walk up a sharp incline, like an escalator, but it isn't. Madam holds onto a side rail as we walk, so I do the same. Suddenly the walkway dips down and we have to steady ourselves to adjust to the incline, and I am glad I followed her lead, copying her movements, especially when the walkway abruptly swishes sideways to the left where we halt by a large, heavy door.

The door is opened by a strange monkey-boy dressed in a Star-trek-like bellboy uniform. He is like a creature from planet of the apes but with kind eyes and thick brown fur on his head and hands. He is very polite and leads the way down a dark corridor lushly decorated in a dense, plum, flock material.

He graciously opens a door into a large, busy office where people and beings pace up and down calling to each other in strange languages. She indicates for me to wait and walks away in her graceful high heels, promenading towards a set of waiting, empty chairs, where she sits down and proceeds, like a deflating balloon, to collapse and disintegrate inside the long cape zipper at the back of her clothes, leaving a neat black parcel. I stare dumbfounded! A friendly voice addresses me-

"Never seen one of those before? She's our latest Fembot android model. You are privileged they sent her as your assigned guide."

I am relieved, realising her behaviour is purely that of an extremely sophisticated machine obeying orders from a higher authority. It is also re-assuring to know that her beauty is synthetic. I was totally convinced she was human, except perhaps for her blank eyes which were emotionless. It explains everything -no wonder she appeared such a perfect specimen and it makes me feel better to know that she wasn't deliberately being nasty, rather, it was just that she wasn't designed to interact on a personal level.

"When she is needed again she will inflate and return to her assignment." The voice informs me.

Turning, I smile at a young, efficient man in a dark suit, who further states:

"The panel will see you now."

I have no idea what he means and open my mouth to question his statement but it is too late and feeling like Alice in Wonderland about to be put on trial by the Queen of Hearts, I stand in front of a table

where a panel of three beings sit staring at me. I feel you evaporate into the ether as I wait in judgement before the strange creatures. The first is a round, obese man in a chequered suit, like tweedle-dum with a tiny, bald head grossly out of proportion to the rest of his body. His minute head sits inside his shirt collar, hardly visible. The second has a body which is genderless and headless and its body is shaped like a caterpillar with tentacles for arms. The third is a grotesque caricature of an old-fashioned headmistress with purple skin, bulbous green eyes and pink fronds bobbing up and down around her head. The situation reminds me of a job interview and when I enquire the purpose of the grilling, they are surprised at my ignorance and inform me that the post of Ambassador to represent earth would not be suitable for me and dismiss me abruptly. Like Alice in Wonderland, I wonder if they have mistaken me for someone else as I didn't apply for the job, so I am not disappointed, but confused by the situation.

The young man appears again and makes no comment about the job interview, as though he expected me to fail. He leads me towards my Fembot who is all wired up again and I am no longer intimidated by her, knowing that she is a robot. The young man announces: "Galieelia will show you the way." It is an unusual name for a very extraordinary human-look-alike. She turns and commands me to follow her. I now realise that her voice has no distinct nationality because she is a machine and her attitude is not rude, just functional and the reason why she didn't want me to follow too closely is because my vibration could interfere with her delicate, electronic signals. We leave the busy, jostling office and walk down bland curving corridors, brighter and lighter than the others and stop outside a white door with gold numbers inscribed in the centre-299. Galieelia flashes something in her hand and the door opens. She informs me in her automated way:

"You will find everything you need. Call for service if necessary. Goodnight."

She turns and leaves me to inspect my room. I marvel at my situation. At the start of the day, I was an outsider-survivor with little food and no direction as to where I was heading and now I am in the lap of luxury. The plush, white room curves round to the left, where an opaque glass door leads to an amazing, luxurious, black and white bathroom with expensive toiletries, baby-soft towels, white robe and slippers. It is glorious to feel pampered, having forgotten the feeling of self-indulgence. I slowly walk back into the main room which is round, pristinely white and sumptuously decorated. A hand control hangs by the door and I press the top button for service. A hidden door slides open and two white and black plastic robots glide out ; "Good evening madam my name is Roberta. It is my pleasure to be of service during your stay."

The other robot echoes the same speech, except his name is Robert.

"Please press the appropriate button for service. Is the colour to your liking, if not we can change it?" Adds Roberta. How about purple?" I enquire.

"Purple!" they both respond mechanically and everything changes in one flick of a switch to purple and I gasp at the transformation. Just for fun I call out all the colours of the rainbow and watch the whole room change swathed in whatever colour I wish, but then Robert suggests a mood change and I ask him to demonstrate the choices.

"Certainly Madam." He obeys and turns on the virtual reality mode where I am transported to an Hawaiian beach with white sand, blue sea and soft guitar music. Next I am transferred beside a waterfall in a rainforest surrounded by tropical jungle sounds, and then we take a trip up a mountainside and stand looking down an amazing rock face covered in snow.

"Thank you Robert!" I decide I have seen enough and wish to retire in a normal white bedroom and flop onto a luxurious bed. I look around the room but I can't see a bed anywhere.

"The bed Roberta, where is it?"

"Single, double, king size, princess, water bed?" She enquires.

Normally, any kind of bed would suffice but I opt for the water bed, never having slept on one. From a corner of the round room a bed slides out, beautifully made with soft fluffy cushions balancing on the top of an undulating mattress. It is tantalizingly inviting. Here in the touch-button world of imaging anything I desire, it is overwhelming, even more so when Roberta offers me a choice of nightwear ranging from silk pyjamas to flowing nightdresses. I choose pink, silk pyjamas. Robert holds out a menu for me to choose my evening meal and states: "We have a wide selection Madam but we also cater for individual taste."

The menu is wonderfully detailed but I am too tired to browse through the plethora of dishes, so I ask Robert to order a selection of fish dishes and he immediately exits to implement my wishes.

While he is gone, Roberta turns down my bed ready for the night and I take a glorious bath and completely cosset myself with all the treats available. I think I must be in heaven. Dressed in my silk pyjamas and smelling overpoweringly of jasmine, I enter the bedroom where Robert has laid out a sumptuous meal complete with sparkling wine. I cannot remember the last time I dined so extravagantly. I am not sure where to begin as the wide variety of dishes are all my favourite and I attempt to help myself, but Robert insists that he must serve me.

"I hope everything is to your satisfaction Madam?"

I smile, and nod. It is strange to be served so efficiently by robots, although before the first lock-down, my visit to China revealed amazing technological progress on all levels, including hotels purely run by robots. The food is delicious but the indulgence is overwhelming and I only manage to eat half of what is presented. Not being used to the luxury, I suddenly feel insecure and begin to panic wondering where I have been transported.

"Where are we exactly?" I enquire nervously. My question seems to stump both robots and they look at each other to verify their reply.

"We are on target to leave satellite moon in precisely two minutes." Robert affirms.

"Moon satellite?" I question, "You mean we are on the moon right now?"

"Correct!" He confirms in his mechanical manner.

"You mean, this morning in North Yorkshire, I stepped into a lift which transported me to the moon?"

"Also correct Madam?"

"I er, don't understand?" I stammer.

"Madam, on your earth, space and time travel have been kept secret from your people, because the expertise and technology came from aliens from the beginning of time and who, in return for their knowledge were given permission to take DNA from humans to research and understand the species, with a view to creating hybrids and improving the human genus to adapt to your earth's atmosphere."

Suddenly, the front wall of the room slides away revealing a gigantic window and a magnificent view of the galaxy. I glean we are travelling in a space ship, as information of our travel, speed, destination and temperature, appear on a screen.

"Please allow me to assist you?" Robert offers, as he places a safety harness around my waist which is attached to my chair. Then both robots retire to the cupboard leaving me alone to watch the take off. As we soar into space leaving the moon behind, I wonder why we are told so many lies on earth about the true nature of the moon and almost immediately my query is answered. Words flow in my head explaining that: *"the moon is a satellite base, placed in position as part of the tri-structure of earth's creation. The moon, sun and earth are one concept and are interdependent on each other. Many species of aliens inhabit the moon and there are wonderful minerals and precious metals to be mined, that is why so many major countries on earth have a station on the moon."*

The voice fades and memories beyond the beyond return. I remember the moon. I recall that parts of the far side are wondrously beautiful with radiant colours far in excess of earth, with sweet perfumes of flowers and plants that could never be imitated anywhere else and where breathing apparatus isn't necessary. The scenery is intensely powerful drenched in shades you cannot imagine with magnificent forests, purple mountains and stunning violet sunsets. People on earth are misinformed and have named the far side of the moon, the 'dark side' which, in fact is a complete travesty. Humans have a natural fascination for the moon and some have come to realize that it is not a planet but a hollow satellite which has many different layers and levels inside its basin. There are so many secrets earth leaders harbour and moon travel has been one of them for a very long time.

Through the window there is a swirling, misty mass of energy which filters slowly into the ether and as the engines decelerate, the vista clears to reveal the galaxy in all its magnificence. My robots return and Robert unlocks my safety harness. I rise and walk to the screen where earth appears so very, very far away. I am in awe at the exquisite blue planet floating in space, which to my surprise, is not totally round but flat on the top, and similarly it is flatter at the bottom of the planet, where there is a large dark hole at the base of Antarctica and I realize why flights are forbidden to fly directly across the frozen pole because people would become aware of a secret entrance to the earth's crust. Admiral Byrd discovered undisclosed confirmation of strange lands and alien beings beyond the ice wall, but he was killed and his diary locked away with all the evidence of such a nirvana destroyed. Gazing at the beauty of the blue planet, I can't believe that my day had begun on that azure sphere and now I am not sure where I am or where I am going, or what I have to do?

"If Madam pleases, it is time to retire," half commands Roberta.

I nod in abeyance and watch as the food is cleared away and the room is made ready for sleeping.

The only light filtering into the room is the faint glow of the engines' flares. As I wait for sleep, my mind wanders to the mysterious person who floats in and out of my consciousness. She seems so familiar. I know her well, yet I do not know her at all. Perhaps one day I will discover who she is, but now I am tired and my eyes are heavy and I allow the darkness to swallow me in a swirling vortex.

Suddenly alert after a short asleep I am wide awake in the dark. Banging, clanging and noisy disturbance echo down the hall. Lights flash and in the bright glare, I see I am lying on the bottom bunk in a large dormitory. Someone is banging a tin mug on the end of my metal framed bed, shouting;

"Waket auf! Waket auf!"

I rub my eyes in disbelief and watch the mayhem swirl around me. Men and women in army uniforms are rushing to dress and collect their gear. A kind girl in the next bunk hands me my clothes, whispering; "better be quick!" I jump out of bed wearing rough, army issue pyjamas and quickly dress in a black jump suit with a black peaked cap. I don't have time to wonder about my beautiful silk pyjamas, or the luxurious water bed, as I have to hurry to get in line with the rest of the platoon. A back pack is slapped on my shoulders and I look down, surprised to be wearing heavy black, army boots. I can't remember how I got them, or how I joined the army, it's all very confusing.

"Right, left, right, left...!" commands the sergeant as we jog out of the dorm in two parallel lines in the dark. We trot down a long black tunnel and vaguely in the distance I spy a light where everyone is exiting. A breath of cool air wafts over us. Nearing the end, I see the hatch where we are all alighting and I follow everyone down a ramp leading into organised commotion. There must be some kind of mistake or I am dreaming but everything seems so real. I wonder if I can talk to a superior officer to explain my situation? I look around in desperation and catch a glimpse of purple light streaking across a dark mountain range. Unable to do anything but obey, I trundle into the back of an army truck and sit tightly, squashed with others.

No one speaks or attempts to make eye contact. Locked in our own worlds we are transported to an unknown destination.

Suddenly you return-my dark mysterious lady and witness my changed circumstances. It is as much a surprise to me as it is to you. You have become a companion in my lost times and I wonder if you are me from the past or I am you in the future? It is a strange thought but not impossible. A memory fights to filter through my confused mind. I remember at six years old, I was taunted by many dismembered and terrifying spirits that would haunt me at night time. I did not know or understand that my house was built on an ancient Druid burial ground and I was plagued by horrific nightmares, seeing dead bodies buried upright with their faces poking up through the ground, calling out for help as I trod my way through a minefield of gruesome deceased beings. My family did not have a television, only a radio and by that age I had not seen a cinema screen, but I could create from my mind a large screen on my bedroom wall, edged in a purple light onto which faces would appear. For entertainment, I would stare at them for as long as I dared and blink them away when I couldn't meet their gaze. I had visions of future events and could see through walls. My brother and I, before I went to school, played games where I could see through cupboards, wooden doors and wall-papered walls to see where he was hiding. At night, lying in bed I would be taught by invisible spirits how to leave my body and was shown Tibetan monk meditation techniques by unearthly beings. I remember a vision so clearly of being grown-up and advancing through a dark tunnel and seeing a tiny light at the end, where I entered an unfamiliar bleak, authoritative, military location. I saw myself dressed in a black jump suit with white-blond hair, commanding people and teaching dance and physical manoeuvres. It was a very vivid vision and I remember thinking, as a six year old... "so that's what I am meant to do?" Now I am in that situation and I recognise myself from the vision.

The truck halts and we all pile out onto a hard core parade ground where we are sorted into groups and dispatched. My group is taken to our billet but I am escorted in a different direction by a young corporal. I follow him into an office, where seated behind a large wooden desk is a very attractive lady with shoulder-length auburn hair, and deep blue eyes. Her military uniform is well cut and suits her slender figure.

"Sit down please." She orders firmly.

I sit in front of her and watch her open a file. I wait until she speaks.

"You want answers and we want what you have been given for safe-keeping. So where shall we begin?"

She smiles reassuringly and sits back in her captain's chair.

"I, er, want to know what's happening and why I am here, and how I got here and…?"

"Yes, yes, just a moment, one question at a time." She leans forwards and glances at the file.

"Let me explain something to you about the human brain-you humans, that is most humans, for there are many different levels of human being, but most intelligent homo sapien sapiens have a brain that produces the same chemical when assimilating reality and fantasy."

"I'm sorry I don't understand?"

"It means that to the human brain, the chemical produced by imagination and actuality is equal, to sum up – the brain does not know the difference between the two and therefore it is easy to deceive a human, if one so wishes."

"I see," I reply softly.

"No, I don't think you do see, my dear. The world is much more complicated, calculating and manipulative than you ever imagined. You have no idea the magical methods, devices, processes, systems and schemes which can be executed to achieve whatever goals the hierarchy sets.

Numerous fundamental concepts which you have been taught from birth are lies, devised to prevent you and your human species from knowing your true identity. There are many reasons for this, but suffice it to know for now, that nothing is what you think it is! The idea that the earth was created as a hologram is difficult to grasp and the hypothesis that the universe is a conscious, living entity and everything is connected by strands of energy, are concepts beyond imagining. You are wondering where you fit into all this. Well I can tell you my dear, you can blame it all on your Father for your early childhood training."

"Training? Is that what it was? Holding my head under water at the age of two to teach me what it was like to drown. Being dragged out of bed at night and beaten for no reason and other physical abuse to toughen me up for adulthood," I blurt out.

She strokes her chin, and continues:

"Your Father being a war hero, with his Celtic fiery temper and flaming red hair, with great physical acumen, and will-power, possessed a particular strain of DNA. If this is passed on to a first-born daughter, she will possess special psychic, psionic gifts. It is not the same for a first-born son, it must be a girl and first-born. When he was in the army he was approached by those in authority to let us say, allow the elite to adopt his first born daughter, for a great price, of course."

Shocked, I gasped in disbelief but it was all beginning to make sense.

"Remember he was a young man and had no concept of what it would be like to be a Father and the idea of receiving a great deal of money for virtually nothing, was very appealing to him."

Nothing? Money? Yes of course, money. I remember the time, the place, the day when he told me he was going to sell me!

"Don't look so shocked, it happens to many young girls and still continues. Gifts like yours are used in many different ways and are very useful."

Tears fall silently, I begin to see the picture clearly, even the comments from my Father's death-bed – "I am sorry for what I did to you," now makes sense.

"Come, come my dear, he did not have the heart to sell you. He redacted his contract. Instead it was agreed you would be used on a training programme."

That also made sense of all the strange things that happened to me as a child, "so all the visions that I saw and experienced were they real or fantasy?" I tentatively enquire remembering my Mother taking me to the Doctor when I was little, thinking I was insane for conversing with invisible presences for hours. The Doctor assured her that I had an over-imaginative mind.

"The training involved being part of a military unit on Mars."

I am astonished. "But how could that be?" I enquire.

"Very easy my dear. Time on earth is not the same as time elsewhere. You were taken when you were six, that is six earth years, and when you were transported to Mars, your time accelerated so that you grew into a young woman very quickly and worked there for many years. When you returned home into earth time, your Mars time would only account for a matter of minutes and your memory on Mars would be erased."

Now I understand the vision of the tunnel and the black uniform. Snippets of remembrance would sometimes filter back at odd times but I thought I was imagining things, but now I comprehend the biological reason that the brain cannot distinguish between reality and fantasy and accept how everything can be muddled in a child's mind.

"Look we are running out of time and we need you to do something for us." She places the file in a cabinet and leads me to the door.

"Of course there is much more to discuss, but I am afraid it must be for another time. Come this way."

I follow her down a corridor leading off to lots of small offices and out across a courtyard to a large community hall, where important officials stand to attention as we enter and a packed audience graciously waits. I expect to take a seat near the back of the auditorium but I am lead to the front and escorted up onto the podium. I turn to look at the lady commander and she whispers, smilingly, "they're waiting for you!" I gulp and panic not knowing what to do. Everyone seems to know me. A figure approaches dressed in purple and white robes and tall hat like a druid priest and suddenly we are all clad in the same sacred robes and are congregating in an ancient temple made of fine marcasite, glistening and sparkling in the dim, hallowed light. Sweet, silent chanting pulses as the priest holds out his hands towards me. I reach for the golden square around my neck and unhook it from the simple shoe lace handing it carefully to him. A wonderful high-pitched note resounds from the community and echoes around the temple. The priest places the golden square inside a bright golden chalice and it miraculously transforms into pure molten liquid, which he pours into a gilded bowl. The amethyst stone slides into his hands and he gives it to me to keep. As the golden liquid settles in the bowl it slowly turns into tiny shards of dust, like fairy sprinkles from a magic wand. As the dust shards are stirred, they metamorphose into tiny golden keys and when the bowl is filled to the brim with them glistening in the light, the chanting crescendos into a glorious, powerful song of joy.

The priest elevates the chalice spilling over with tiny golden keys and the roof of the temple evaporates into pulsing, cosmic energy. Telepathically, the priest asks me to blow on the keys. I open my mouth and an electric breeze enthuses forth, raising the keys with a gentle, powerful push out into the universe to ride the clouds and settle in the air to land in the conscious minds of those ready to receive golden opportunities, to unlock their higher conscious channel to receive new teachings, to become a wiser and better soul.

I don't know why I was chosen for the special mission, I just accede graciously to all that has been revealed to me without judgement. I now have a greater understanding of myself and events that have shaped my being. That is all anyone can wish for. I am glad you are with me and in time we will learn much more together, for you will also learn about yourself, and who you are and where you came from and where you are meant to be. I do not know what lies ahead but I know there is a universal pathway leading onwards and I will be guided, for I am Lucky.

CHOOSE YOUR DRAGON

Where am I? I open my eyes and sit up in a wooden bed, cosily covered by a home-made crocheted blanket. How did I get here? In my conscious state I was last in an army encampment somewhere in the universe but now all I hear is crashing surf pounding against an emptiness as I spy grey, white-topped waves rushing to a deserted shore. I am inside a compact cabin where everything is neatly set out with military precision. What am I doing here? I am lost in a 'hollowness', like the time of the first lock-down, waking day after day to a smudged routine of nothing. I am not used to a blank canvas or being suspended in limbo struggling to forge a pathway towards a new horizon of survival. Newness and change can be terrifying and wondrous -like giving birth, and birth of the new world was certainly painful, especially for the elderly. The planned World Reset, slyly and surreptitiously, like a thief in the night, stole lives. People were fed the bitter kernel of fear so they were afraid to speak out when they were cheated of their civil liberty rights and without realising it, before it was too late, became prisoners of their own choosing. Now, in a different situation I have to be the change, embrace the newness and work the challenge. I have long abandoned my security crutches to stare worthlessness in the face-accepting 'aloneness' rather than loneliness. The cruelty of 'self-isolation' for the aged during home imprisonment, where many had to die abandoned and separated from their loved ones was horrendous. A gentle voice in my head reminds me, that however alone we think we are, there is always someone listening to our thoughts. My whisperers tell me:

"You need strength to die and courage to release the past, for when you are closest to death you are most alive!"

During the first lock-down my whisperers gave me a mantra to repeat when I felt depressed and lonely – *"I am magnificently alone!"*

The notion of glorification of 'aloneness' is inspiring and something I try desperately to adopt, but I still deeply mourn the loss of my family, friends, dancers and students.

Now as I climb out of the cramped bed, shouting my mantra: "I am magnificently alone" my words echo around the cabin and fade into the vacuum. Memory seeps back and I am drawn to my last assignment and wonder if it was a dream. The Commanding Officer's words echo in my head: "the chemical produced in the brain is the same for fantasy and reality and therefore the brain does not know the difference between the two – consequently it is easy to deceive humans."

So was the mission real or fantasy? I touch my neck where the golden pendant hung, recalling it was turned into myriads of minute golden keys unleashed into the atmosphere to help unlock higher conscious truths to those ready to receive the knowledge. The trip to the Moon and Mars – were they real? Is reality an illusion? Einstein thought so. I ask my whisperers if my experience was real and there is silence. Then a soothing voice in my head replies;

"Yes and no. It was real in the sense that you executed the mission, but you must understand that it is possible to be out of your body and accomplish other things at the same time as being in your body elsewhere. Understanding the laws of a parallel universe is important when trying to unravel such mysteries."

The voice fades and I am left pondering the reality of the experience.

Standing in the centre of the compact chalet I wonder who owns it? It is a well-equipped survival outpost, with pots, pans, and wood-burning stove and even books. I spy a note on the tiny table addressed to 'LUCKY' and read it out loud:

"TO LUCKY – as indeed you are!

Thank you for your help in the last assignment, you might say – mission accomplished. You will have all you need for the time being and contact will be made later. In the meantime enjoy your holiday."

The note is unsigned and I wonder if I am being used, or guided by my people as part of their plan?

My whisperers have answers but aren't always forthcoming with explanations. I understand a little about laws of parallel universes because I have had experience of such. When you take on an obligation in 'world service', your duty is to help people whenever and wherever you can, whether you are asleep or awake. In such service you give yourself permission to go out of your body at night to help the living or recently deceased who cannot accept that they are dead and who need guidance to be escorted to the stairway beyond. I remember one night finding myself out of my body and wandering to the top of my street where I found a neighbour's little girl out in the cold in her nightdress. She said she was waiting for her Father who hadn't returned home. I was worried about her and she was getting cold, so I persuaded her to go indoors where I escorted her back to bed, assuring her that all would be well and stayed until she fell asleep. A week later I saw her mother, who was a nurse and she said, "I don't understand – but I have to thank you." I looked puzzled, then remembered her little daughter being out late at night by herself. She continued;

"Sara told me she was out looking for her Daddy when you found her and took her back to bed and stayed with her until she fell asleep. Thank you but I don't understand how you…?" I told her not to worry and that my only concern was for the safety of her child. She accepted this and never questioned it again.

Similarly, one night having given myself permission to travel out of my body to help those in need whilst asleep, I found myself on board a Russian submarine which was in trouble. The captain with his crew were stuck inside the vessel not able to rise to the surface or escape and they all drowned. I saw the Captain very clearly with his strawberry blonde hair tucked underneath his cap and his cloudy blue eyes searching for answers. There was commotion on board until all was silent. There were many of us helping the lost souls to enter a new world. I helped the Captain and he followed me obediently to a portal of glorious, glowing energy, where we, the light workers had to stay back until all the men sailed safely into the radiance and were greeted by shimmering beings on the other side. On waking the next morning I remembered the episode very clearly and told a friend. In amazement she asked me if I had read the news about the Russian submarine disaster, where the captain and crew were all drowned and she showed me the headlines and a picture of the captain with his strawberry blonde hair tucked under his cap and his deep blue eyes just the same as I had seen the previous night.

Souls who have died in traumatic circumstances often have the most difficulty in transitioning and one shocking case in particular happened when I was working in Barcelona and had invited my fifteen year old daughter for a short break, to show her the magic of Las Ramblas street performers and the magisterial architecture of Gaudi's Sagrada Familia. Our hotel was situated in a very old part of the city, where there had been many ancient Churches, where Moors, alongside Spanish kings had left their mark, together with persecuted Jews and Indian princes. It was strange that our room was in an annexe far removed from the main hotel and being alone in the wing, we had to walk through a myriad of glass fire doors to reach the foyer. It didn't matter because we were excited to see the sights and returned later that evening exhausted. My daughter got into bed and soon drifted off to sleep but woke startled, crying, "Mum, Mum, someone touched my arm, they did, they did, I felt it! Please stay with me until I go to sleep".

I sat on the bed next to her and stroked her hair. I was puzzled because it wasn't like her to be so distressed. When she was soundly asleep, I got into my own bed feeling uncomfortable as an eerie presence descended. I was used to dealing with lost souls, helping them to cross over, but the manifestation of something so forceful and powerful closing in on me was terrifying. The hairs on my left arm stiffened and stood on end like the bristles of a harsh toothbrush and my head locked in fear facing my right side. My body went rigid. The air grew cold, like the icy atmosphere in an antiquated church and I tried to hide under the covers but couldn't move a muscle. I could only stare as spirits approached. An old man peered over my bed wearing long robes and a young boy, also in long hand-woven clothes stood by his side, while others glided stealthily behind them, banding together in a tribe.

I must have passed out in terror and woke the next morning trembling at the thought of the encounter, but dared not tell my daughter as it was they who had touched her arm. That day we were meeting my son who was studying in Barcelona and I told him about the visitation. He explained that in the city, centuries ago, there was great conflict between, the Moors, the Jews and the Spanish and many Jews were burnt to death in Churches. He suggested that the souls of the dead were still trying to escape but needed help to cross over, saying, "who better to help them Mum, they've probably been waiting a long time for someone like you!"

I heeded his advice and was determined that night to overcome my fear to help the long lost souls.

When my daughter was asleep, knowing they were waiting in the shadows, I lay down to go under in meditation and encase myself in a protective bubble to prevent being sucked into a vortex with the spirits. In deep concentration I placed myself in the sacred silence where the thick, musty scent of religious ritual surrounded the dead souls who were imprisoned in their time-warp, pleading to escape. The old man, the boy, women with veiled heads, mothers, daughters and elderly folk gathered around me. I listened to their tragic story of abuse and their attempt to flee the city and locked themselves in a Church but were burnt alive. The strength and power of their communal faith and belief that they would all be saved, held them captive to their earthly condition, preventing them from naturally passing on to the next life. In that way they remained trapped. In the action of becoming a conduit for their freedom, I was not afraid, for I was trained for the purpose and gave myself over unconditionally to the mission.

Purple energy surged above and around me opening a portal in my solar plexus which reached beyond into the cosmos. Purple the highest healing energy with the strength of a panther curled and coiled around my body creating a starlit stairway home for the lost ones. The old man approached first with all-embracing gratitude thanking me for my help, then instantaneously he passed through my body, sailing out on translucent energy where he escaped beyond. The exodus happened quickly as the spirits sailed through me one after the other, shaking my body uncontrollably as each soul passed. My daughter in the next bed convulsed as though they were also passing through her too.

Lightning bolts of electric tentacles flashed around the room whipping the celling, exploding with flashing pink streaks as thunder rolled joyously, celebrating the departure of spirits fleeing through a tunnel of glorious light. Outside a storm raged lighting up the night sky with fiery flares cascading past our window. Gradually as the first new flecks of dawn speckled the horizon, all was calm and still. Our room was silent and no longer icy cold. As daylight crept into our bedroom my daughter woke and smiled. We both knew the disturbing presence had disappeared and I was relieved that the souls were finally at peace.

Now I accept my situation in the cabin awaiting another assignment. Clothes are laid out on a small table and a waxed, green weather-all coat hangs on a peg behind the door. Everything is my size. I need a walk to clear my head. I lift the little green latch, bracing myself to face the cold wind, when I spy an open book on the dresser with an underlined quotation in green ink: "*She washed, dusted and cleaned in the company of angels.* "I read it out loud and laugh. I understand the message. No matter how menial the task or how great the assignment or how leisurely the vacation, we are never alone, as there is always a celestial Presence. The message accompanies me along the seashore as I childishly splash the edge of the waves in my green wellies. Therapeutic sploshing and splashing spontaneously break into joyous jumping and I twirl into a magnificent leap and land in the squelching sand. The moment is all embracing, pacing, picking up speed like a race horse freed from the race. Unhindered by living, unbound by expectation, no longer suppressed or repressed by outside forces, I rejoice in my freedom. Buzzing to hold earth's dynamism close, knowing that the potency of the earth is the earth itself, not the people, for they are merely guests who will arrive and depart, my body tingles, gulping in air and my head spins. Taking in earth's diurnal life force, I am content. I have not been able to run for a long time and in this new situation, in a different setting I am given a new lease of life and I am grateful, for now I can run with the wind and leap over puddles.

A solitary beautiful shell glistens in the water and I retrieve it, noting its exquisite mother-of-pearl opalescence shimmering in the light, but on wiping it dry, it loses its striking charm. Is this life? Do we only sparkle for a short while before we are hauled into the dockyard to dry out and left to rot?

To see beauty in a vision under water – is it an illusion if it vanishes when it rises to the surface? I stare across the choppy sea pondering the human condition. Is it possible for humans to live in peace and happiness? I remember the riots and the shocking violence during the first pandemic arising from the murder of a black man by a white American police officer. The whole world, like a coiled spring let loose, retaliated, fanning the flames of racist hostility. It was a time when the world drastically changed with radical protestors rioting and rebelling against centuries of racist abuse. But racism of what kind? Do we ever see the full picture, the complete truth of any situation? The whole world like a wall of dominoes crashed down because of the murder of one black man, but what violence had that man perpetrated against a pregnant woman, threatening her life and that of her unborn child for the purpose of obtaining drugs? The picture changes when the truth is unravelled.

Turmoil upon turbulence, upon layer of havoc and confusion exploded – it was as though Mother Earth was cleansing the sins of the world's immoral lineage. I recall standing in the entrance hall to a masonic lodge, sensing the licence for evil wrong-doing given to those embracing the power of infused ritual masonic ceremony. The black and white tiled floor represented the eternal struggle between good and evil, which according to the cult, is a necessary force behind their secret code, where everything has to be revealed in plain sight, in order that members do not receive karmic retribution for any malevolence pledged in their name. Earth planet, is a unique sphere where Gaia watches her children make choices for better or for worse. Choice is everything and makes an eternal difference to spiritual growth.

Slowly, I make my way back to the chalet along the desolate shore and feel your presence descend like an old friend. Once again you are my only companion and I know you are here to watch and learn, but my friend I cannot vouch to give you what you seek. I have been placed here to take time out and I wonder what benefit you might glean from this situation. My whisperers interject:

"Break through the stone to find the gem; break through the dark to know the light; breakthrough the lesson to learn the truth!"

I understand the message and feel chastised for my lack of insight. I know that the treasure we seek lies within and that we must always have our antennae for good on red alert and our 'dream machine' running at all times. As I contemplate the shoreline wondering in what part of the country this beautiful coastline is situated, I spy other abandoned chalets, derelict like ghost shadows lurking in the sandy dunes, as the wind wistfully invokes the memory of children's laughter rolling across the deep. Drawing close to one of the beach huts, still maintaining a lived-in appearance, I creep along the veranda and the door nudges open with a little push, releasing the smell of long lost family life lingering in boxes of toys, tattered puppets and children's paintings displayed on the wall. A few postcards remain on the rusting fridge door with little magnets saying 'Welcome to Cornwall.' The views show tourist attractions of the Cornish coast, ice-cream and white sands with holiday – makers having fun. My query is answered. The Cornish coastline as I remember is truly picturesque. The time of year I guess, is late September as the trees are resplendent in their glorious red and golden canopies, but I do not know the year. It seems many years have passed since the third pandemic and the cataclysmic disasters that struck the planet, but time now, in this moment is inconsequential and I saunter back to my chalet collecting drift-wood along the way to make a comforting inferno in the wood burning stove.

Back in my cosy cabin, I check the fridge and am delighted to find all my favourite food stocked neatly in categories, from vegetables, cheese, eggs, fish and other treats. Someone knows me well.

The note said 'holiday' and I am puzzled. Why would I be given the chance to have a vacation by the sea in Cornwall? I ponder this as I sit by the fire with hot melted cheese-toast and a glass of sparkling wine. Gratified, I watch the flames soar and flicker casting shadows on the freshly painted walls. The cabin must have been recently renovated with its fresh clean appearance and as I look around I notice a control panel by the kitchen sink and study it. I press a green button and watch the lights automatically dim as a hologram of a man glides from the wall. He is tall, with light blonde hair, matching beard and moustache, wearing an American Colonel's uniform.

"Hi there. My name is Colonel J.R. Gerald. I'm here for the purpose of your training."

And I thought it was to be a holiday – there had to be a catch somewhere?

"Training will begin tomorrow at 9 am sharp. In the meantime please acquaint yourself with material to be studied in the book, 'The Men Who Stare at Goats'." The apparition wavers and fades like a shimmering mirage in the desert and glides back into the wall. I wonder if the chalet has been fitted with all kinds of modern technology especially to be used as a training outpost? I glance at the neat book shelf and note the paperback has been marked for my attention with a message:

'Please engage with this non-fictional work. It is based on a true account of a group of men with paranormal and psychic gifts who are assigned by the American army, to use their talents to help the military in their espionage reconnaissance. The group of men have psychic skills such as remote viewing-that is using paranormal insight to travel to a set place to observe events from a distance.

But of course you are acquainted with this technique. Also listening to conversations far removed from the listener – which of course you already have experience. The book gets its title from one of the men who claimed to be able to kill a goat by staring at it. Of course you will not be required to do this, but we trust you will find the content interesting.'

I am very interested in the content of the book and very surprised to learn that the American military placed such credibility in paranormal and psychic skills. Ever since I was a small child I had psychic ability and naturally used my gift to 'remote view' as a means of entertaining myself, although I never knew others did it, or that it was a recognised phenomenon.

I settle down with the book and become totally engrossed, relating it to my own psychic experiences and begin to see connections as to why the military might want to use me. Long before the first lock-down I had alarming extra-terrestrial encounters, which some might term as 'alien abductions' but I somehow think that I had given my permission to be taken when I was a child and so the word 'abduction' seems inaccurate. I know that the American military did tests on me using Grey Aliens, but I always felt they were robots and not real beings. One evening when I was remote viewing, I involuntarily travelled to an underground military base and entered a large warehouse, where I watched two men sitting at a desk dressed in black uniforms and black caps.

They were security officers watching multiple tv screens. I floated past them, entering a massive storage space where many costumes of Grey aliens hung on rails. I realised that the outer suits of the Greys shielded and protected robotic androids and that the

American Army were using them in their reconnaissance work. I was taken many times, but on one occasion I was approached by a senior military official and offered some work, but I refused, as I was uncertain of the implications.

I wake early, having devoured the book and am reasonably equipped with background information ready for the Colonel. I am both nervous and excited for the training ahead, so seated, I wait for the hologram to appear at 9 am and true to form the Colonel appears from the slot in the wall. You are with me and watch from a distance. He greets me with military politeness and I note his film-star good looks as he parades up and down walking and talking. "I have been chosen to pass on higher knowledge to you, which in time you will teach others. The information will be paramount to your understanding of events that will take place later. It has nothing to do with the military at this point and you may meet me in the future for further elucidation."

I nod and he proceeds:

"It is a soldier's primary goal to save his or her life at all costs, so that he or she may save others. This is ACTING FROM PRIMARY MOTIVATION." He accentuates his statement by pointing to the board with his parade stick where the words are heavily underlined.

"Primary Motivation should be the core of your life's mission; that is everything you do, say or think must spring from your primary motivation source. Now this may sound selfish and contrary to religious teaching, but you enter this world alone and you exit alone and during the interim battle you fight for your survival alone. It is not being selfish, but merely sensible. It is vital that you wish the best for yourself at all times. To help you to achieve this you must think 'Golden'. Surround yourself with golden energy from your higher consciousness and you will find that everything will stem from the purest motive. When you begin to trust to your higher purpose there will be a change in your perception of the world... you have a question?" He pauses.

"What if I saw a child about to be hit by a car and jumped in front to save her – would this be wrong?"

He laughs. "I knew you were going to ask that question. Your actions when they are initiated from your primary source will be correct. Nothing is ever wrong when you are living in your Primary skin.

Whilst you are in the highest state of love, your reaction to the child would be to save her. If you were killed in action then you would have been doing your duty as a soldier. If you died, then it would mean that your primary source lead you to that moment, which was of your choosing."

"I sort of get it." I interrupt him but he continues regardless.

"Acting from a secondary source or motive is selfish."

Puzzled, I am moved to ask another question but the Colonel pushes on.

"An action undertaken with secondary motives usually feeds the ego and is self-aggrandising, which brings down spiritual energy into a denser, darker place. If you, for example give away a lump sum of money to charity and want other people to know about it, or do it for tax exemption, or for courting popularity-your motives are secondary and not springing from your primary source. Do you understand the difference?"

I nod and wonder where the instruction is leading.

"And you wonder where this is all leading?"

I nod again.

"Understanding the concept of being your best at all times encourages you to live every day of your life like a warrior, believing each day is your last and so giving it your best shot. Remember think 'golden' at all times."

His last words echo as the image flickers and fades inside the wall and I remember my experience of the golden, Adonis who gave me a key to pass on to others in order to open their minds to higher spiritual teaching. I mull over his lecture and decide to take a walk by the sea. The idea that all actions, thoughts and words should spring from primary source and to think 'golden' at all times is a new concept and one which I resolve to try to adopt.

Outside the air is fresh and I breathe deeply enjoying the sharp spray swept inland by the light breeze. I wonder if this strange period is a spiritual sabbatical? Did I lose all sense of self during the pandemics, and become lost and confused as the outburst of riots and chaos infectiously spread across the world? It was the hoax of the century. I stood by helplessly as my life evolved into an existence I never imagined. Perhaps I died a long time ago and have transitioned away from earth?

But as the sun breaks through the cloud, spreading a glorious haze over the white sand, creating a golden pathway, I smile recalling the Colonel's 'think gold' motto and want to bathe and steep myself in the bright yellow sunshine. I am very much alive in the moment. Perhaps I didn't die; but what is death? "There is no death;" the wind sings and my whisperers speak of powerful, invisible forces ready to help from beyond, some of whom reside in a realm long discarded and relegated to stories, mythology and fantasy. Creatures who were once an integral part of all human existence now walk invisibly side by side on earth with humans, but being of another vibrational energy can only be accessed by those with special antennae to receive their signal. Cornwall is renowned for its folk-law and I remember pictures from my childhood of Cornish mythical creatures and ancient tales of dragons, Kelpies, and Faeries and felt their presence and heard their pan-pipe music, especially when my night terrors descended.

The golden pathway fades as the sun darts behind the cloud and I make my way back to the cabin. I need hot soup, warm bread and to rest by the wood burning stove to wait out my time. Loneliness can be cruel, like the torture of a slow drip, dripping tap, but I know there is purpose ahead and all I can do is be grateful for the present. Feeling drowsy by the fire with the gentle crackle of burning logs, I momentarily dose, drifting into a world I loved, in a time when my family gathered around the dining table to feast, drink and laugh.

As I sink into the contentment, treasuring the memory, lights flash and a 3D screen appears on the far wall displaying photographs of Antarctica with bright white ice mountains and floating icebergs set haphazardly adrift in a dazzling blue ocean. As the pictures are presented one by one, a monotone voice drones in the background:

"Your remote-viewing trips to Antarctica have been noted. It has also been drawn to our attention that you strayed, on occasions into unauthorised areas. For this reason a blocking code was issued preventing you from further visits. For the present this code has been erased as you are needed to make a return call, but firstly you are required to answer a few questions."

I do not answer in the deafening pause.

"Very well, we will begin by asking you the purpose of your visit?"

"I was just fascinated by the idea of a secret continent and wondered what was hidden there." I reply nonchalantly.

"Who sent you?"

"No one sent me. I sent myself!"

A terrible sharp pain pierces the top of my big toe. I shriek. I know the hurt because they have inflicted the same puncture torture before.

"I told you I went there myself, no one sent me!" I gasp.

The stab is repeated and sustained. I suck in my cheeks fighting the pain. Then it stops abruptly.

"What did you find when you ventured into the unauthorised cavern?"

This time the intense pain pierces my right heel and I reel in agony. Then it ceases and I struggle to speak but manage to continue:

"I wandered past a section of glass cases with bodies floating in liquid. Some had pipes leading from their stomachs with bubbles ballooning upwards, others were static. There were humans and non-human-like creatures that looked like unfinished experiments."

"Go on!" They prompt.

"Well I didn't look very closely as they frightened me and I hurried on towards large black doors engraved with an enormous black sun which opened into what looked like an ancient temple. There were, I think, eight gigantic, whitemarble sarcophagi placed on pedestals."

"Did you look inside?"

"Yes."

"And what did you see?"

I gulp and pause and they prod my heel again. The sharp intense pain shoots to my stomach.

"I saw a giant man, regally dressed like a king. He had long, ginger curly hair, splayed out on a white silk pillow and a golden crown rested on his brow. He had a thick ginger moustache and long beard.

He was wearing fine woven garments in the style of a Roman ruler. His face was beautiful. He looked peaceful. I think he was in stasis. I stepped to move away and suddenly his eyes opened. They were startlingly bright blue. I was afraid and brought myself back very quickly."

I wait in deadly silence. It is as though my answers are being dragged through a sieve. "Thank you. That will suffice for now. We will discuss your other visits later. Wait for further instructions."

The screen slides back into the wall in the early evening darkness. The fire has almost burnt itself out and I open the stove door to pile on more logs. I am glad they did not probe further into my clandestine visits to Antarctica because I know some terrible secrets and have seen some astonishing scenes that are too shocking to reveal. During the World Reset Programme (W.R.P.) people world-wide became accustomed to a new global police state but they did not know that World Governments answer to a higher alien intelligence based in Antarctica. A few years before the first lock-down world leaders were summoned to Antarctica in secret, the purpose of which was never disclosed. Thirty nations operated research stations there and were not allowed to reveal any of their findings. The fact that no plane was ever allowed to fly over the secret area, (and still are not) was suspicious and that when Admiral Byrd discovered the truth about Antarctica and Middle-earth with giant inhabitants, he was murdered. The Nazis built a base in Antarctica and Hitler paid visits there and on one occasion took with his entourage, forty German virgins. When Buzz Aldrin, a well-known astronaut of his day, was invited to pay an unofficial visit, he became seriously ill and had to be air-lifted out. Later he tweeted: "we are all in danger, it is evil itself." Was his sudden illness caused by the shock of learning the intended plans to cull humanity? The ruling Alien intelligence has inhabited Antarctica since time began and claims that humans are part of an on-going experiment, which is why they have no conscience about culling humanity. Yes, I know secrets and they know I know!

In the distance the sea crashes pounding a gentle rhythm and an old song slides into my mind … 'the rhythm of life is a powerful thing….feel it in your fingers, feel it in your bones…' I rise and want to dance…imagining the music, I sing out loud and parade around the tiny cabin. Suddenly the song plays from speakers strategically placed around the room, resounding in a magnificent acoustic blast. I am surprised and try out another just for fun… 'Oh I do like to be beside the seaside…' it picks up the tune and an old-fashioned brass band thumps out the melody. Then I request a classical favourite and it immediately responds. I cry. I love the music. It brings back so many wistful memories. Realisation dawns – I am imprisoned in an advanced techno world encased in a rural, basic shack by the sea. I am probably under constant surveillance. Perhaps I have always been watched by other worldly beings? I walk outside and sit on the porch gazing up into the star-studded night and search for signs of my people. Inadvertently, I begin deep breathing and go under in meditation and find myself remote viewing a large stretch of open sea with massive floating ice blocks bobbing on the water. I recognise the icebergs of Antarctica. They said I would return. I am travelling inside a black triangular craft flying stealthily over the mountains, but I am also outside the craft watching it dip low to a cave opening inside the ice which is cleverly camouflaged by large mirrors reflecting icy mountains. The aperture is also triangular shaped and the ship glides inside the ice, banking to the left, then right and flies out into a large lake where the air is warm like a summer's day. In the middle of the lake there is an island with square buildings constructed from a dark-brown substance-not bricks. It appears to be a landing station where craft take-off and land and I watch the black ship descend and disappear rapidly underground. It is as though it is swallowed whole in one gulp. I float inside one of the dark buildings through a glass door which slides open and shuts like an automatic airport door. From the darkness of the arrival bay I enter a bright, white monorail encased under a massive crystal-like dome. A pod swishes forwards to the platform, shaped like a bullet made from a Perspex-type of material. I enter the pod. There are two blue seats inside facing each other. The doors swiftly close then the pod speeds downwards, suddenly submerging into a deep water marine world with luminescent dancing corals twirling through waves and electric blue fishes darting and spinning in shoals. The underwater monorail ride is a short sea adventure and soon I arrive at a platform where a conveyor belt transports people and beings to a strange machine with fairground-like mechanical octopus arms. I step into a small cubicle and the arms begin to move simultaneously in different directions dropping passengers off on designated floors. I alight at the third floor which leads to a plush hallway decorated in red and gold Chinese symbols. Although I am travelling in my ethereal body, I am still acknowledged and can be seen as energy in the shape of a body, rather than a body housing energy. I am met by a small Chinese lady dressed in a red and gold sarong. She guides me quickly to a lavish apartment but I do not have time to appreciate it as another young Chinese girl with a long black pony tail ushers me to a lift which takes us to an underground cave. I stand at the top of steep rocky steps where the dark, damp air clings to my clothes. I look upwards but can't see the top of the cave, only overhanging bleak clefts of stone jutting out in all directions and the sound of dripping water echoes softly as it falls miles below. The smell of wet animal fur, like that of caged animals in a zoo wafts on a cool current of air sifting from an invisible vent. The young girl beckons me to follow her down the jagged steps adding, "you will inspect the dragons?"

"What? Did she just say dragons?"

I stop in my tracks horrified, paralysed with fear, but the girl ignores my reaction and in a matter-of-fact manner shoos me along the steps and makes me follow her to the bottom. Nonchalantly, she glides along as though she is giving me a guided tour of a furniture store. Our footsteps resonate in the emptiness as we round a dark, bleak corner to where a high steel barrier is erected. I stare through the steel cage and sense something lying at the back of the enclosure. Hazily, I spy a dark, damp rocky wall but then as my eyes grow accustomed to the gloom, I make out the form of a gigantic creature. I am alarmed. I stare in disbelief and am rooted to the spot. It moves slightly and turns its grotesque head towards me, opening its eyes baring its fanged teeth and then it grunts and coils back burying its head by the side of its scaly tail.

"Blue dragon" states the girl.

I shudder with disgust and step backwards finding my feet. The blue dragon remains asleep and I am relieved to be lead away to another cage.

"Red dragon!" She states indifferently. The beast is on its feet, with its head scraping the high rocky roof. It snorts scratching its claws along the stone floor like a bull in a ring preparing to fight a matador. I cling to the girl and she laughs. Its fierce, powerful reptilian green eyes bulge and glare at me through the bars and my stomach twists in revulsion. The monster is a horror, made from movie nightmares. I turn away repelled by the stench of its scaly body and am lead to the next cage.

"Green dragon." She sighs, bored with the tour and unimpressed by my cowardice. The green dragon lies asleep curled with its head under its tail and doesn't respond to our presence. I am relieved it is peaceful. The tour seems to be over as the girl leads me back towards the stairs pausing, and enquires: "You don't like any dragon?"

I am dumbfounded and don't know how to reply and have no idea why I was given a tour of different dragons, furthermore I have no interest or experience of dragons, other than that of cartoons or animated films. Dragons in my understanding are ferocious mythical beasts, with a history of eating and tearing humans to pieces or burning them alive with their fire-flaming breath.

"I'm sorry," I reply apologetically, "but I have no idea why I am here!"

"You will choose a dragon, or rather your dragon will choose you!" she states.

"But I don't want a dragon!"

"Like I said your dragon will choose you!" She states impatiently and leads me back up the rocky steps to the red apartment where the first Chinese lady waits. On seeing her, the young girl shakes her head in dismay and leaves the room, making me feel like a school child being summoned to the head's office. "So you do not like any of our dragons?" She smiles insincerely.

"Er...no, I don't really want one, thank you!"

She laughs and signals me to sit down.

"Ahh you have much to learn and understand. You are being guided onto a new vibrational level of spiritual learning. You have proved yourself as a light – worker, spiritual teacher and healer and now you are being given the chance to step further into understanding, knowledge, and higher consciousness. Previously you had two familiars looking after you – your precious tiger and your beloved black panther. Now you are ready for your dragon. All light-workers who reach a certain level of awareness are given a specific dragon because, you see dragons are powerful teachers and guides with unbelievable knowledge. You will choose a dragon to enlighten you, but most importantly your dragon will choose you. You must prove to be worthy of a dragon's attention. There are many different kinds of dragon and each has its unique colour for specific reasons. You are not drawn to any you have just seen?" She enquires.

I ponder her words and assess the dragons I have just witnessed. The blue one was aware that I was there but wasn't interested. The red one certainly didn't like me and the green one slept on blissfully unaware of me. The dragons I was shown were fully grown and to my palate were repulsive reeking of rotten cabbage – I cannot envisage a relationship with any of them. The little lady stares at me and explains:

"Working with a dragon is not to be undertaken lightly. It is not fantasy. It is a grave responsibility and is more real than reality itself. The vibrational sequencing of planet earth is shrouded in a deceitful mist where you are ridiculed for unorthodox ideas and accused of being illogical and mentally unstable for adopting anti-social philosophies. You must learn to ride through mocking derision, realizing that you will gain much knowledge and superior understanding with your dragon by your side. You will be greatly tested in order to be accepted, but one day you will know all. There are those who watch and seek to protect and guide you and it is their wish for you to acquire Dragon Knowledge."

I think of my whisperers and nod. Suddenly, I have no idea what I am saying but I open my mouth and ask: "Where is the golden dragon?"

The lady smiles sweetly, whispering, "Ah, now I understand. You have been chosen to encounter the teachings of a Golden Dragon. Golden Dragon is most special and very precious. Those who are selected for this knowledge are very, very lucky. Only the Emperor of China was allowed Golden Dragon. He loved the golden ones more than his children. Only he was allowed to wear gold or yellow garments, for these colours are viewed as the most lucky colours. You are indeed lucky!"

Yes, I am indeed Lucky, for I am Lucky.

MIMI AND ME

The little Chinese lady wastes no time in ordering her young girl to escort me to the 'golden realm' to find what I most desire. The young girl reverently bows and beckons me to follow her transporting me through a time vortex into to a maze of caves deep in the mountains of Tibet. From afar I hear gongs chiming and drums beating with voices chanting, resonating through the maze. The girl runs ahead and I try to keep up with her until we arrive in a dark, warm, colourful room with bright mandalas painted on the walls and sand paintings like iced cakes, spread out on the stone floor.

Mischievous young boys with their trainee monks play gleefully, hiding and catching each other, racing around huge, ancient terracotta coloured columns. The seated monks in prayer smile with their eyes and a senior priest nods and motions a young Tibetan girl dressed in a beautifully embroidered tunic, to escort me to a mysterious place beneath the temple. She has a cute face and large dimples in both cheeks.

"How old are you?" I whisper as we quietly step away from the temple.

"Eight." She replies confidently.

"What is your name?" I enquire.

"Xian." She adds, almost defiantly but quickly moves along and picks up a goat's wax lamp which eerily lights our way through dark corridors, where finally we step into a vast, heavenly cavern.

Peace and unworldly tranquillity reign in a golden magical atmosphere as we perch on a small wooden Chinese bridge overlooking a gentle golden river. Huge golden pillars line the river bank supported on golden square plinths and tiny bright lights sparkle and twinkle in the dim glow. Gold shimmers and gleams everywhere like Aladdin's treasure trove and I wonder what Colonel

Gerard's reaction would be to this blissfully, golden retreat with his "think gold" motto.

"This is special secret golden world for secret golden dragon." Xian proudly states. "I am baby dragon keeper" she continues with import, "we have baby dragon eggs from many, many dynasties ago as they were rescued from the Emperor's keep to be nurtured here in secret Tibet. The Chinese want to conquer our land and find our secrets but they will never, never do that."

I smile and nod in agreement and ask, "How long does it take for a baby dragon to hatch from the egg?"

She stops to answer my question and places her delicate little head on one side and replies:

"If the egg is with Mother dragon, then it is much shorter time, but if egg is incubated then perhaps many thousand years."

I am shocked but accept her superior knowledge.

"We have four baby juniors for you to see, their age equivalent to humans maybe around six years old. From egg, baby dragon grows from level one to three. These are all level three."

Finally after walking by the golden riverside for about a mile, we reach glass encased pens where the back walls slide open onto a beautiful paradise for the dragons to play and roam freely. In the first cage we approach, I spy a little plump bundle huddled in a corner. She is the colour of a muddy duckling. Xian explains that yellow-golden baby dragons are born the colour of dull green grass but as they grow their colour changes until they are bright yellow and when fully grown are golden and only Emperors were permitted golden dragons and were allowed to wear yellow. The junior I view is still quite green in places and on her neck and tail her scales are like leaves turning gold in autumn.

Immediately I warm to her and like viewing a new puppy, I want to cuddle her. There is something vulnerable and sad about the way she is hiding, as though she is hurt.

"I like her!" I whisper.

"But you have not seen the others yet. Dragons come in many shapes and sizes, some reptilian, some like fishes, some like horses and some like hippos," recites Xian. "She is like horse," she informs me, pointing to the first cage. I observe this to be true. The creature has four legs with the hind ones longer than the front and her head is shaped like a foal's. Her tail is stubby and her claws are long and sharp. Xian moves to the next cage and motions me to follow where there is another stumpy creature, the same age as the first, but as soon as it sees us, it charges in a fiery temper, squealing like a new-born piglet. She is not for me.

In the next cage is a peaceful, sweet male contentedly snoring. His name, I am told is Toby. But he is not for me as I do not immediately feel a connection with him. The last junior dragon, Damian, I dislike instantaneously as he stomps from one foot to the other, grunting arrogantly.

"I really do like the first dragon," I smile. "Can we see her again please?"

Xian looks slightly vexed as I think she wants me to choose Toby, but she complies with my wishes.

"Do you want to go in?" she enquires.

I am momentarily flummoxed as the thought hadn't occurred to me to go inside.

"It's alright, she won't bite!" urges Xian.

I agree, not really wanting the challenge but I feel it's expected.

"You can ask her questions and talk to her and she will answer in here." She points to the top of her head. I understand she means telepathically.

The door opens and I enter apologetically, afraid to make any sharp moves.

"Hello, what is your name?" I ask timidly.

She doesn't reply and snorts.

I hear myself attempting to make small talk... "I would like to make friends with you."

"I don't like you!" She retorts, telepathically, in a very sophisticated manner, and I gather I sound patronising. Realising I know absolutely nothing about dragons and even less on how to address one.

I attempt to make a better impression saying, "Oh I am sorry but I er.." She impatiently doesn't allow me to finish and vehemently adds:

"Well just look at you-you're frumpy, uninteresting and your dress sense is appalling and you're overweight!"

I am stunned and shocked into silence. I hadn't imagined a junior dragon would be so astute, intelligent, forthright and outspoken. I admit I am a little hurt by her outburst. I turn to Xian waiting outside the cage and she shrugs her shoulders as if she expected the outburst. I had been told that my dragon would choose me and this little lady doesn't want to know me at all. It was explained that for a bond to exist between human and dragon there had to be a strong connection. The human is known as the dragon's connector and has to pass individual turgid scrutiny.

"I don't want you to be my connector. Go away!" the junior dragon cries, "My connector will come for me and she will be important like a princess and she will have style and grace and love me greatly."

I can see so much of me as a child in her and want to take away her pain, to comfort her and soothe away her insecurity. Her hurt calls out to be consoled and I want to be the one to do it. She catches my thoughts and dragons being telepathic, understand and know your every intention. They can never be deceived. She is disgruntled and offended by my opinions of her because she is so proud and can't bear for me to feel sorry for her. Xian intervenes and asks me to leave the cage. I obey and want desperately to say goodbye but the little dragon flies outside to play in the beautiful paradise garden and part of my heart goes with her. Xian nods, bows, smiles and says, "I will see you next time." But I am doubtful whether there will be a next time. She disappears into the ether and I, suddenly without warning, am back sitting on the porch with the ocean receding into the distance as the tide turns and the sun, like a large orange ball sinks down below the horizon.

You are still with me and have witnessed a world of mythical creatures beyond imagining. Outside ourselves lie other selves waiting to be discovered and if we allow exposure into the unchartered landscape of our minds we will uncover the truth of who we really are. We must take gentle steps into the unknown and my voices whisper:

"Align yourself in time with the universe and take baby-steps towards your goal – for small hinges can open large doors."

You understand and I know for now, we must part but it is certain you will return, for we have forged a bond and you are here to learn, as am I. Beyond the beyond lies an unfathomable world of unexplored magical beings who wait for alignment with us and now I am drawn into that world, for I have to do what I can't not do, as my life extends beyond the limitations of me and that realm is also open to you. I will wait for you until the next time, being lucky to share journeys into unknown lands.

I have to do what I can't not do, for my life extends beyond the limitations of me and since being informed that I am ready for 'Dragon' knowledge, I have not been able to think of anything else!

Days have passed in quiet solitude with lovely walks and tranquil evenings by the fire with good food and wine and calm restful nights waking to sweet music, but all the time at the back of my mind a little stumpy, stubborn, lovable junior dragon plagues my thoughts. I have never delved into the realms of mythological creatures before, only in folk tales and fairy stories have I ever entertained the notion of such beings, but to have been transported to a very real place where dragons exist is totally insane and I constantly battle with myself yearning to return to see the little being and then convincing myself that it's a crazy thing to do.

In the stillness of the days there has been no teaching, no messages, no direction, no signs or signals absolutely no contact from anyone. I miss my loved ones; I miss human contact; I am an empty vessel without love pouring in and flowing out and in the void my mind is saturated with images of baby dragons. I dream of baby dragons and the need to make friends with one baby dragon in particular. I have become obsessed with the idea of making a beautiful connection with a magical creature and perhaps being totally alone has played its part in making me seek someone or something to love, like during the first lock-down when the 'aloneness' was almost unbearable, especially when my business collapsed overnight and there was nothing left and naught ahead but uncertainty. I have learnt that to be a human means being part of a whole and that the 'desire and pursuit of the whole is love'. People need to love and be loved. I argue with myself that I could end this situation and surrender to the nearest city scape and have some form of social interaction with people, albeit sanitised and manipulated, but I know my fears are temporary and I just have to get through the desolate emotional desert and my fortitude will be rewarded. I know my people will take care of me. I place my total trust in them. Now, strolling in the sunshine, gazing out across the ocean I wonder what my little dragon is doing and if I could try again to make her acquaintance and gain her trust. I know she is seeking to connect with a princess, or high ranking royalty, or someone close to her regal lineage and I know I disappoint her and have offended her dignity by suggesting our friendship, but I sense she is hurt and I want to help her. As I stroll back to the cabin the bright day changes into grey monochrome dullness. Inside it is cosy and warm and I spy on the bookshelf, strategically placed for my attention, an antique book on 'Dragon Law'. It is as though everything I do is planned and pre-ordained. 'They' are watching and monitoring and guiding me towards something. I pick up the book which is beautifully bound and illustrated and has lots of pictures of many different species of dragon, all various colours for diverse purposes. It contains interesting facts and general information about dragons and how certain types prefer specific areas with particular energy in which to make their lairs. It seems that Cornwall is pertinent to Golden dragons, besides their homeland in China, especially in Beijing in the Forbidden City. As I digest the information, things begin to slot into place and I wonder if being in Cornwall has a bearing on connecting with a golden dragon and Colonel Gerald's teaching about 'thinking gold at all times'.

I had chosen a golden dragon, not through any prior knowledge, but perhaps I was inspired by my whisperers, who keep me informed of many secrets and I need to understand why the Golden Dragon is relevant to me so that I know what is required of me. Before the first lock-down when travelling was a normal, healthy activity, I had undertaken a massive journey exploring China. I had no idea why I craved to place myself in a potentially dangerous situation in order to accomplish life-long ambitions such as walking the Great Wall of China, visiting the Beijing Opera, sailing down the Yangtze river, standing in the great hall of the Emperor in the Forbidden City and stroking a real panda – all I know is that I needed to do it. Just as I ponder these questions, the holographic screen appears and Colonel Gerald stands life-like before me, not in uniform but dressed like a lumber-jack in a check shirt and jeans.

"Hi there!" He salutes, smiles and states, "Yes, you made the correlation between 'thinking gold' and choosing a golden dragon. Thinking gold is the best energy for your spiritual development and a golden dragon is the strongest, most majestic, most powerful of creatures amongst all the dragon species. You chose well and in fact it ties in with the sun deity who entrusted you with the golden key". I remember the spaceship rising out of the sea and the golden craft landing on the beach and the golden Adonis forming out of pure liquid gold handing me a golden key, which I wore around my neck, until it was time for it to be transformed into myriads of micro keys to be unleashed into the atmosphere to help unlock pathways to higher knowledge for those seeking enlightenment.

I nod, understanding another 'golden' connection and watch the Colonel parade up and down with his hands in his pockets as he continues to explain the reasons for my choice:

"You see the Golden dragon, apart from being a symbol of strength and wealth, is a dedicated Creature-Warrior battling against evil and will fight to the bitter end against injustice and foul-play. This type of dragon is highly respected for its fairness, knowledge and its quest to promote good at all times. This golden creature is the apex of the draconic species."

I am truly impressed and feel unworthy to be a golden dragon connectee. The Colonel reads my thoughts and laughs saying:

"I know all this sounds pretty crazy right now and a golden dragon is not an easy choice, but it's your choice and so it's good to be armed with knowledge. Facts are the best way forwards."

I agree with him and want to learn more as he explains some of the characteristics of the Golden Dragon.

"This will interest you, as a dancer," he reads from some notes," Golden Dragons are graceful in their movements and appreciate finer, cultural qualities in a human."

My little dragon's words come tumbling back – "Well just look at you-you're frumpy, uninteresting and your dress sense is appalling and you're overweight!" I flush bright red and feel embarrassed recalling the moment of her judgement.

"They are very wise creatures with great healing knowledge and skill." He continues.

I smile at his words, for being given a healing gift and not wanting it at first, I feel humbled by the thought of learning more from a Master.

"You will like this one," he states, pointing his finger at his notes, "it is said that they like pearls and gems in their diet, but in my experience, such creatures often do not have the need for material sustenance. They can breathe under water and are very good swimmers as well as graceful, swift creatures of the sky. They have full night vision and have two types of air weapon. One is their fire breathing capacity and the other is their exhalation of a gas which can weaken an enemy."

The information is very interesting, but a bit scary as I wouldn't want to get on the wrong side of a fire-breathing creature.

"Now aspects of their personality," he added, "which you will need to be aware of when dealing with a golden dragon and that is they are highly intelligent, sagacious, and will need an elevated level of intellectual interaction with a human. They will not suffer fools gladly and will be blatantly blunt when expressing their opinions, oftentimes quite savagely, which can make then appear rude and arrogant. They also seem to be grim and without humour and very dismissive of humans if they don't like them."

I had already experienced that with the little dragon who told me directly she didn't like me and didn't want to make a connection with me, as she had someone far superior in mind.

"Shu-li, what else does she need to know?" enquires the Colonel.

I had not noticed a small Tibetan lady standing behind the Colonel. She is delicately beautiful, dressed elegantly in a golden-yellow sarong.

"Step forwards Shu-li", he motions explaining, "this is Shu-li who is overall caretaker of the Golden Dragons in Zanscarr where you will meet your dragon again."

My heart skips a beat to think I am going to have the chance to see her again.

"Shu-li what advice would you like to pass on?" The Colonel asks politely.

She steps forwards courteously and says: "You should have a clean mind at all times, as dragon, knows your thoughts always. She is psychic and will telepathically transmit her thoughts to you. You cannot know her thoughts unless she wishes it. She is stronger than you in this way. Do not try to outwit her for she is always ahead of you."

"Thank you," I sigh, a little overwhelmed by the gravity of the advice and she continues:

"Never, never treat dragon as a pet. They will not bow to anyone's will. In this way there must be a generous balance between human and dragon. You will have preference for dragon but dragon will choose you. When relationship is established you will be privileged and learn much and be protected. One day you will have special place in dragon kingdom."

She bows politely and I bow awkwardly in return. I thank her for the advice and then pluck up the courage to ask why I have been chosen to make a connection with a dragon. She looks at me sharply, and pauses before she speaks as though listening to an outside voice and addresses me directly:

"You have in your memory a moment which you have forgotten."

I look surprised and puzzled. She continues quietly, "When you were seven years old you were told by your people, your whisperers as you call them, to look very closely in the mirror to study your right eye. You took your Mother's hand mirror and looked very hard. What did you see?"

I struggle momentarily trying to remember, then the memory floods back. I see myself perched on a dressing table with a small hand mirror peering into my right eye. They tell me to look closer and closer into the centre of my khaki green eye. I see the clear outline of a yellow dragon. I can't believe it and keep staring and staring. The amazing yellow dragon is in my eye, there is no doubt.

"Yes," she sighs, "this is so. This was shown to you when you were young to explain that you are a child of the yellow dragon family and now it is time to re-connect. On this new journey you will see and hear things in a totally different manner. When you remove all limitations of 'self' then you will be limitless. Now is the time for daring, to dare."

With those last words she and the Colonel fade into the holographic screen and disappear into the wall. Contemplating the information, I am determined to return to the secret underground caves in Tibet where secrets are power and as much as the Chinese force the people to subjugate to their will, they will not claim the soul of the Tibetans, for their secrets are sacred and will remain forever in their hearts.

Caves and underground networks from Antarctica to Tibet through Middle earth and throughout the planet exist. Back before the reset of world government when freedom was taken for granted, I had a very strange experience which opened my eyes to the reality of secret underground tunnels with advanced rail network systems connecting the whole world across a secret grid.

Looking back, I believe I was set up to meet a stranger who was a professional tunneler because he wanted me to write his story to tell the world what was really going on beneath the earth. At the time I was a columnist for a well-known popular paper which had a wide readership. Every Friday morning I had coffee in a small art gallery and one Friday, two men sat opposite the table where I normally sat and struck up a conversation. One man left and the other joined me. We chatted about occupations and I was intrigued to learn he was a professional tunneler. I was fascinated as I had never met a person highly skilled in that profession. He explained they had special hi-tech machines that could tunnel anywhere and cut through hard rock to produce beautiful, polished surfaces. He intimated that the technology was not of this world but had been introduced by alien beings. He asked me if I would undertake to write his enthralling story and in essence I agreed, not realizing how dangerous the mission might be. He told me how he had been threatened and cajoled into undertaking secret assignments that were illegal and described how men had been murdered in front of him, executed and buried under cement on building sites because they wouldn't do what the bosses wanted or had been disloyal. He had witnessed mafia gang leaders running horrific operations for top world leaders and was prepared to whistle-blow operations that would shock the world because, as he explained, he was going to disappear and that he hadn't much time left and his conscience plagued him about his involvement in evil operations. I genuinely believed all he said and was curious to learn more, so we agreed to meet again the next day when he would give me his lawyer's phone number to verify his identity and to arrange money. When we met, he was very nervous and stated that he was in a hurry to have everything contracted and ready to sign, adding that his lawyer would transfer written documents and information that was top-secret. Naively, I agreed to undertake the assignment. I followed his instructions and contacted his lawyer to find he was telling the truth.

The following evening, late after my dance class, driving home, I took small rural lanes to avoid traffic on major roads. My two children were in the back of the car asleep and so from the outside it appeared that I was driving alone. From nowhere, a car pulled up behind and I slowed down for it to overtake, but it didn't. It stayed close behind, almost on my bumper. I speeded up and so did the driver. The car tailed me in a menacing manner and drove up by the side of me at one point where the road widened, then it dropped back. I was afraid and raced to get home but the car stayed close behind. On arriving home it parked opposite my house and two men got out furtively watching the street. They thought I was alone but when my children suddenly jumped out of the car laughing and shouting they scarpered back to theirs and sped away. I was frightened by the experience and the next day I received a phone call threatening me and my family if I went ahead to write the story. I was terrified and being alone, immediately retracted my agreement. I phoned the lawyer to inform him that I was not going to write the story. I never forgot the tunneler and what he revealed about the existence of underground, hi-tech transport across the world, hinting I would be shocked to learn the truth about what lay beneath the earth and the alien inhabitants who dwelt there since time began! I never heard from him again but from that time on, I was aware that something massively secret was being constructed for clandestine reasons below the earth across the world.

Ancient scripts and tales tell of secret underground tunnels and it is said that the Tibetan monks have passageways leading to many continents.

In almost every culture throughout the world, dragons have a place in folklore and many people believe they still exist, albeit in a different vibrational field. I am told that in the future, in the Shannon Mountains in China, dragons will exist cloned from a frozen corpse. Similarly, I have been informed that a secret island has living dinosaurs roaming the forests and a new species has been created. I cannot vouch for the truth in these predictions but can only evaluate what happened to me as a real experience and am driven to explore further possibilities. Now, sitting in the gentle calm of the evening on the porch, listening to the waves' rise and fall, sweeping a dying sigh across the still sand, I begin to meditate, breathing in and out to the call of the sea. I go under, deeper and deeper below the ocean; deeper below the earth where the atmosphere changes and I see little Xian waiting for me with a big grin.

"I thought you would return." She chirps gleefully. "Number one dragon is inside. You want to see?"

I agree and humbly go inside the cage. Number one female dragon stands with her back to me in the corner. It is obvious she doesn't want to see me. I try to remember what Shuli said about dragons knowing all thoughts, but as she turns and stares with her yellow/green eyes I can't help but think she is sweet and dumpy but as soon as my thoughts register, she flies at me with her claws and hovers above for a few seconds beating the air with her outstretched wings before dropping down with a clatter on the floor. I sense she is proud of her mock display of anger. Then in a composed indignant manner she states:

"I told you I do not like you, and you are rude to call me dumpy!" With a final glare she turns and flies out to the garden paradise and is lost in the trees. I am mortified to think I have hurt her feelings when I wanted so much to make friends. Xian enters the cage clicking her teeth and shaking her head in dismay scolding:

"You made a big mess of that!"

I am lost for words and lose my concentration and open my eyes to find myself back on the porch.

I am ashamed to fail so miserably at befriending my little dragon. I want to go back and make amends but I know it is not possible. The evening turns into night and with a heavy heart I try to sleep. Days and nights roll and I wait. I try many times to go under in meditation but the energy evades me. Now it is late afternoon and feeling sleepy I lie down on the bed and close my eyes. In a flash I am standing in front of little Xian who is sweeping the floor.

"Hello," I greet her with an apologetic smile.

"She doesn't want to see you and she is not in her cage." Xian replies, still sweeping.

"I am so sorry I upset her, I didn't mean to, it's just that..."

"It doesn't matter. When dragon makes up mind, it is difficult... she is stubborn and high-born stubborn is worst," she warns.

"I understand," I plead, "but I want to make amends and I am sure we could be friends...I mean... I don't even know her name. What is it?" I enquire.

"I cannot say, she will tell you when she is ready."

"What can I do Xian to get to see her again?" I implore.

She stops sweeping and looks at me. "You really like her don't you?" She half smiles. I nod and she continues, "She is very special. She was hatched here by the monks from a collection of Emperor's eggs. The Emperor treated his clutch of golden dragons better than his own children you know, so when the revolution came the eggs were hidden in secret and given to the monks to breed here. She has unique royal lineage directly from a long line of Emperors. She has high expectations of her connector and you do not meet any of her royal requirements, so she is not interested in making friends with you."

I am grateful for her explanation and understand the little dragon's reaction to me. Xian is sympathetic to my disappointment and continues as though she is reciting from a ledger:

"Every dragon is different, with diverse personalities. Do not presume to understand them, they understand you better. It is not your place to think you know more, for they have knowledge that you may never fathom; do not patronise them. Each dragon is a glorious gem, multifaceted like a diamond and they will always choose whom they wish to befriend."

"Couldn't you just try to persuade her to come back for a few seconds please, please," I plead.

She looks at me sideways and perches her arm on the top of the broom and then waves her arm for me to stand by the cage. A few moments later there is a flurry of wings and my little dragon is standing inside the cage. I tentatively step inside and she immediately states scornfully:

"I told you I don't like you!"

"Er...yes. I know I'm sorry but I thought we might just be friends... that is if..."

She flies at me with her claws and hovers above me for a few seconds beating the air with her outstretched wings before dropping down with a clatter on the floor. Like a coward, I hide my head in fear of her attack and curl up on the floor. I hear a faint giggle. I guess she is testing me, teasing with her superior power. I am embarrassed by my cowardice and she knows it and snorts down her nostrils. I almost expect to see flames shooting out, but she is too young for flame throwing.

Swallowing my pride, I address her directly, looking into her beautiful duckling yellow eyes, "my name is..."

"I know what your name is!" she retorts.

I am surprised by her response but then not, as dragons know all. "What is your name?" I ask standing nervously by the door.

"It is not for you to know as there is no reason for you to know. Please go!" She commands.

I turn, hurt, not being able to get near her and feel sad to leave her, when she states nonchalantly:

"I like peaches. White peaches!"

I turn and smile and ask if I can bring her some when I next visit. There is an awkward silence, then she deigns to answer.

"You may and they must be ripe and soft and very white."

"What is your name?" I politely enquire.

There is a deep silence and she turns away and looks up into the air as though she is plucking a name from the universe and whispers... "Mimi".

I restrain my laughter. I expected a grand, Chinese name from a prestigious dynasty with many titles rather than a cute French name. Immediately she knows my thoughts and it is too late as she indignantly flies out of the door. Again I have hurt her feelings. Xian enters the cage scolding:

"Well, you messed that up again! You will never get her back now! She is very proud and you made fun of her name which she chose to shorten so you could pronounce it. Mimi is little name for a very big, long name. She is right...you don't deserve to be her friend-now you must leave."

A vortex swirls around me and I am hurled down a dark tunnel until I am thrown back into a different reality at the cabin. I am so ashamed and shocked to have made a terrible blunder.

I was given a second chance and had inadvertently mocked Mimi's name, hurting her pride and now my stupidity hangs heavy, made worse by my lonely existence, with no one to share my grief and no one to tell me it doesn't matter and not to give in, and to try again, but I feel abandoned. I just want to sleep and lock out the world. I want to be back with people. I want to be loved and give love. In the bleak darkness I cry myself to sleep.

In the morning I wake to the sound of rain pelting on the tin roof, like glass marbles dropped into a biscuit tin and you are there. You are a comfort in my dark days and I am a little ashamed that I have nothing to share with you, only sadness. I am marooned by the sea with nothing but hollowness and I cannot escape. There is nowhere to run, only to the cityscape which is far away and I know I have been placed here for a purpose and I believe that my people will come for me, for I am lucky. I hold onto that thought as I rise to prepare coffee. The rain ceases and a streak of sunshine hits the coffee table through the cracked kitchen window, highlighting a picture on a magazine. The cookery page shows how to make a delightful fruit salad with white peaches. I recall Mimi's voice stating: "I like white peaches!" I smile and resolve to take her some. In the realm beyond, the manifestation of things happen automatically, so all you have to do is imagine and focus on what you wish to manifest and it appears. After breakfast I sit on the veranda and gaze out to sea. The heavy rain has left a dense earthy smell permeating the salty air and I breathe in deeply ingesting the briny atmosphere and go under into meditation quickly and find myself standing outside Mimi's cage which is being cleaned by little Xian who looks at me disapprovingly and says,

"She doesn't want to see you! You know this!"

I nod and tell her I have brought Mimi white peaches just as she asked.

"She won't come. Just leave them there!" She points outside the cage.

"Where is she?" I ask plaintively.

"Outside!"

I stare into the lovely paradise garden where many young dragons are gathered, but Mimi is not there, my gaze roams until I spy something moving by the trees. It is Mimi but she has changed. Xian stands by my side and observes my surprise at her development and adds, "Yes, she has grown hasn't she? Junior dragons grow very quickly. She is now about the age equivalent of a nine year old child and her green patches are turning yellow, especially on her neck and she is taller and less wider." She laughs and continues her chores.

I notice all the changes in her and perceive she is not so dumpy with a longer neck and larger head.

"She will not come so you had better go!" Xian commands.

I obey and leave the peaches and return disappointed. During the next few days I repeat my visits and each time I leave a little basket of white peaches for Mimi, always with a note to say I am sorry and would like to try to make amends, but my efforts go unnoticed, until a few weeks later a strange thing happens. Time in another dimension has no meaning and so a few weeks here can amount to a few years there and vice versa and being Lucky, I never give in to the notion of defeat, because I know that if I think lucky, I will be lucky and I will find my little Mimi dragon again.

—◦◦◦◦⟨⟩◦◦◦◦—

THE DRACONIC PATH

It is late and a full silver moon gleams bright orbs of light around the cabin. I am tired and fall asleep listening to the surf beat a timely rhythm along the beach. In a dream I hear Xian's voice echoing through a dark tunnel. She is distraught and implores me to visit. Waking from the dream, Xian's urgency stirs me to transfer my consciousness to a meditative state where I teleport to the dragon caves to find Xian waiting for me outside Mimi's cage. She speaks in a hushed tone:

"I am glad you have come. Perhaps you are her only hope now?"

I am shocked to hear her sad words and ask her to explain.

"You have to understand that because of Mimi's heritage she expected to be connected to royalty or a person with wealth and so when a very auspicious opportunity arose from a very wealthy lady to be her connector, we all thought it was a good idea. Mimi was glad to go with her and she seemed happy."

I am miserable to hear she was taken by a rich woman, but Xian motions me to peep into the cage where I am shocked to see how much she has changed and how she has grown. But she is curled up in a corner and is despondent, looking thin and gaunt. Xian whispers:

"Mimi is now equivalent to teenager. She has lost almost all of her green spots and is nearly all golden."

"Yes," I whispered, "she is beautiful. But what happened?"

"Do not be surprised that there are many who seek dragon knowledge for evil purposes and come here with false intentions to master, tame and claim ownership of dragon. But dragon will not allow this. They have strength and force whenever necessary to resist. Wealthy lady wanted young dragon to train from early age to be a malicious guard for her rich possessions and she chained Mimi and whipped her until Mimi was forced to use her fire weapon for the first time and burnt down lady's home. Monks freed her and brought her back here. That experience was terrible for her, but she recovered and a nun from prestigious convent came to claim her. She seemed very good woman but outward appearances can be very deceptive and it is with the heart we must learn to see the truth.

Mimi agreed to try again but there are those who only want dragon knowledge to twist into selfish greed. The nun was not a good lady and tried to suck out secret knowledge from Mimi by torturing and starving her. Dragon is pure in nature and carries no guilt of sin. A dragon has no need of self-denial and self-harm and such religious fervour has no place in dragon law. Poor Mimi was enslaved into a religious prison but she refused to co-operate with the mother superior and was left in a dungeon to die."

I am distraught to hear such awful news and want to go into the cage to console her but Xian continues:

"After the first disastrous attempt to house Mimi the head monk decided to check on her in her new home and was appalled to find her half-alive in a cell. He brought her back here and ever since she has hardly moved or eaten anything. She needs someone who is pure of heart and kind in spirit because that is her nature and her counterpart must be the same." She looks at me intently.

"Can I see her?" I whisper.

Xian nods and smiles saying, "she said it was alright to contact 'White Peach' – that is what she calls you."

I laugh and ask: "is it because I bring her white peaches?"

Xian smiles wryly, replying, "partly, but mostly because the white peach is special and pure and has no other nature than to be itself."

I understand and am flattered. Xian adds, "Mimi has learnt from her terrible ordeals, that what she was taught to expect and what she came to expect is misleading, as treasure is often hidden deep."

I understand and creep softly into the cage. Mimi does not stir. She remains coiled and curled in her corner with her head hidden under her tail. Her skin gleams golden in the half-light; she has matured so much since I last saw her. I place my hand gently on her back and she does not resist. I gently stroke her and hum quietly. Suddenly a deeper voice commands from her hidden head below her tail:

"Don't make that noise!"

I stand back abruptly. "You mean sing?"

"Is that what you call it? It's a noise, it destroys sound!"

I am amused, relieved and shocked all at the same time, being careful not to think negative thoughts.

"All sound is music. All music is emotion. All emotion is vibration. Dragons live on emotional vibration. Dragon Law number one."

I gasp. I am in awe of her knowledge and want to learn more. She gleans this and with an air of great importance rises from her hunched position and stands tall and straight looking me in the eye. She is much taller than before and more magnificent than ever and continues her speech:

"All vibration is frequency. Every fibre of every pulse has a purpose, like each note in a musical scale is different but part of the whole and has a special place in the creation of harmony. So too does frequency."

I understand completely. We speak the same language of music.

"Where are my peaches, my white peaches?" I laugh and she laughs too. Happiness floods my being and I am one energy with her.

"I am so sorry I hurt your feelings Mimi, I did not mean to and if you will accept me, I will try to be more like the person you wish me to be...I will lose weight..." "Stop, stop!" she interrupts, "I am not the same as before. It is only in the darkness we see the stars and I have been to a dark place and now see the light of truth. I did not like you because I was taught to expect something that does not exist. I did not like you because you are like me."

Tears roll down my cheeks. I did not expect to be so moved by her and to feel such a close connection.

"Now stop that immediately!" she commands. "There is no room for idle sentimentality. We have work to do together. Next time you visit please bring white peaches."

She said 'together' we have work to do and she said 'please'. I smile and hug her chest.

My arms only reach a proportion of the way across her frame but she responds and licks the top of my head leaving my hair wet as though I have stepped into a light shower of rain. From outside the cage I see Xian's beaming smile and as the golden dawn streaks in through the window I wake to a bright new day in the cabin.

As I rise I feel your presence hovering around me. It's as though you are trying to communicate through electric interference. I close my eyes and strain to see you down a long dark tunnel but we cannot move. You are with me and I you but the force between us is too strong. One day we will meet and we will know all, but now you fade and I am once more alone in the cabin. I recall my wonderful meeting with Mimi and remind myself that there is much to learn about dragons and dragon law and look forward to my next visit.

I rise and look out of the window where everything is shrouded in a white, cloudy veil as a sea mist swirls around the cabin blanking my view of the ocean. All is enclosed in a dense haze and my chalet prison is encapsulated in a timeless cloak. I hear the ocean breathing and I know I am alive. Just when I think I have been abandoned by the Colonel, his hologram slides from the wall.

"Hi there! Bet you thought I'd abandoned you?" he smiles.

He must have read my thoughts?

"Well, you did good there, taming your dragon!" He adds enthusiastically.

I rise to Mimi's defence – "a dragon cannot be tamed! She chose to befriend me!"

"Ok, ok, take it easy. You are right of course! Sit down, relax. Look they want me to fill you in on some scientific info to help you understand the mechanics of how you and Mimi connect. Is that ok?"

I nod and sit down ready to listen. I watch him take out a file, adding:

"It's hard to understand that creatures, such as Dragons exist and I know you will question your sanity when faced with this reality, but planet earth is one dimension surrounded by many dimensions that can and do co-exist all at once within the same vibrational frequency. It is only those with a certain type of brain who can access this electromagnetic field, allowing them to tune into otherworldly wave-lengths and enabling them to interact and communicate with beings outside earth's vibrational field. Does this make sense?"

I nod and he continues.

"Scientists tell us that everything is 'vibration'. All particles of substance are vibration. All that we know, see, hear and touch exists because of the vibrational current passing through everything.

Human beings are an energy form which is harnessed to the human shape. Our human vibration triumphs amidst a whole maelstrom of resonance surrounding us, isn't that amazing?"

I nod again.

"How we use our mind and brain determines how we view the world and our own unique individual perception of it is influenced by our upbringing, education, social influence and personal preferences. Ok so far?"

I understand the scientific principles and wonder where the instruction is leading as I watch the Colonel produce an interstellar map with a red arrow pointing to a tiny microscopic earth amidst myriads of other tiny specs representing galaxies beyond galaxies.

"Our earth here," he points to the tiny spec, "is a minute particle in a multi-verse of multi-verses.

Everyone generates energy, albeit positive or negative and according to what level and intensity of good or bad inner energy we engender, our personal vibration mirrors it."

"So what has this to do with Mimi?" I enquire.

"Well quite simply everything!" He claps his hands triumphantly and continues," being aware of many differing layers of existence, either negative or positive, residing parallel with each other is tantamount to accepting her existence. Do you see? So with your individual capacity to be aware of other vibrations, you are able to see Mimi and interact with her on an unearthly level. Many people do not have your ability and therefore will mock you and make you feel mentally unstable, but you must not pay heed to them if you are to spiritually progress. Remember this world is an illusion...beyond is reality!"

I sigh and nod once more, acknowledging his teaching.

"Oh, and by the way, before I forget, you might want to know that in the future dragons are found high up in the rocky mountains in America and also in the Shannon mountains in China. It's true soldier, so take comfort in that piece of info. Bye for now!"

I watch his hologram slide back into the wall and walk towards the window pondering the Information. It is wonderful news that dragons return to earth and I wonder in which year they are discovered. But now, I am glad to see the mist separating and fading into the clouds leaving a glimpse of a silver-grey sea. I shiver and light the wood stove and curl into a thick blanket on the sofa to close my eyes to find my way back to Mimi.

This time it is easy and I swiftly find myself standing outside Mimi's cage with Xian washing down the glass frontage. She is pleased to see me as my visits have helped to cement my friendship with my beautiful dragon and helped her to recover from her nightmare ordeals.

"She is waiting for you beyond in the garden," states Xian busily engrossed in her chores, "you may go through!"

Hastily I enter the cage, being careful to leave a small basket of white peaches on the floor before I slip out into the amazing paradise. Mimi who is now almost fully grown is magnificent. She is the species which resembles a horse. Her long neck is elegant and graceful as she holds her head high revealing her long jaw line and flared nostrils. On the top of her golden head are two small stumpy horns and behind her tiny ears flair two, webbed small wings which fan the air as she moves. Her front legs are longer than her back ones and her long tail coils around her feet. Her two large golden wings open and close in the sunlight and her green eyes sparkle like dew drops in the early morning clover. When she spies me racing ungainly towards her, she nods her head up and down welcoming me to her lair. We have made a wonderful connection and our friendship grows stronger each time we meet.

"You are grossly unfit and overweight! You must rectify this!" She scolds haughtily in her superior manner. I agree with her and promise to try to get fit again and am willing to make sacrifices to please her as she is after all, my mentor. She reads my thoughts.

"Don't do it to please me...it must be for yourself!" She scorns... "and don't give me that age nonsense? Humans are far too preoccupied with where they are in their timelines and what they should be doing and achieving at which age and stage of their earth time before the decline of old age sets in. In our Kingdom progression is forever moving forwards, never backwards."

I gather my breath and agree with her observations of humanity. The gentle breeze quivers the reeds by the waterside and shards of bright sunlight skim across the lake like sparkling diamonds in a secret treasure chest and I breathe in the moment knowing it is forever; for time here is timeless and I am One with the Oneness of being. I look down at a leaf fluttering by my feet, becoming sharply aware that the leaf is the centre of my universe and its 'leafiness' is a harmonious vibration with mine. All colours here sing tones beyond belief, while on earth the brightest most magnificent scenery is dull because it is dying.

"Don't be sad about your world, it is as it is. Your earth is a special zone for learning and you chose to be there to be educated spiritually and your life experience will shape your next level of consciousness. Now climb on my back!"

I am not ready for her shocking command and step backwards in horror at the thought. Mimi laughs making fun of my outburst.

"It is a simple trust task. Why are you so afraid?" She admonishes.

"Because I can't reach up and I am afraid of falling," I whine hopelessly.

"If you trust me, you will never fall. All fear is a false emotion to trick you into believing you cannot do, or have, or achieve that which you desire. Fear prevents you from realizing your potential. Now climb on my back!"

I do not have time to procrastinate as her tail whips around my waist and hoists me up at the base of her neck, where I dig my legs into the side of her scales clinging on desperately with my arms. I feel her pause to check my safety, preparing for take-off, then she gracefully glides into the air with her body cushioned on clouds as we sail across the purple ocean to rocky, orange outcrops of gigantic boulders topped with strange, stone pinnacles pointing into the skyline like ornate Church spires. In the distance a peak juts out across a valley and we land softly on a patch of flat rock as the sun sinks below the horizon. I stand close to the edge of a great chasm and watch Mimi flap her vast wings beating the cool evening air across a blue forest. She hovers, as though waiting and watching for someone. Suddenly a dark silhouette glides towards us, with magnificent wings spread out against a purple twilight glow and I gaze in awe as two magnificent creatures beat the air with a powerful rhythm in a courtship ritual, then gracefully land either side of me on the outstretched rock. Mimi whispers:

"This is Draco!"

I look into his beautiful compassionate eyes and I know he is a perfect match for Mimi. His shiny scales are golden-green and he has a ridge of small scales from the tip of his nose to the back of his head and where Mimi has small wings behind her ears, he has curled horns like a goat and tiny scaled ridges for eyebrows. He is a mighty and powerful dragon. Suddenly the two soar above me facing each other, pausing momentarily in the silence until a flash of lightening streaks the darkening sky and Mimi is engulfed in golden, red-orange flames which flare up and consume her body. I am alarmed as her head rises above the blaze and her mouth gapes wide as she lashes out with her tongue, flailing the air like a crackling inferno. Opposite her, Draco combusts into electric blue and purple flames igniting the sky with firefly flashes, roaring and crashing with streaks of bright indigo sashes flaring into the cosmos. Together their flames mingle and burn each other. I am both in wonder and terror to witness such a spectacle. Yet I know it is a sacred joining ceremony, which I am humbled and privileged to observe. As the flames mingle and devour each other, forming a myriad of different hues, the two dragons merge until nothing is left of their magnificent bodies and the last sparks of their fires dart into the ether, leaving me alone in a heightened silence, where I drift back to my earthly reality and fall deeply asleep.

I wake in the late afternoon and it is as though, like Rip Van Winkle, I have been away for many years in a zone where there is no time limit or concept of schedules or rigid keeping of minutes, hours or days and where time has a different value. I could be in Mimi's time locality for many years and return back to earth and it would be as though I had only been away for a few minutes. Now the light has dimmed and it is time to rekindle the fire and turn on the soft side lights. Through the window I spy, where the land meets the sea, dark shadows of a mysterious underworld swimming through the waves, becoming one with a black mass of tangled seaweed, like phantom mermaids dancing a ghostly waltz. Below in the depths of the ocean are many hidden secrets and it is easy to become lost in the forever changing apparitions forming under the water. Watching the dark ballet, I am reminded that there is so much I don't understand about my own planet and the revelations I have been shown so far are mind-boggling and difficult to digest. Pondering the mysterious underworld, I pour myself a glass of burgundy wine as the holographic screen slides from the wall and the Colonel appears relaxed, sitting by an open fire in what seems to be a log cabin. Sitting next to him is a younger man casually dressed, drinking a can of beer.

"Hi there!" hails the Colonel. "Thought you might like to hear first-hand from a retired super-soldier about different time zones beyond earth. Meet Daikin."

"Hi!" Daikin greets me with a wide smile.

"Better drink that wine and sit down, Daikin has some fascinating encounters to share with you, don't you Daikin? You're gonna tell the little lady what you know."

"Sure!" affirms Daikin.

"Go on tell her what it means to be a super soldier – she's read the book we suggested about killing a goat with just a stare, so she understands a little of what you are about to describe," explains the Colonel.

"Well, er, it's very hard to believe anything I tell you because it's so far removed from your experience of reality and for that matter most peoples' – but you have to realize that reality is an illusion and like a magician convinces you that his trick is real, the 'unseen' can manipulate your mind into believing anything!"

"Yup, that's correct. The so called 'unseen' controls everything. It's easy you see because here on earth we're encased in a matrix, that is a simulated reality – computer generated by intelligence, way, way in advance of the human brain," adds the Colonel.

"I was part of an experiment," continues Daikin, "which was created to produce special babies to be trained as 'super soldiers', not here on earth but on the Moon and Mars, born with brain implants that are telepathic transmitters. From the age of four we are instructed how to use our psychic super powers and coached in super physical skills which are activated on the Moon and Mars to give us super power strength to fight strange alien creatures. Those in charge have the technological skills to replace and regrow lost limbs, broken bones and even bring us back to life from the dead if we are killed or injured in battle and even transfer souls from one body to another."

"Wow, that's amazing! Really?" I question.

"Yes, it is true. Once in battle against these grotesque creatures, which are like giant crabs and spiders, almost thirty feet wide, I saw one of our soldiers eaten and torn in half and months later he had grown a new body."

"That's a tall tale to swallow isn't it? But I can vouch that he is telling the truth; for I have witnessed similar things myself," assures the Colonel.

I remain silent trying to assimilate all the information.

"I was a soldier in the Marine core sent to Mars to defend our people who have been there for decades. Eventually we made a treaty with the Reptilians and Insectoids to help fight the Draconians who were invading sacred places, in return for the security and safety of our base."

"The Draconians...you mean Dragons?" I gulp.

"Yes, Mam,"

"But Dragons are good creatures?" I question.

"Yes, on the whole, but there is an evil species on Mars. I am sure there are many kinds of dragons who benefit humankind and are wholly good creatures, but the ones we fought were malevolent."

I thought of Mimi and her wonderful healing powers and her benevolent alignment with the human race and could never imagine her being anything other than compassionate, kind, generous and caring.

"Eventually we managed to bring peace to some zones as the Draconians fled to places further afield and when it was my time to return to earth I was age regressed, using an age reversing process which everyone who is taken to Mars or the Moon, undergoes in order to return to earth the same age as when they left. It is as if hardly any time lapsed."

What he says rings true and I believe him, feeling a strange understanding of his experiences as though I connect with being taken when I was little.

"Do you want to ask any questions before we depart?" asks the Colonel earnestly.

I feel I do, but am unable to formulate any in the moment as I am still assimilating the information.

"I hope this has clarified some concerns about time inconsistency in the Universe and has helped you to understand a little more about your own adventures into other worlds?"

I nod and thank them both for their expert advice and wonder about the strangeness of it all, thinking that perhaps sometimes it is better to live in sweet ignorance of what the world is really like than to be troubled by the horror of the truth.

After their departure, the chalet is deeply quiet, surrounded by the echo of crashing waves rising and falling on the shore and I decide to take a walk along the stony pathway leading down to the beach. I need to clear my head to grasp the new information. The cold night air, stings my nostrils as I take a deep breath looking out across the navy-blue vastness, which hypnotically dances to a secret force beckoned by the moon. In the moment I know and feel the truth of all that has been revealed to me and I wonder how I could have been so blind, naively accepting everything. Facing the greatness and magnificence of the ocean I feel small, insignificant and helpless like a tiny ant attempting to roll a boulder up a hill, realising that the 'Unseen' play us like puppets and we allow our strings to be pulled and manipulated according to their command. Daily we suffocate in a cycle of eat, sleep, work and never emerge to pause to take a look beyond the stars. It is a shock to know that humans have been involved in interstellar wars and have bases on the Moon and Mars and many other planets. The Colonel sent me evidence that America has three deep space star ships that have been in action since 2003 and have D.P.Q.T. techniques, that is Deep Protocol Quantum Tunnelling devices, which means that each star ship can shrink space time and can arrive at far distant destinations in very little real time. The information is verifiable and the names of the ships were revealed in a secret document which was leaked by a whistle-blower. The USS Curtis Lemay apparently has travelled to twenty eight different star systems. The USS Hoyt Vanderberg has the largest team of Tall White Aliens crewing the ship and the USS Roscoe travels between the star systems providing supplies and other needs. I am angry that we are not deemed trustworthy to share the greater knowledge of the privileged and made to feel foolish if we question the untruths which the world is fed concerning Aliens, space travel and inter-planetary facts. Back in the chalet I fall into a troubled sleep.

Days roll into one another and I exist. I have had no visits from the Colonel and have not been able to visit Mimi as my entrance into her world has been blocked, but I am certain it is for a good reason and know she will soon contact me. Since she has been in my life, she has enriched my understanding of many things. How can you ever be the same after you've found your dragon? I never thought my life was incomplete without one, but now Mimi is always at the back of my mind offering comfort and support in whatever I do. Her knowledge is vast and impressive and we have much to learn together – me to know and understand dragon law and apply it to my higher consciousness and her to learn about human nature and how best to give support. I am lucky to have a golden dragon to help me progress onto the next level of spiritual understanding. The wait for Mimi to contact me seems endless but a strange tingling of excitement in the pit of my stomach tells me she isn't far away. As I close my eyes and relax into night's darkness, I am swiftly transported to the side of a purple lake leading out to sea. Draco is waiting for me and nods politely as I stand by his side. The lunar landscape pitted with red and lilac rocks etched with golden, magical symbols is densely quiet. Under Draco's magnificent, powerful chest I stand looking up into his face and ask about Mimi and he telepathically replies, "she is waiting for you. She sent me to take you to her. You must understand that it is unusual for a human to visit at such a time, but she specifically asked to see you."

I don't have time to question him, as within a second I am transported to a nearby cave where I spy Mimi hunched over a nest. Draco vanishes and I stand before my beautiful dragon lying peacefully over a layer of soft sand. Her face is yielding and gentle and her eyes less piercing than usual. She seems tired and moves slowly to one side allowing me to glimpse into the nest where five eggs nestle.

"I had no idea you were going to become a Mum?" I whisper excitedly.

She slides back onto the nest and replies caustically: "Do not equate Motherhood from your earth zone with ours. Motherhood is different, so do not wallow in sentiment. We do not use the term 'Mother' like you. We do not weigh the word with so much emotion. It is our job to bring others into our realm and once they are able and capable of fleeing the nest then we never see them again because we have done our duty-that is the way and law of it, like birds and other creatures on your planet. Once the fledglings have flown the nest there is no recognition of a relationship. In our simple and unique way life's miraculous cycle continues. Draco, I have chosen as my partner and you witnessed our 'pairing' that special night and we will bring many new dragons into being and not know any of them in adulthood. This is Dragon Law and it is important for you to understand this."

I nod and can't help asking: "what about the relationship between 'connectors', I mean like you and I? Will you forget me one day?"

She gently laughs sleepily, replying: "I am not your Mother. We chose to be of equal benefit to each other. I am not responsible for you, but I can be your advisor and protector. I will be in and around your higher consciousness for as long as you wish and we do not have to communicate often but suffice it to know, I will be there for you. Now you must go!"

Her eyes close and I can't help asking one more question: "can I see your babies when they arrive?"

She briefly opens her eyes and replies: "if you must!"

Swiftly I am transported back to my earthly bed and am filled with a wonderful warmth knowing that Mimi and my whisperers will always be there for me and I feel so lucky, because I am Lucky.

CITYSCAPE ESCAPE

The weeks at the seaside chalet have fled and the golden autumn has faded leaving stark skeleton trees quivering in the icy sea breeze. This morning the Colonel left a message stating that my holiday had served its purpose and that it was time to move on and I would be contacted and taken to my next operation, but he didn't disclose details and told me to sit tight to be ready to move at short notice. I drift along the seashore wondering what my next mission will entail, realizing that it may be my last walk before I leave my sea world bubble. My people said they would come for me. They are my family from another planet and sometimes I yearn to return, but having made a promise to come to earth to help raise the higher consciousness of humanity, I have to complete my mission.

When I agreed to come to earth, the planet was a very different place and for over half a century I played my part as a dancer, choreographer and teacher, until everything changed and the first pandemic set in motion the great re-set of world government. The planned culling of humanity happened almost imperceptibly without a struggle, as everyone was duped into believing everything they were told was the truth and for their own benefit. Extreme fear was generated as a mighty weapon into making the populace comply with all the new rules and regulations when Covid 19 changed the whole world.

Now I am a fugitive, on the run from the controllers of the cityscapes, refusing to be vaccinated with their monitoring tags and micro-chip implants which manipulate all behaviour, thoughts and actions and have the capacity to annihilate anyone at any time. The 'self', as far as the new-reset community understands, no longer exists and is not encouraged. Individuality is forbidden and long before the first lock-down, education played its part in destroying the finer principals of learning, preventing the nurturing of unique, original thought. The primary goal of education from the Greek word 'educere' meaning to 'lead out' was smothered and strangled in the exam cult, where simply regurgitating the correct answers and ticking the right boxes was all that was required for an exam pass. Teachers were pressurised into making sure that most students obtained a grade 'c' or more in order to keep their jobs and were forced to falsify grades, which lowered educational standards in general throughout the country. Out-going inspirational, creative ideas became unlawful and students turned inwards, locked inside their computer cages. Now a nightly hypnotic mantra plays in the cityscapes during sleep time brainwashing the populace. I know this because I heard it once when, over-night I was hidden in a medical supply box waiting to escape the cityscape boundaries and heard the mantra played repeatedly everywhere in the city... "there is no self...self has no identity..." and it was subliminally flashed across tv screens. The mantra, I understand, brainwashes humans into believing that transmuting into robotic humanoids is best for them in the new world.

The groundwork for this process began long before the world re-set with the chemicalizatiin of food, toothpaste, washing powder, soaps, cosmetics, drinks and almost every popular commodity and life-changing additives were designed to work in conjunction with 5G electro-magnetic frequencies pulsing from power points in streets, thoroughfares, outside schools, hospitals and shopping malls. Some of the chemicals were created to dull the mind and suppress brain activity such as fluoride, which is a rat poison and dries up the pineal gland, which is said to be the engine room to fire imagination and ignite spiritual understanding. Also, earth's atmosphere was gradually altered through chemtrails and weather modification programmes and HAARP mind control weapons, to enable alien species to live and breathe on earth without synthetic aid. Robots and artificial intelligence of all kinds began to take over the world under the dictatorship of alien beings residing in Antarctica, who, it is reported, have ruled the planet surreptitiously since time began.

Surviving outside the cityscapes, is hard for everyone and I am grateful to exist from day to day without compromising my life's purpose, enjoying the liberty to roam freely and admire the natural world claiming back its life-force. But, in order to survive and exist in this strange, changing environment, it is important to keep a positive outlook on everything and adapt the Colonel's teaching of 'expecting the very best for yourself at all times and thinking 'Gold' in every situation.

This way, you protect yourself from the 'shadow people' who dwell in the dark-lands of the spirit realm. It is easy when faced with fears of everyday living to slip into the darkness, allowing a sense of hopelessness to invade all thoughts. Thinking 'gold' dissolves the lurking grey shadows to dust and I remind myself that golden light always penetrates the darkness, like the sunlight scatters sparkling gems across the vast blue ocean. Waiting for my next assignment, I resolve not to sink into dark, oppressive thoughts and I lift my head to bathe my face in the bright, golden sunlight, rejoicing in the freedom of the moment. Ahead just over the hills a black vehicle races down the country lane making its way to the seashore and my stomach churns, knowing it is time to move. I race back to the cabin to collect my bag in readiness to depart. My holiday has been fruitful and I leave the chalet with sadness, but the thought of seeing friendly faces and chatting with people after being in the wilderness for so long is exciting. Standing outside the chalet breathing in the salty air, I am empowered to take on a new challenge and have gained confidence and self-assurance with Mimi as my compass. On visiting last, she showed me five precious eggs which will be her first batch of baby dragons and I hope to be allowed to see them when they hatch. Her advice was to be stronger in my thoughts and actions and not to be afraid to speak out and assert myself. She said: 'take the dragon power with you – it doesn't have to be loud…sometimes it is more forceful when it is quietly silent.'

I watch the shiny black vehicle glint in the morning sun racing down the empty beach to the sea. You appear by my side, ready for the new adventure and I am happy to see you. We wait together for the sleek black vehicle, which is a strange combination of a police van and army truck with blacked-out windows like a secret operations car, yet it has sports-car features and speeds like a bullet.

Two Darth – Vader beings stomp out. They are cold, emotionless, robotic soldiers. They do not speak but open the back door and motion me to climb in. I obey and one of them throws my bag inside, while the other jumps in opposite me and secures a harness around my waist and shoulders. I am a little shocked as they are not what I expected and I wonder whether they are human, as I cannot see any facial features under their facemask and headgear. I am treated like a prisoner and my suspicions are aroused when the one sitting opposite takes out a gun and lays it across his knees.

I look away to watch my little chalet fade into the distance as we race along the seashore to the open empty roads. It is not how I thought it would be. My journey to the next mission should be exciting but it is not. Fear rises in my stomach and my hands sweat. I reach down to open my bag for water but the guard blocks me with his gun. "Water, I want water...!" I plead. He allows me the water and I sink back in my seat to drink slowly, whilst advising myself to think positive and I pluck up the courage to ask the guard where we are going but he blanks me. I watch and wait in silence noting the motorway miles monotonously whizzing by. Suddenly the road leaves us and we are air-born. It is strange to be flying so high in a car but to cityscape dwellers it has become the norm, like many changes brought about by great technological advances. Virtual Doctors now perform major surgery through highly skilled robots with high precision instruments and robot lawyers undertake the vast majority of cases normally handled by humans. Food is prepared by robots and cyborg bar tenders mix amazing cocktails, so I'm informed by one of the 'leakers' who is an informant residing in the cityscape and has secret contacts outside the city, exchanging new high tech gadgets with outsiders for farm reared meat, fresh eggs, cereal crops and home-grown vegetables.

Everything can be manipulated through an A.I. system – even cars can be stolen, houses robbed, money lifted from bank cards and with the hi-tech knowledge virtually everything is attainable.

Eventually we touch-down on a reinforced landing strip in front of a massive red brick fortification, which opens like a fortress draw-bridge as we drive through. My view is deliberately blocked, as black shades slide over the windows and we crawl along on a smooth road until we come to a standstill, where the guard unlocks my harness and I follow with stiff legs, wobbling after the long journey. Without speaking, he returns to his seat in the front of the vehicle and drives off with the other soldier. It is dusk. I am alone in a strange place. The soulless street is empty, totally silent; not even voices or cars stir in the stillness of the unfamiliar, cold, new world where I have no understanding of living. I am hollow in a hollow architectural greatness. I stand nervously in front of a gigantic glass skyscraper which disappears beyond a grey-lidded sky. Abandoned in a futuristic city, and unsure of what to do, I debate with myself whether to walk or wait. I am certain that someone must know I exist? I sense invisible eyes watching, testing my patience. Just as I decide to move, a glamorous woman appears through a glass door in the crystal building. She has dark blonde hair swept up in a French pleat and is wearing an off-white two piece suit with a white blouse. She has white high-heeled shoes and is carrying a red folder. She smiles as she approaches. I immediately distrust her feigned, false, over enthusiastic welcome and reluctantly shake her outstretched hand, meeting her stark blue, guarded eyes with scepticism.

I follow her inside the amazing glass and steel cathedral-like structure and am reminded of gigantic glass buildings on the far side of the moon with huge glass towers, miles high, erected by ancient aliens. Our footsteps echo on the white, highly-polished marble floor and although no one is in sight, I perceive the presence of many beings busy behind the scenes as we step inside a shiny steel lift and alight at the eighty seventh floor, which I am told is only a third of the levels and that the building is one of the smallest in the vicinity. She leads me into an open corridor where rows of empty glass cubicles are lined side by side. They are small single rooms with a bed and a compact rail on which to hang clothes and as we enter, white walls automatically descend forming a white boxed room. The clinical bed is ready made with clean white sheets and white cotton pyjamas hang on a paper coat-hanger on a small rail.

"I am Doctor 329." She opens the file as she speaks. "This is your room for the night."

"What is your name?" I enquire.

She looks puzzled and replies: "I am Doctor 329. Please undress and put on the pyjamas supplied. I will leave you and the night staff will return shortly with refreshment."

"Hey wait a minute!" I demand holding onto her arm, "where am I? What I am doing here?"

She ignores my questions pushing away my arm and states: "Please comply with the regulations as requested. You will be informed," she states mechanically.

"Wait! Wait!" I shout trying to find the door which disappears into the walls leaving the room seamless. I am locked inside. I am a prisoner. I have walked straight into their hands. A crease of light pushes through a tiny long window in the corner of the room, where, if I squint I can glimpse a little of the outside world where lights blaze from myriads of massive skyscrapers and the night buzzes with life from a motorway high in the sky where flying cars dart in and out like dodgem cars in a fairground. The vehicles are so different from the cars I knew in an era when driving was a skill performed purely on the ground. Pressing my nose to the window pane, I can make out flashing neon lights chasing in sequence across the cityscape showing glitzy stage performances projected onto buildings and small saucer-like craft cruising above the highway in the sky.

I remain squashed and folded into the corner to glimpse the outside world, until I hear someone enter and turn to see a middle-aged lady in a white overall place a portable, small table on the floor with a plate of food and a tumbler of water on a white tray and she smiles nervously adding, "The biscuits are dry but the cheese is ok, if you like that sort of thing?"

"Where am I? What is this place?" I plead with her to tell me, but she just smiles. "Where's the Doctor?" I enquire.

"Oh they're all switched off for the night!"

"Switched off?"

"Cyborgs!"

"Yes, dear, they look like us, but they're not us – they're better than us. They've got all the answers. We don't have many ordinary humans left, mostly workers like me. They're all cyborgs now you know." She stated patting the sheets and plumping up the pillow.

"Wouldn't you like to be one of them too?" I enquire casually.

"Oh it's not for the likes of me dear. I'm not clever enough; I'm happy just being a night-worker."

"What's your name?"

"We don't have names, well not when we're working."

"What is this place?"

"Don't you know dear? This is the Sequester Suite for visitors."

"The what?"

"All visitors are invited to stay here first before they are given the all-clear to enter the city. They have to make sure you don't bring any nasty diseases into our beautiful city."

"But where are we, what city is this?" I urge.

"Everyone knows this cityscape dear...!"

"I don't so what is it?"

"Well, now, you must have been out of it for a long time, why it's the epicentre of..." she stops abruptly as the door slides open for her to leave. She looks at me quizzically and rushes out leaving me staring at the four white walls. I sit on the bed and try a dry biscuit. The cheese is synthetic and plastic but palatable. Outside the city seems vast and I can only imagine if it's the epicentre of the country then it must be the new Londinia. Folk I met outside, other outlanders, spoke of the new Londinia and how the old historic monuments and buildings had long been demolished, along with the abolition of the monarchy. I need to use the bathroom and stand up panicking. Someone reads my thoughts and a screen lights up behind the bed informing me that a small green button on the far wall gives access to a bathroom. I press the button and the wall slides open to reveal a tiny bathroom with a toilet, hand basin and a corner shower. When I return to the white box room, the lights have dimmed and the screen on the back wall wishes everyone 'a good night one and all' which in a Dickensian way, is out of kilter with the high-tech, ultra-modern society. Lying down in the tiny bed with the screen glaring brightly behind me, I sense I am being observed and I distrust the screen, which I fear will transmit hypnotic messages throughout the night. I close my eyes and hear a soft droning, electronic pulse travelling in circles around the room, like the ones used to hypnotise me into a deep sleep when I was taken many, many years ago by alien beings for investigation. I try to fight sleep, but like then as now, the mesmerizing pulse takes me under and I enter a forced sleep until morning.

At dawn, a siren stirs everyone into action and the screen on the back wall declares 'a very good morning to one and all'. I stand and rub my arms where there are indentation marks on both wrists as though I have been restrained. The marks remind me of the times when I would find strange and unusual marks on my body after a night of terror in the hands of unknown beings. A wave of fear coils in my stomach and I shudder at the thought of pain inflicted torture. I call out to Mimi, my beautiful golden dragon, and see her eyes full of love and sympathy. I hear little Xian's words explaining that "your feelings will become intertwined with hers and she will feel your anguish. Do not worry because it is part of her job to do so. In fact she will expect this and will help you." In my mind she tells me to be strong and fearless and to 'drink in Dragon strength' and a curved glass bottle full of vibrant green liquid appears in my mind and I drink it, imagining a warmth spreading throughout my body leaving me with a glow of confidence.

Feeling better, I dress in a set of white clothes hanging by the door with white socks and sneakers lined up in my size. The door glides open and a guard dressed in a black uniform motions me to step out and follow the others. I obey and walk in line with other men and women all dressed in white.

No one speaks. The sound of plates and crockery being set out on tables echoes through the vast glass dome and the smell of unrecognisable heated food permeates the corridors as we parade down a gigantic escalator and line up at the entrance to a vast cafeteria where we are handed a tray.

Mechanically we approach a long counter lined with unfamiliar food, which I suspect is chemicalized and created to look like breakfast food from the past, such as cereals, milk and omelette. I take a few unappetizing things that resemble yogurt and a pancake and watch some others choose a red pill rather than eat the synthetic provisions and then I sit down at a long white table with many others. We are not allowed to speak or communicate. A black woman sitting opposite stares into my eyes and I warmly return the gaze. I gather from her expression that she is as shocked as I am to be in this strange situation, but a guard catches our interaction and walks purposefully towards us with his laser, so we dip our heads to avoid his scrutiny. There is a constant flow and flux of movement, like airport lounges from the past and I am surprised all kinds of aliens and strange beings enter and exit in every direction. It's a nightmare scene from a horror film with insect-like creatures with human features and slimy, bulbous organisms with gelatinous bodies rolling and slithering along the white floor. A bell resounds and we all rise and walk back to our box cells where a history of Londinia is playing on the screen.

I sit down on the bed to watch the documentary presenting Londinia as an amazing cityscape with all the amenities and facilities of an ultra-modern society. I watch appalled at the changes in modern living in the cityscape and the augmentations humans are adopting to become transhuman. The adverts are constantly feeding the community's lust to become super human on every level, which is the ultimate achievement of the new human prototype. Keeping up with technology is now a constant ongoing goal and the companies offering the transformations relentlessly push their latest physical conversions further and further into the robotisation of humanity. The film is interrupted every couple of minutes to advertise brain enhancements, super hi-tech communication implants, and body augmentations transforming people into super-human athletes. Clones with super human abilities are devised to take the strain and stress out of ordinary life. Clips show the clone becoming a person's avatar going to work and enjoying social events, while the original person stays at home controlling the dummy with an electro-magnetic device. Humans with enough credit can buy youth, super-human powers and immortality.

As the door slides open, the screen fades and a young man in a white nurse's uniform enters with a tray. His face is plastic and his hair fake, like one of the androids on the adverts.

"I would like to take your temperature if you don't mind?" He states apologetically.

I nod and stand in front of him as he scans my body with a neat instrument which takes my temperature and records it for future reference.

"That's fine," he adds then promptly exits.

The screen flashes on again this time advertising the ultra-modern living space – organic pods in the shape of large eggs where a being, human or otherwise can rest, sleep or play interactive games and have virtual reality experiences with five sensory encounters where you can see, hear, touch, taste anything you desire and you can be soaked in colour vibration, drenched in sensations and have the ultimate corporeal indulgence ever created. The organic pod provides all that is necessary to live a fully contented, happy life. The screen fades again as the door slides open and a man enters who is the replica of a gentle professor from my university days. I am aware that he is a character rather than a real person, devised to gain my trust.

"Hello my name is Professor Alton and it's my job to help ease you into your new surroundings. I know it must be difficult to adapt to the new world after living a primitive existence for so long.

Come with me if you please?"

I take offense at the word 'primitive' as my world, as I understand it, is far from crude and full of beauty, albeit hard, unlike the sterile, unnatural, monochrome fairground in the cityscape.

I follow him out into the corridor, which is now a bustle of all manner of beings scurrying along, some even have electric shoes transporting them at great speed through the crowds. We pause looking down at the endless glass and steel floors below, as multitudes of alien species interact with humans, cyborgs, robots and androids. The professor proudly states:

"See down there, it makes you feel honoured to be part of all this, to witness intergalactic forces all harmoniously residing side by side in a wonder world of technological genius. The future is here and now and more so!" He exclaims enthusiastically.

I remain silent as we continue towards the lift.

"You see what we have achieved is a cityscape paradise where everyone has what they need for their level of existence."

"Level of existence?" I question.

"Yes my dear, there is nothing so unequal as everyone treated as equals!" He scorns.

I sigh shaking my head as the Professor continues.

"You see the planet was dying, heaving under the strain of supporting far too many inhabitants and the only kind, reasonable action to take, was to relieve the world of a percentage of its population and divide the remaining populace into three categories- the workers, the thinkers and the innovators."

"But how can you segregate people into three classifications?" I enquire.

"Quite easily my dear. Every person has a place, a mission, a purpose. Everyone is happy with their position and status. Every being is part of the whole and that is how it works."

"But when a baby is born how can you be certain about its status?" I probe.

"Again, easy my dear, the concept of parents from the old ways and parenting, no longer exists. Sex is for sexual pleasure only and reproduction is performed entirely in our labs so that we have total control over the entrance and exits of our population."

"Exits? You mean you determine the death of people?"

"Well it's not as shocking as it sounds. When the workers and the thinkers come here they enter into a contract specifying their arrival and departure dates, which are then recorded and processed by our computers. Departures are activated automatically."

I listen and know it all, have heard it all, seen it all and the 'brave new world' is now, as I learnt it from the past. "What about the 'innovator sector do they get to choose their departure date?" I enquire.

"Well, that is slightly different – they have a choice of our immortality programme, but we won't go into that right now."

We step inside the lift which glides smoothly, flying silently to the top of the building. "You see it's all so well balanced. We don't have a government to make silly, uninformed mistakes. We have the tip-top best Artificial Intelligence which can never be destroyed."

"You mean the country is run by a computer? What if it breaks down?"

The Professor laughs and shrugs his shoulders explaining, "Our higher intelligence is self-regenerating, there is no such thing as a 'break down' it just can't happen!"

We exit the lift and walk into an amazing crystal dome with a panoramic view of the city. I gaze out across the clean, clear lines of the mass high-rise towers built of glittering glass and shiny materials erected in fantastic shapes, reflecting rainbow colours emanating from multi-coloured fountains and waterfalls. Neat synthetic parks divide the city into sections which are unsoiled, sanitary, dirt-free recreational areas, where no pets, or stray animals or insects ever roam because they have long been eradicated. The Professor explains that people still have pets but they are essentially robots-cyber-pets. Animals in general, in the cityscapes have been phased out long ago, as they were deemed non-essential, useless devourers of nutrients. Everything is planned, calculated and sanitised leaving no room for error or disturbance. I ask if police patrol the city. He is shocked and replies: "My dear, the police force and the idea of policing a state was long removed from our civilized society. People automatically conform to the rules. We have no need to rebel against anything. We have a flawless system and if anyone has any defective thoughts or steps out of line, they are called to the chamber of Justice to be questioned and are given the choice of staying or leaving to eek out a terrible existence in the cold, crude outlands beyond the cityscape walls. There are no prisons because we simply have no need of them."

"You mean they have to answer to a computer?"

"Of course, what else my dear? Higher Intelligence is far wiser than we mere mortals!"

"But what if a worker wants to progress to become a thinker, what then?"

The Professor heartily laughs stating, "well my dear, that can never happen. You see worker food reflects their situation and station in life containing, let's say, brain suppressants which control mind activity..."

"You mean you drug them?"

"Well that sounds harsh, but it's for their own good and for the good of everyone!"

I am uneasy and suddenly yearn to be back in the outlands. The Professor senses my anxiety and invites me to step outside the dome explaining "there is something I would like you to witness outside on top of the world, so to speak. Come, it isn't cold, our weather and temperature is always regulated so we have no insecure battles with unwelcome weather bouts."

I follow him and step onto an amazing balcony, the likes of which I experienced standing at the top of the Eiffel Tower in Paris and the Empire State building in New York, many years ago.

"I see you are impressed my dear!"

"It is truly an amazing sight which I haven't experienced since... since my travels." I add.

"Ah yes travel. There was a time when many humans travelled across the globe I believe, but of course we have no need for that primitive activity any more, every cityscape is the same, even the cityscapes in the sky are built exactly the same across the planet, so what would be the point of going somewhere that is replicated elsewhere? We have virtual reality scopes that can give you any travel experience you desire. So we have no need to tour when everything is at our fingertips. You see our world is complete."

"There are cityscapes in the sky?" I enquire.

The Professor laughs adding, "Of course, there are many cities built on islands in the sky. Now I will leave you here for a while to ponder your future. You can stay here and work with us in your specialist psychic field and become part of our forwardscope team, or you can return to rot in your primitive cave and probably die from one poison or another or some obnoxious disease roaming out there. The choice is yours. If you leave, you will return back to the past where last we found you."

"Past?" I enquire.

"This time is now in the future. Here you are part of the imminent present."

"I wasn't aware that I had flown into the future."

"The vehicle you were transported in is a time transcender, capable of travelling through time, out of time, beyond time and around time."

His last words drift into the synthetic air as he leaves me to make a choice. The light dims from an internal switch signalling the city dwellers to prepare for evening and from fake twilight hues, the light technicians fade to black.

I stroll over to an extraordinary telescope and peep out beyond the lidded dome into the real galaxy. Here is the future amongst the stars. Here are the galaxies of forever. The telescope is an amazing feat of engineering and can penetrate universes, beyond multi-universes where time has no meaning or debilitating rhythm or restrictive imprisonment and where time is a nothingness not a word. As the telescope draws me into a swirling mass of purple gas, I enfold into it and am sucked into a vortex of frothing smoke, eddying into another universe where I arrive on red soil looking up into a violet sky towards the place from whence I came. A voice greets me but I see no one. In a dream-like, hypnotic state I ask: "Where am I?" and the voice replies: "In another universe, away from yours."

Gaining awareness I look around. I am standing in a red sand arena and a black silhouette of a matador promenades in the far right corner. I move closer to see him and he transforms into a Mexican Indian who tells me to lie down. I obey him and as I crawl to the floor I note black mountains outlined against the darkening night sky, like menacing giants. With my ear to the ground I hear the beating pulse of creation throbbing, flowing, flying, flipping, sighing, whispering –
"ONE. All IS ONE. All life is ONE! ONE! ONE! And on and on only ONE."
In that moment of infinity I know and feel with all my heart and being that I am part of a whole much vaster, more intense, more alive than life itself, and I grasp that as an energy, as a form of life I can never die. My body is on earth and yet I have travelled out far beyond to another universe and I am the same. I, me, myself are one but without my body and I am not alone – I am part of one energy. I have known it all along but never really understood it and now passionately feel it. I want to return to my body to connect with it and tell everyone what I know. I ask the voice: "Where is my planet?"
"See that black swirling mass over there?"

I look and see a blob of black energy wriggling, writhing and pulsing. I do not understand why it appears so angry.

"That is your universe."

"Why is it so disturbed?"

"Because it is a universe of choice. It is a universe of conflict. It is a universe where battles are fought between light and dark forces. It is a university universe where souls seek enlightenment through selection and adversity."

"It looks a harsh energy." I add.

"It is, but you chose it. If you reach out beyond the angst, beyond the fear and doubt you will find Peace, for you are not alone and never will be, or have been." I take comfort from the words.

"Walk towards the black mass and you will be taken back. Take time to view your planet for you will see your world as it is." And with this advice the voice fades.

I follow the directions and am swallowed back into a gyrating mass of kaleidoscopic energy which spirals into a small bright hole through which I glimpse a beautiful blue planet – the earth, my world where, through a misty veil gazillions upon bazillions of silver-stringed energy, coil and spiral from the masses of people, like tiny optic fibre snakes twisting, grasping, clutching at the air in vain to return to the truth of their origin. As a child I was aware of my own silver thread anchoring me to earth and that when I left my body, the silver string always brought me back. From a distance I clearly see the silver fibres anchoring souls to earth but each is fragile searching for answers, chasing clouds beyond rainbow spheres, seeking secrets hidden in deepest space and chasing shooting stars with firefly flashes, yet returning, knowing that 'ashes to ashes, dust to dust' is the legacy of human mortality. I hear the thunderous roar of questions pending doubt and worth from delicate souls seeking to know 'what is reality?' I feel the rising fear of humanity, uncertain that when the sunsets on each day are they ever sure if they will wake again to open the door to new opportunities. I am horrified to witness the churning energy of emotion which cries out in anguished agony searching for comfort. I behold the searing pain of love lost and lost loved ones as the planet screams under the weight of its sorrow and destruction.

So why return to earth? From the depths of despair a light shines, a golden light of love cascading with powerful explosions of sparkling energy enveloping all. It is always there and has been and always will be. Through the ether I spin and suddenly I am back inside my body. I am weary but strong. I know what I must choose. I cannot stay in the future. I must return back to the past with my new strength and knowledge to share my experience. I look around the cityscape and view an amazing technological feat. The new world buzzes engineering magic, the likes of which I had never imagined possible, but I need to return to the world I left. I think of Mimi and she appears in my imagination. She smiles acknowledging my choice and tells me she is waiting for me and that we have much to accomplish together. The professor is not pleased with my decision but accepts it reluctantly, dismissing me as though I have thrown away a precious gift saying; "return then to your primitive world, you may regret it when your planet collapses. Go, go back to your time of hardship and disease. I have shown you the best you will ever know and you wish to turn your back on the future. Go! Returning is easy, all you have to do is wish it and you will be transported back to an era of your choosing." With his final words he reveals his true self, slowly transforming into a Mantid-like creature with a human body and gigantic praying mantis head. As he fades out of sight, I am left standing on the edge of the brave new world of tomorrow but I wish to return home to a time of great contentment.

You are here and have witnessed it all. It has been a strange journey and one in which I never envisaged travelling to the future and I am lucky to have shared it with you. Now I am going back.

We are going back. Let us jump together. We are lucky, for I am indeed – LUCKY.

POSTCARD BACK FROM THE FUTURE

I am on my way back to the past from the future and my brain is inundated with high-tech, artificial intelligence information, having glimpsed an unbelievable, space-age world with technological advancement and machine computerisation, the likes of which I never imagined possible and where robotised humans and transhuman beings live side by side with aliens and hybrid human-aliens. After the trauma of the mind-blowing experience, I need to find an oasis of peace and calm with conventional humans residing in a haven of natural surroundings like the time when I lived in a beautiful log cabin in a forest.

As I travel back through my memory bank, I am drawn into a tranquil scene, which forms as I arrive.

I stand on my beloved veranda as it assembles before me just as I remember it. I am home. Log by log, walls of recollection build. Here is stillness. Here is nature. Here is earth's diurnal round of night and day and day and night in a sky of bright stars unblemished by light pollution. Birds call each to each and the little Jenny Wren nest bustles with three hungry, squawking chicks, impatient to be fed. My beautiful purple buddleia tree in full bloom is set alight with a cascade of red admiral butterflies fluttering in the gentle breeze. I step inside my lodge where my two cats wait to be fed.

Have I been away for a long time? It seems I have just gone shopping and returned with your food.

Have you missed me? Curling around my legs and nudging my feet with your heads you show me love – oh how I have missed you! I fill your bowls with food just like before. Can I have been away and witnessed so much to return in the blink of an eye? Was it all a dream or can time loop itself in and out of existence? Silence is the hushed pause I remember and peace is the tranquil calm that harmoniously reigns here. Alone with my two cats I am back in a time of contentment. I breathe again. I have returned to a time when life was uncomplicated. Where are the others? I see my own cabin and the immediate surroundings but not beyond. Can it be that I have only enough power to create my own vibration, but not that of other people? Is this a holographic experience where I can plug in and out of a timeline at will? Do I create my own existence in this memory and having walked into it, can I enter others?

"*You can.*" My whisperers reply.

"But how?" So many questions bubble and rise to the surface.

"*By using your inner energy, as you have just experienced.*"

"Explain please?"

"*Firstly you have to understand that your perception of the world is determined by a collective consciousness ; that is the general consensus of the world's structure. You were born into a configuration which all earthlings accept and understand as their reality, whereas in fact reality is like a shimmering mirage, mirroring what you wish to see, which is both deceptive and limiting.*

Humanity has the capacity to create a life reality span for a limited period, which is a coded reality.

Human DNA contains lost codes and hidden memories from the beginning of time and a multi-dimensional awareness is optimum for rescuing those lost codes, together with secrets which you have been brain-washed to forget, but when you remember, you will realize you are much more than your body or a physical resonance. You are energy which can migrate into other energies, therefore you can travel into another memory."

"But a memory is only a memory, not a living organic process, is that so?" I enquire.

"*Correct*", my whisperers confirm.

"So I can't stay in a memory?"

"*You could, but you would be stuck in a time lock.*"

"Would it be difficult to get out of the time lock?"

"*It depends on what type of memory you are locked in,*" my whisperers state firmly.

I am surprised by the implication of different types of memory and probe the idea further and receive a very detailed reply, as they whisper the information on a sound vibration which tingles in my ears-

"*You see a memory is an event recorded in the mind which can be played over and over again at will.*"

"And of course everyone has this facility," I interrupt abruptly.

There is an admonishing silence, before they begin again and I promise not to interrupt the flow of the information.

"*There are four main types of memory. The first is 'Fleeting Recall', which is just a momentary glimpse into the past, such as a flash-back or an association recall, or a sensory recall and the mind does not delve too deeply into the recollection. The second is 'Memory Search Engine' when you search your mind to remember information or recollect a person's name, or reconnect with knowledge learnt from the past. The third 'Event Reinvent' is when you go in deeper into your memory bank to relive, revive or reinvent a specific recorded experience or happening. In recalling the memory you do not have the intention to stay there but may linger there for a while and therefore the brain does not become attached to it and you are free to dip in and out of the experience. Then there is a dangerous zone where a person unwittingly enters a memory and stays there, triggering the brain to believe you are actually living the memory , not just recalling it, and this situation can loop and loop, especially when a person has dementia or suffering from trauma, both physical and mental.*

I understand the information and wonder about other psionic data, asking: "Are apparitions and ghost energies, people who are stuck in a time lock?"

"*That is also correct.*"

I remember the beings I freed in Barcelona who had been burnt to death centuries ago and were trapped in their earthly dogma, believing they would be rescued, remaining perpetually locked inside a time loop waiting until someone like me, with insight beyond the norm to free them. I recall a harrowing experience I had when I was pregnant with my first child, relocating from London to North Yorkshire to live in an old farmhouse. It was a daunting prospect, especially moving to a cottage that had been the centre for black magic rituals and child sacrifice, of which I had no prior knowledge, until my days and nights were haunted with frightening paranormal disturbance and terrible psychic attacks. Being heavily pregnant, I was highly protective of my unborn child and fearful of malignant spirits caught in an earthly prison of their own making. My spirit protectors revealed terrible information about the devilry and occult mal-practice that had been initiated in the cottage and many people who visited witnessed shocking paranormal phenomenon. A local tiler who was employed to re-tile the kitchen floor came one afternoon to remove the tiles and never came back to complete the job. His wife telephoned to explain that he had seen and heard horrifying things that he couldn't discuss and would never under any circumstances return. Just having moved, to my dream cottage, I was not going to be ousted by anyone or anything, so I endured the psychic onslaught hoping it would vanish when my baby was born. A month before the birth I had retired to bed early and lay awake thinking about my unborn child, when my attention was drawn to a corner of the white ceiling where I thought I saw a flash of light. I concentrated on the spot where a small round yellow light was slowly advancing across the ceiling, flickering like a hand-held candle and suddenly floating into focus was a young woman with long black curly hair, wearing a Victorian white nightdress holding a burning candle in a pewter candlestick holder. I was alarmed and mesmerised as I stared at the heavily pregnant woman who was gaunt and terrified. She seemed to take forever to walk from one end of the room to the other before disappearing through my built-in wardrobe.

My whisperers informed me that she had been the victim of a black magic, sacrificial ritual where her baby was cut from her womb and sacrificed for devil worship. What I saw was a time loop memory just before her terrible ordeal. The trauma and pain of her murder caused her to be locked in a time zone until something or someone could free her.

Sitting on my veranda, wrapped in my memory of long, lost summer evenings watching the sun sink below the trees and sipping clementine whiskey sour, I recall another time-loop experience. It was a period of my life when I organised Performing Arts trips for young people across four different European countries. I loved the job and the travel opportunities but in order to create the right material for the pupils, it was important to visit schools and meet the students who were going to participate and perform in the country of their choice. On one such visit I had to travel across London on the underground and not knowing my way around, it was stressful as I had a time schedule to meet. It was fine taking the mainline tube, but when I had to branch out to other lines I became nervous, especially when the line I was supposed to take had been closed for repair. As I stood on the dim, dusty platform with the wind whistling through the black tunnel, I began to panic.

I didn't know how to get to the school and I dreaded the thought of losing the contract. Looking around in despair, I realised I was alone on the platform as everyone else was familiar with alternative routes and had dispersed. Tears of frustration welled as I hoped with all my heart to find someone who could help me. I turned and behind me was a frail, small lady, wearing a headscarf and a drab mackintosh, who reminded me of an old Indian lady I once knew when I lived in India, but the lady on the platform was unhealthily pale with skeletal features and sunken eye sockets. I asked her if she could direct me to a line which would take me to my destination. She smiled meekly and answered in a distant, far-away tone, explaining she was on her way to the hospital and was going in my direction. I followed her to another platform noting her painful walk, carrying a flimsy plastic carrier bag which seemed to be a burden for her. I asked if I could carry her bag but she declined adding that her hospital visit would only be short and the bag wasn't heavy. It was only a short wait before the tube train rumbled into the station screeching to a halt and we climbed on board the empty carriage.

I sat opposite her feeling extremely grateful to be travelling in the right direction and smiled, but she was distant and locked in her thoughts. We quickly thundered to the next stop and as she stood up to leave, she pointed to the stop I had to take on the tube map above me. I nodded and studied the map and realising I was no longer lost, I suddenly had the urge to thank her and rushed to the door, but she had disappeared. As the tube juddered into action to leave, I searched the platform to wave to her, but she was not there. I sat pondering the meeting. She couldn't walk very fast and so could not have left the long platform before the train set off. Then I recalled an unusual fact about the ride. I had stared at her watching my reflection in the black window opposite but couldn't see her reflection in the reverse window. At the time it didn't seem strange but on considering it, I realised it was odd. All the way to my final destination I pondered her timely appearance and her strange disappearance. She was like an angel who had come to help me when I most needed it. Later after my successful meeting at the school, I asked my whisperers about her and was told she was in a time loop and having died alone without any family, she had continued to take the same tube train day after day, repeating the journey like the repetitive events in the film Ground-Hog Day. They further explained that not everyone would be able to see her, it was only people like myself with second sight that could encounter her. Also because she had spoken to me, and helped me, her time loop was broken and she was free at last to move on from her incarceration.

Now I am gloriously pampering myself, eating my favourite food, drinking sparkling wine and indulging in the peace and harmony of my cats asleep on my feet and shoulders. Time inside the memory is whatever I wish it to be and stress-free. Inside my memory I can re-charge my batteries at will before I move on. Gratitude overwhelms me. I am so grateful for my life; for my children; for my loves; for my contentment and happiness. I wish I could kiss and hug all my children and grandchildren and tell them how much I love them, but I am inside a memory and can't reach beyond. I look towards the vast universe beyond the forest, aching for all that was and I yearn to see my children again. Where are they now? My whisperers feel my pain and advise me:

"*Living inside a memory will only give you the limited experience of that time encounter. It is dangerous to stay inside the past, you must move on.*"

I understand. I know that the essence of a memory is limited and repetitive and the quality second-hand. I also realise that I have no free will to manoeuvre the present and I must precipitate a shift of consciousness in order to move on, but I am lost and not sure how to heave myself forwards.

"*Focus!*" They command. "*You must bring your point of attention to the front of your mind and forget the memory.*"

"But what is the point of having a memory if I can't use it?" I ask.

"*It's a yard-stick, something by which you measure your life's worth. You can look back and see how far you have journeyed and what experiences have formed your inner energy. It can define who you think you are and help you outline future goals. It is a record of your daily existence. A memory can help you analyse your mistakes and guide you to learn from them and maintaining a memory helps you to complete the full picture of who you are today, but you must measure who you will be tomorrow by the present – so you must return.*"

I had never thought about the function of 'memory' and knew I had to return to the present but a question posed itself and I had to know the answer. "What happens to people with dementia?"

Without hesitation they replied:

"*Their brain steers them back to a time of safety where they are secure, which is quite often a memory loop from their childhood and they live inside that time, cut off from their present reality not knowing or recognising their own children or husbands and wives.*"

I accept the information, recognising how the brain is eaten away, leaving only a slight resemblance of the person who once inhabited a body – a person like my Father. It is comforting to remember happy times and it is good to have a memory bank to dip into at will. I listen as my whisperers explain: "*The brain is a very special machine, more powerful than you could ever imagine and it hallucinates conscious reality, imagined or real. The mind is the navigator and the heart is the barometer monitoring emotions, all of which drive the physical body, but in order to have full control of all faculties in the present you must travel beyond your memory. You have the power to fight through!"*

"Return...fight through" I hear my words form from a distance echoing from far away.

"Listen, she's trying to speak..." a voice from a dark tunnel whispers.

"Fight to return..." I repeat plainly and open my eyes.

"She's opening her eyes," another voice whispers.

Where is the now? Blurred faces slowly fade then slide into focus. I close my eyes. Voices whisper.

Muffled sounds of movement distantly reverberate through a void, then return to my head. I struggle to recognise simple words. I open my eyes again and the faces become clearer.

"Well hello there, welcome back. Don't try to sit up too quickly, take your time. Don't worry you are among friends. You are safe." A large woman reassures me.

I sit up slowly feeling my head swathed in bandages. My head throbs, my eyes ache. My body is bruised and battered.

"Here drink this slowly. You are lucky to be alive."

"I am lucky. My name is Lucky," I croak.

"She's suffering from amnesia" a voice whispers.

"What happened?" I ask meekly.

"It was an accident dear, a bad crash."

"I remember getting into a black vehicle with two black-guard soldiers and arriving somewhere in the future!"

"Poor dear, she's confused...?"

"Don't you worry yourself right now, it's more important for you to get well." A friendly voice assures.

"But I...I was taken to Londinia."

"No dear, you're here in Wales, in a beautiful place far from any cityscape."

"Wales?" I question. "I was in Cornwall on my way to Londinia."

"You were on the right road alright, but in the wrong place at the wrong time!" A male voice states.

"Don't try to move dear, you've been in a coma for ten days and your body is weak." The large lady explains.

Coma? I struggle with the word and yet it all makes sense. My subconscious steered me to my memory bank, to a time when I was happy and contented. There I was able to recuperate and summon up energy to return to the living present.

The man moves forward to speak and sits on the end of the bed. He is middle-aged with greying dark hair and beard, wearing old-fashioned army combat gear. He speaks softly; "I am sorry you were caught up in all of this. The ambush was meant only for the blade guards, we didn't know there was a passenger on board."

I look blankly at him and cannot speak.

"There are still some of us left fighting on the edge and…" he continues but is interrupted by the large lady.

"Later, later, explain later, right now let's leave her be and let her rest."

She ushers them all out leaving me alone to ponder my new situation.

Placing my feet on the old, uneven cold stone floor I know this is now and not a memory. The vibration of the present is dynamic and energetic. Through the window the sky is real with sunshine blinking through clouds. The farm is lovely set amongst acres of undiluted farmland and is, as I have been told a special haven for outlanders. From my window I can see children playing and the sound of their laughter ignites a lost flame. Here is a slice of normality carved in the countryside.

Here is a lifestyle from the old ways. The door flings open and a young teenage girl enters with a tray of food and a bag of clean clothes.

"I am glad you are better, well getting better. We were all worried about you. They sent these."

She places the tray down on a small table and puts the clothes on the bed.

"What's your name?" I enquire quietly.

"Rebecca," she smiles sweetly, "What's yours?" she asks.

"Lucky!" I reply.

She stifles a laugh and places her hand over her mouth, embarrassed at her truthful reaction.

"What's wrong?" I question. "Oh, er nothing, they said you would be suffering from amseizure and probably wouldn't remember much!"

"Amnesia!" the teacher inside me corrects her.

"You will like it here, it's a very nice community and we are safe from the city dwellers and marauders. We've been left alone for a long time now." She turns and jumps on the bed adding enthusiastically; "and did you know that this place used to belong to a very famous pop star, a long time ago when they had pop stars and film stars in the world outside? My Mum told me she used to watch them on her mobility phone,"

"Mobile" I interrupt.

"Yes, one of those and in the common room there is still the organ he used to play,"

"Ooh, wow!" I reply, "I used to play the organ many years ago in the old life!"

"That must have been a long time ago?" she adds, chattering aimlessly, until I am finally released by a large lady who orders her out of the room.

"I am sorry if she has been bothering you, she is curious to meet new-comers from the old life. Oh by the way my name is Lydia and yours is...?"

I pause, remembering Rebecca's reaction and I fall silent.

"Oh never mind, it doesn't matter, I'm sure you'll tell us when you remember?"

She leaves the room and I peck at the food and get dressed in a long white caftan decorated with multi-coloured beads dangling from the neckline. A pair of blue flip flops just fit and I venture out of the door and walk carefully down an old medieval corridor. The farm must be very old and was renovated to a very high standard by the pop star in the old days when celebrities had plenty of money to buy outlandish places.

My wobbly legs take me down a winding staircase into a homely entrance hall with a distinct smell of rubber rising from a mass of raincoats, outdoor wear and wellingtons. I hear voices in the kitchen and the clatter of pots and pans. As I enter three women preparing food and two dogs stop and stare. The younger one speaks : "Well now, looka who's here? You should na be on your feet you know. Sit down." She places a stool by my side. "My name's Gael and this is Margie and..."

"I'm Helen!" A middle-aged lady chips in, "and yours is?"

"It's Ezianne!" calls out Rebecca, as she enters happily skipping, munching an apple.

"And how do you know young lady?" enquires Helen, pointing at her with a large wooden spoon.

"She told me!" scorns Rebecca.

I remain silent, wondering if Rebecca prevented me from saying my name in case the others also found it funny, or whether she had made it up on the spur of the moment?

"Ezianne is a lovely name," added Gael, "and where does it come from?"

"Italy!" shouts Rebecca, knowledgably.

"You know a lot, little miss nosey parker!" scolds Margie, placing a large pie in the oven.

"Well, it's right, she told me, didn't you Ezianne?"

I remain silent. The women busily continue their chores explaining that in the community they have some very talented and skilled men who fix generators and mend almost anything electrical and that they are very fortunate to run their own electricity.

"Rebecca, make yourself useful and show Ezianne the common room. She can rest there!" states Margie forcefully.

Rebecca reluctantly obeys and slides down from her stool and motions me to follow. She walks painfully slowly allowing me to catch up and eventually pauses in front of wooden double doors which open inwards, revealing an amazing room the size of a mini concert hall, with a magnificent church organ on the far wall complete with steel organ pipes and wooden foot pedals. I guess the pop star had created the entertainment area to play for guests. The organ is truly magnificent and I eagerly clamour on the beautiful polished seat to inspect the notes. Rebecca switches on a light and then another switch by the organ which whirrs it into action. Elated, I cautiously play one note which reverberates around the room, echoing sweetly as the tone bounces off the walls. Little by little I add more notes, experimenting with the stops – swell to great-dulci-pianissimo and finally I plunge into a piece long forgotten. The notes wake up under my fingers and call to each other claiming the moment and I am lost in a miraculous melody from the past. Pausing before the final chord, I float back to earth amidst thunderous applause from the community who have gathered to listen to the music. A man steps forwards with long silver hair and beard and reverently addresses me: "That was beautiful. It is so wonderful to hear such sounds again. My dear wife use to play, but since she died no one has taken up the art."

I smile and thank them all for their kindness and promise to play again later that evening after the communal supper.

Rebecca adopts me and takes pride in giving me a tour of the compound. It is a wonderful place for re-settling outlanders and I am fortunate to have been saved by them, although the same people set the trap in the first place causing my injuries. Their plan was to ambush and kill the black guards and to take the vehicle but the explosives were too strong and exploded wrecking it, killing the guards and throwing me onto the verge. They had, however, managed to salvage parts from the vehicle to use on the farm, so perhaps my accident wasn't in vain? As we walk, one of the young men approaches and introduces himself as Dale and apologises for causing the accident, assuring me that the crew had no idea I was in the back. I thank him for his concern and confirm I am well on the mend. He smiles and returns to the tractor he is fixing. I do not remember the moment of the explosion, but am told I was thrown from the vehicle by the roadside and taken to the farm where I lay in a coma for ten days. I ponder the power of the mind still able to function when the body falls into disrepair. I know my mind travelled to the future to encounter earth changes and was given the choice to stay or return to the present. In doing so, I was still me, still the same spirit energy but without my physical body. I travelled with my light body and making the choice to return to the present, I needed to heal my mind, so it was necessary to revert to a time of peace, which was stored and filed away in my memory bank. My watchers did not want me to stay locked in a memory and encouraged me to fight to journey back. When the time was right I could feel myself drawn into conscious rising, and sucked through a tunnel into to a new pitch of resonance.

Walking with Rebecca the relief of being alive in the moment is overwhelming and I pause to breathe, taking a big gulp of air. Tears fall silently and I surreptitiously wipe them away not wishing Rebecca to see, but she does and gently steers me back to the main house where everyone is gathering for supper. Everyone introduces themselves enthusiastically, welcoming me into the community and I am ushered to a place at the table next to Rebecca. The women are great cooks and the food is delicious made with real food, home-grown and harvested by hand, not chemical, synthetic sustenance I had encountered in the future. There are twenty people at the table, not including myself, with four children under ten years and three teenagers, enjoying the meal and recounting their day's events. It is beautifully peaceful and ordinary, like a loving family. After supper we all assemble in the common room and I give them a little recital which they fervently appreciate, and then around the fire, stories are exchanged from the old days-the pre-pandemic era before the world was thrown into a new order-a chaotic disorder! As it grows dark the young ones are taken to bed and a little later the teenagers disappear leaving the senior members of the community to sit and ponder the future. Leonard brings out the potcheen and hands a wee dram to the elders who reverently down it in one gulp, laughing heartily as he refills their glass. Gael looks at me intently as though searching her mind for an answer and triumphantly states: "Ah there it is, I knew you reminded me of someone!"

"Oh?" I reply.

"Yes, a woman, just like you came through here last year with her husband and they stayed a few months before moving on to Scotland. She does, doesn't she Helen, remind you of that woman, oh what was her name...?"

"Oh you mean Estrella?" replies Helen.

"Yes, that's it Estrella, she was just like you!"

My heart skips a beat. Estrella is my eldest daughter's name and she married a Scotsman. Excitedly I question the group in the hope that I might ascertain if the woman in question is my daughter. The group tell me of her natural healing gift and how she healed one of the sick children with her knowledge of herbs and natural medicine and they praised her artistic ability and were proud of the picture she painted for the community.

"Oh please may I see it?" I enquire.

"Run and get it Marge."

"So you think she might be your daughter?" queries Helen.

"Who knows, but it would be wonderful if it was – I haven't seen her for many, many years, not since our world fell apart and we were scattered across the country unable to reach one another."

Marge scurries in carrying a small painting. I recognise the work immediately with its magical, mysterious, spiritual undertones and lyrical shapes.

"Well what do you think?" urges Helen.

I am unable to speak, drinking in the essence of my eldest daughter. I know it is her work. I kiss the frame. She is alive I am sure. Overwhelmed with relief, I hug the painting and a warmth seeps across my heart. I want to go to her – "I must find her, I must…!" I cry rushing to the door but my legs collapse and my head spins. Someone catches me and the lights go out.

I wake in the dimness and turn to see Rebecca asleep in the armchair next to my bed. She makes me smile and I am grateful for her devotion. My thoughts race to my daughter-she is alive! I begin to plan how I can find her, but inwardly I know as yet, I am not strong enough to travel. They said she was making her way to Scotland with her Scottish husband and that was at least six months ago. I get up quietly, trying not to disturb Rebecca but she stirs and asks if I am feeling better. I tell her to go back to sleep as I shuffle downstairs to the kitchen for a drink of water where I find Lydia drinking tea.

"Well, well, well!" she utters, surprised to see me up. "Who would have thought you would come across your daughter in these parts?"

I nod and pour a glass of water.

"You know you are not yet well enough to leave?" she affirms.

I nod in agreement and take a sip of water and sit down next to her at the kitchen table.

"I know how hard it is not to just get up and go, but you have to think of your health. Look, Tom is leaving here in a month's time to take some pigs over to the border and you could go with him. From there you might find another lift further into the Highlands, who knows where she might be or if you'll be able to find her at all?"

I know she is right and agree to her plan. I watch the night fade into dawn and a watery grey sky turn golden as the sun rises above the woods and I tell myself -there is always a reason why things happen. My voices whisper and echo my thoughts explaining:

"*You are not able to see the thread interwoven and intricately stitched behind the tapestry, all you see is the end result of the framed picture. Wishing and wanting something to happen will not always bring the desired results because what you want is not always what you need. The universe drip-feeds everyone's needs and YOU must be patient."*

I only know that as long as there is hope that I might be reunited with my daughter, I will be patient.

The voices whisper – *"dum spiro spero...while I breathe I hope."* I remember well the title to one of my special performances when I was asked to choreograph the Church of England's history through the form of Jazz dance. It was performed at Walsingham and was very well received. My small company of dancers loved it but hidden in the choreography was the power of the high-priestess healer, the pagan goddess alive and well, thriving amongst the pomp and ceremony of man-made Christianity. I was honoured for the piece and invited to the House of Lords for high tea to celebrate my artistry. How I laughed to myself knowing my little joke against the establishment. I now look back at the turn of events which destroyed of the House of Lords and Parliament and the monarchy-all burnt to ashes like a pile of books thrown on the fire ...ashes to ashes, dust to dust, all accounts for nothing when there's nothing left.

Lydia rises, leaving me to my thoughts. The now is in the moment of the present and that is all we have before we depart this world and all I have in the here and now is the will to survive to find my daughter. The community is so kind and caring and a small committee approach me to perform a special task before I leave, explaining that a woman, Bergita, who recently joined the community was living like a hermit in a small dilapidated cottage behind the barn, preferring to keep to her own council as she believes she is possessed by a demon and will not put others at risk. They fear she is wasting away and need someone they trust to perform an exorcism, so that she might integrate fully into the community. They believe in my strength and ability to perform the sacred task on hearing my experiences of banishing evil. On recounting my many battles with evil forces, one in particular was horrific and invasive and the elders were most interested to learn more. It was during a time when I was in India with my son travelling on a mission after raising money to give to an orphanage and we were also making a pilgrimage to great

Granny's grave on Tiger Hill. We were staying in a small house in Coonoor in the Nilgiris which was notable for its connection with Shri Baba, a famous Indian healer and guru who used to stay at the house and after his death, ash was often mysteriously found beneath his picture. Prior to going to the house, my son and I had stayed in an amazing sanctuary by the sea, dedicated to artists, writers and musicians. The small community with its own eco system supported itself entirely from farm and agricultural produce. I took yoga classes in the evening in a specially built hall situated on the edge of the jungle and made friends with the yoga teacher who misread my friendliness. He was a small, wiry, slithery man with a face like an untrustworthy snake charmer. When we left, he hung around saying goodbye, pacing up and down like a caged tiger. During our conversations together he had intimated connections with black magic, which I didn't take seriously.

Travelling onto our next destination I forgot about the Yoga teacher. One night, just before our return to England, in the early hours before dawn, I was asleep lying on my stomach when I was rudely awoken by something shaking my legs vigorously. From my feet upwards an energy juddered my legs, shaking them involuntarily as I gained consciousness. I wondered how my legs were quivering by themselves and fighting to understand what was happening, I reached down to touch my legs hoping it was part of a bad dream, but it wasn't. Energy waves shot up through my legs, up my body, into my pelvis and up through my spine. Horrified, I realised it was a physical attack and that it was from an outside force. My whole body began to shake in the grip of a powerful entity, invasively molesting my body. I fought to shake free but suddenly as my shoulders were pummelled, music was unleashed into the air with a full blown orchestra reverberating through the ceiling, accompanied by a beautiful concert piano romantically playing a haunting melody. I had forgotten that I had told the Yoga teacher I was a musician and that one of my greatest loves in life was music and my favourite instrument was the piano. I didn't know at the time that people working in black magic often used a victim's love of something to capture and enslave them in order to entice them into a receptive mode for sexual abuse. As the heavenly music played my mind wanted to drift with it, whilst at the same time fighting the physical assault, which was growing stronger and more invasive. As my attacker's brutal force toughened, I became aware of a masculine entity pushing his way into my body, lying over me and on top of me with his hand pushing my left hand down, forcing my head into the hard mattress. I struggled to lift my back up and shake him off, fighting to breathe against the weight of his chest on my back. Suddenly in sheer desperation I screamed: "I hate you! I hate you! Leave me alone!" Strangely, the presence responded in a surprising manner. It paused in mid-air, as though surprised and hurt by my cutting words. It seemed to recoil in disbelief at my anger and passionate hatred of it. As the attack ceased, an image of the Yoga teacher quivered like a mirage in the sun, then spun, rotating like a Katherine wheel before shrivelling into a tiny ball which rolled upwards into a corner of the room and vanished as the music faded, spiralling into a vortex out into the bleak, blackness beyond.

I was terrified and shocked by the whole encounter and feared it would follow me back to England and my fears were justified as the "thing" returned a few months later. I was asleep and rudely awoken in the same manner as before, but living alone there was no one to hear my screams.

This time the obnoxious energy screeched and cackled like a demented banshee. Again I fought and shouted "I hate you! I hate you!" This time the energy didn't pause but slithered away squawking maniacally. The next day I began extensive research into the banishment of evil entities. I read many accounts of peoples' experiences displaying similar characteristics and one of the most successful banishment techniques was to repeat "in the name of Jesus Christ be gone!" Also to invoke the help of Angel Gabriel and Archangel Michael. During a meditation session I was also given a mantra to chant – "I seek light, love and knowledge in the highest realm." I was also told that the entity fed off of fear and that I had to try to remain calm when it appeared. The next few nights were peaceful but somehow I knew the night it was going to attack and I was prepared. Lying on my back in the dark, with pounding heart, I asked for help from Angel Gabriel and Archangel Michael and had the sensation of protective wings covering my chest. I repeated my mantra visualising a white light surrounding me. When the air grew cold, I knew it was approaching and I waited, hardly daring to breathe, then without warning it sprang from the dark attacking my legs, rougher and harder than before, pummelling and pushing, racing to get to the top of my thighs. From within a tremendous inner strength exploded and I screamed, "in the name of Jesus be gone!" Fear drained and mighty power from within, lashed out at the grotesque evil monster which stopped and sidled away from my body. I sat up determined to beat it and stared at it with disgust as it ogled back at me from the end of my bed morphing into the image of the repulsive yoga teacher, cackling in a high-pitched tone before evaporating into a grimy mass of energy evaporating down a gaping black hole. It never appeared again.

Now I am walking with Rebecca who has become a constant companion and treats me like a second mother, although oftentimes it is she who is the mother figure. As we approach Bergita's ramshackle cottage, with its cracked window panes and crumbling white pebble-dash walls, a great sense of loneliness and despair hangs like a dark cloud before rain burst, over the tin-lid roof. I feel sorry for Bergita's predicament and am glad she requested to meet me, because without her invitation to heal her, the task would be impossible. True healing only takes place when the healer is invited to heal and the sick person truly wants to be better. A rickety door opens and I am surprised to see a middle-aged, slender lady with long grey hair waiting for us. Her face is young and her smile demure but her eyes are guarded and troubled. She beckons us to enter. The kitchen/living room is cluttered and untidy with bits of unfinished embroidery, art work and pottery strewn on the table and every work surface, indicating an unsettled and muddled mind. Rebecca's eyes wander everywhere as we both clear a space to sit on the broken couch.

"Please take a seat" she calmly states, her voice soft and faintly foreign.

I watch Bergita carefully as she curls up in her large armchair like a sphinx, bringing her arms up underneath her chin, staring at us over her hands. As we chat lightly about many mundane things, I try to read her eyes. She is very polite and gentle with no outward sign of evil within, but then many subjects who are victims of possession react the same way when confronted with goodness -they hide behind a façade of respectful courtesy to throw you off the scent. Taking her off guard, I ask her directly why she wants my help. Her mood changes and her defence crumbles. Her face and hands tremble. Tears flood her cheeks. She whispers as though she doesn't want to wake a sleeper:

"I need your help. I think there is something inside-eating me, controlling me!"

I take her hand, assuring her all will be well and chant:

"you are a perfect child of the universe; nothing and no one can harm you!"

It is a wonderful, powerful mantra to repeat in any frightening situation which I was taught by an amazing healer in India. I repeat:

"you are a perfect child of the universe, nothing and no one can harm you!"

She snatches back her hand and holds it under her armpit, crossing her other arm on top as though to protect it. Her eyes darken. The loose window panes rattle and the door flings open. A rush of cold air encircles the room and Rebecca screams. I stand and chant:

"in the name of Jesus Christ, depart. Peace, love and light can only reign here. Be gone in the name of Jesus!"

The door slams shut and all is still. I know this reaction and am not afraid, for in the presence of pure love there can be no evil. I also know that for the time being the attack is a warning not to proceed further, but I will not be phased. Pitting my energy against the unknown force, I prepare to fight in the psychic realm, but the dark shadow disappears and a stray ray of sunshine splays across the kitchen sink, highlighting rainbow specs of dust disturbed in the air.

Silence hangs heavily. No one moves or speaks. Rebecca for a change is tongue-tied and Bergita slumps back in her chair. I wait, having experienced the same attack in previous, similar situations. I know the drill. The force also waits, slyly hovering in the conscious realm. I gently ask Bergita to explain how the invasive spirit had conquered her mind. She breathes heavily as though she is summoning up the courage to speak:

"A few months before I came here, I was a psychiatric nurse in a hospital on the border. One of my patients was a young Muslim girl who suffered terrible psychic attacks. I once witnessed one such episode where it appeared she was being raped by an outside force. It was horrible to watch. I didn't know what to do. I just held her and tried to stop it and I think it was then that the thing entered me. Later, the girl said she thought a djin had possessed her and had tried to take over her life."

I nod sympathetically and ask her what had happened. She gulps fighting back tears continuing:

"After that incident I didn't see the girl again as she was removed to another hospital, but I became restless, weary and couldn't settle. I couldn't make up my mind about anything. I became directionless and didn't want to work. It seemed I had two personalities fighting inside me and I could never finish anything I started. Everything seemed worthless and I left my job and escaped here where everyone has been so kind. I have been praying for my release. Please, please help me!"

She sobs folding her head onto her knees.

"Of course I will help you!" I assure her, "but first I need to make some preparation and I will be back this evening with help, in the meantime I want you to rest and keep on repeating the mantra I taught you and say it with conviction... "I am a perfect child of the universe, nothing and no one can harm me, in the name of Jesus Christ."

She agrees and Rebecca and I promptly leave.

"Oooh that was scary that was!" whispers Rebecca, finding her voice again. "Can I go with you tonight?" she questions. I adamantly refuse because it is potentially a dangerous situation and she is too young and inexperienced to handle it. I ask her to leave me alone for a while and she obeys. I ponder the attack and mentally prepare to banish the evil force. My teacher and healer in India had taught me to deny the existence of evil, saying that you need to deplete it of its importance by refusing to acknowledge it. In my experience, the way to squash it out of existence is through powerful love energy, like the light as bright as the golden sun now peering through the trees in a final endeavour to light the world before twilight.

In the beauty of the moment I feel your presence hovering in the light breeze. I am pleased to see you again. It has been a long time since we last met on the ethereal plane. I wonder if you witnessed my accident or stayed when I was in a coma? Now you are here to experience the exorcism. I do not like the word as it has too many connotations of misguided violent acts by perverted religious leaders. I prefer to call it a healing release. Now I must prepare. I am glad you are here. Back at the main house I ask Helen, Lydia and Bob to help me in the frightening task ahead, as they are grounded people with strong inner energy. I prepare some sage stacks, like the ones used on the Blackfoot reservation where I stayed for a while in a tipi, learning Blackfoot traditions such as tying sprigs of dried sage together in a small bundle to burn like incense sticks to cleanse and clear the air. I meditate for a while and call the others when I feel empowered for the mission, then the four of us walk calmly over to the cottage as a golden sun waits behind the dark trees casting a pink/orange glow over the flaking white brickwork as we knock and wait.

"Go away!" Bergita bellows.

We look at each other, questioning what to do.

"Come on, it's only us, we're here to help," states Bob with calm authority.

"Open the door love!" implores Lydia.

"Go away! Go away!" screams Bergita, her voice rising defensively.

Without delay Bob shoulder bashes the door which opens easily to his force. In the dimming light we see Bergita lying on the floor and we lift her onto the sofa and begin circling around her lighting the sage which smoulders leaving a smoky, herbal trail in the dusty air. I chant a sacred verse. Suddenly Bergita sits up with a jolt. Her eyes darken as she draws in short breaths, panting to take in oxygen. I ask her to stand and face me but she runs to the large window on the other side of the room, where in the dimming light her form is silhouetted against the twilight sky. I see her own light body lift out of her physical body and stand next to it. Her physical body begins to cough and splutter, heaving from the depths of her stomach as though she is going to be sick. Grotesquely, her outer body contorts into the shape of a medieval gargoyle as her shoulders round and haunch and her rib cage collapses inwards, while her elbows arch like demonic wings. She leers defiantly in a distorted pose, pausing before she suddenly shrieks with blood curdling howls tearing through the air, hissing and spitting like a teased tom-cat. The others recoil in horror, dropping to the floor, covering their faces and heads with their hands. I stand in front of the monster chanting, hurling my inner energy against it, forcing it to leave Bergita. Eternity rolls on and on forever as I pull black liquid from her body which spouts from her mouth and trickles over the floor. As the black bile spurts out, releasing the evil energy, she regains her inner light body and runs out of the door where I catch her shoulder and push her to the floor forcing out the demonic energy. It hisses, curses, shrieks and spits, hurling obscenities at me. As Bergita lies on the ground with her face turned in towards the dust she gurgles and babbles strange words calling in different languages and speaking in diverse tongues.

Ceaselessly, I drag out the evil energy and hurl it away into the bowels of the earth. I summon the others who have regained their composure, to bring lighted candles to burn around her while I continue the fight. For those lucky enough to have a special dragon as protector and guide will know that in times of dire fear, the dragon warrior will appear when called. I summon my powerful golden dragon Mimi to help and she comes. For some, this is hard to believe but in a situation which is not earthly, other worldly realms open all unbelievable possibilities.

Now Bergita is lying on her stomach with her face turned sideways to the left. Her pelvic area begins to jolt up and down in a simulated sexual assault as though she is being raped. I call upon the strength and power of Mimi who cloaks Bergita's body with her expansive wings as she lifts her up and places her on her back on the ground. The onslaught ceases. She lies like a crumpled rag doll making soft, gurlgling sounds like a baby. A huge sense of release encapsulates the room and we stand motionless like victorious warriors after a battle. The demon has fled. Bergita is calm after her ordeal and Lydia wraps her in a blanket as she is carried by Bob to the sofa. Helen makes a brew of herbal tea which she has brought for the occasion and hands it to Bergita who is calmly grateful and sips it slowly. We stay for a while, ensuring Bergita's safety and Lydia volunteers to stay the night. Bob and Helen return to the house but I need to gather my energy in the stillness of the night and I walk over to the barn where the warmth and smell of fresh hay and newly cut grass wafts through the cattle stalls. A single light at the far end of the barn sheds a golden glow by the window, where I catch the last twilight hues of pink and purple flashes fading into night's black void.

Underneath the lamp is an ancient, antique bookcase packed with congeries of old books which the community have collected and I pick up a maroon covered hard back. A page falls open on a fresh chapter headed – 'We Are the Good Guys, the Good Guys Always Win'. I smile relieved that goodness has triumphed over evil and feel confident that my invisible protectors are safeguarding me from a counter attack. I walk through the barn to a little flower garden where I planted a selection of tiny solar lights and watch them flicker, changing colour in the deepening dark. I sit on a rickety bench near the flower patch and enjoy the colourful light show. Suddenly two new orange/pink lights appear side by side near the geraniums. I sit and stare at them and they stare back. Somehow I am engulfed by their mesmerising power. I know I didn't place them there and I am certain no one else added them to my collection. Puzzled, I gaze intently at their light, drinking in their presence pulsing with warm energy, surrounding me in an armour of pure love and shielding me from dark forces that might return. One light is taller, more slender than the other with a male aura and the other is a smaller, rounder light with feminine poise. The two tubes of electric orange potency give me comfort and I marvel at the intense depth of their power, which is fearless and unquestioning. I sit bewitched by their spell until the mosquitoes begin to bite and I realize I must move. As I rise to investigate the lights they disappear. I can't believe they have vanished and search the flower bed feverishly for them. Perhaps their batteries have failed? Hastily, I turn over the flowerpots, and hunt in between the bushes but there is no sign of the beautiful, mysterious lights. Disappointed I walk back to the house and a voice in my head says...

"We came, you see we came, we promised you we would. You are always in our care."

Of course, I am so stupid not to recognise my people! They came to protect me and I never thanked them, not realising who they were. I should have known their loving energy; should have felt the connection of my family from across the universe. Now they are gone and I know they will not return for a very long time. I am sad not to have acknowledged my own kind but happy they came to show me I am not alone. I am glad you saw them too. Now you have experienced life from another planet and know that only goodness energy can and will prevail against all odds. I know you feel privileged to have witnessed many strange things on our journey together and I am fortunate to share your company on this rocky road, in the knowledge that further adventures await.

Back in my room, my bag is packed for the long journey ahead the next day and I feel sad to leave the loving community. My thoughts are interrupted by a gentle knock on the door which I recognise and smile as Rebecca enters saying:

"I brought you this." Holding out an old navy-blue leather bag, she continues "it was around your neck when they found you by the roadside but they forgot to give it to you when you recovered."

I smile and am happy to see my old friend who has travelled many miles with me, carrying my important documents and a few treasures. I open it and handle my belongings nostalgically, but am surprised to see a postcard with crumpled edges at the bottom of the bag. I lift it out and gape at the picture of a futuristic city, overlaid with the words in heavy black letters 'Londinia'.

"Look Rebecca, this is what the future looks like!"

She takes the postcard and stares at it in disbelief. She hands it back and I am astonished to see an inscription on the back:

'look at this when you return to the safety net of your past – hope you made the right decision?'

"What does it mean?" questions Rebecca.

"Oh nothing, just a joke."

"Is this really what the future Londinia looks like?"

"Yes, perhaps." I reply, "keep it!"

"Oh really? Thank you!" she smiles then her face creases and tears fall.

"Please don't leave?"

"I have to. Perhaps one day I will return...?"

I hug her fervently until she breaks free and rushes out of the door.

Sleep evades me and I lie awake waiting for the dawn to break across the forest. Tom said we would leave at first light and I hear him downstairs scuttling around in the kitchen preparing for the long drive ahead. When we leave there is only a sleepy silence in the courtyard and I am relieved not to have to say goodbye again to everyone. I am so glad to have been a small part of the community's life and happy to have been of service to them, helping Bergita to heal and reinstating her back into community life. I take a last glance at the farm and one small figure appears in her bedroom window. Rebecca waves. A tear slips and rolls down my cheek. Tom pretends not to notice. I am grateful to the universe for my experiences. I feel lucky, for I am LUCKY.

BEFORE THE MOON

We travel all day in the old, grey truck with pigs occasionally squeaking in the back, barely speaking, as Tom is hyper alert to all the would-be dangers on the open road and my mind is back at the farmhouse thinking of Rebecca starting her day without our usual banter, but the anticipation and excitement at the prospect of finding my eldest daughter overrides my sadness. The roads are quiet and Tom explains that the Blade Guards don't often venture far North as they consider the Highlands useless territory and the Outlanders, settled in communes in desolate regions, generally have been left to their own devices due to the arrival of new E.T.'s in the cityscapes. It is rumoured that the recent species of alien have landed in order to use planet earth as a stop-gap station before entering a portal to another universe. They say that planet earth is a cosmic gateway to multi-verses.

I remember the excitement when the Cern accelerator complex was built and the Hadron Collider, the world's largest and most powerful particle accelerator, which claimed to have discovered the God-particle, but it was really a ruse to use the accelerator to rip open a doorway to another world and to research time travel and gateways to other planets.

Chugging on and on down the empty highways avoiding large pot-holes and decimated road signs, we spy in the distance curving hills and rolling mountains like magnificent purple mythical beasts folded in sleep. We churn through jungle-wild forests which were once tended agricultural farmland with low hedgerows and pastures where cows and sheep grazed, but now everything is a tangled mass of overgrown scrub brush and motley vegetation. As we drive past towns long abandoned and whose once beautiful buildings have collapsed leaving piles of bricks, I remember town fairs and the lights and the noise of the rides and the loud music blaring from every stall and the raw excitement of it all. Now mountains of trash and sad burnt-out vehicles line the once thriving streets. Looted, shops and bomb-shelled churches are a reminder that communities were ripped apart by the new regime. Stopping for short rests at safe places to eat our picnic packs prepared by the kitchen ladies, I am thankful to be one of the rebellious Outlanders with a natural body and brain untampered by modern technology and artificial intelligence micro-chips and implants. Looking up to the untainted sky, unblemished by chemtrail poison, watching as it slowly turns pink and yellow in the sunset against the silhouetted backdrop of purple hills, Tom explains; "here and as far as the Isle of Skye and beyond, never gets chemtrailed...we're not important you see!" I am relieved not to be important to the cityscape guards and enjoy the freedom of the wild landscape. Slowing down, we turn off the main road and take a side track up through a steep forest incline where a large fallen tree halts our journey and Tom jumps out to inspect it, but to my surprise he pulls a hidden lever and the massive tree rises up opening like an army encampment gate. The decoy is cleverly designed to detract trespassers from entering the compound. Tom smiles wryly climbing back into the cab as we chug safely under the tree arch. Once through, he clambers out and pulls another lever hidden in a bush to close off the entrance and laughs as we move slowly forwards towards an impressive, lavish stately home with large Roman pillars magnificently shielding the entrance with giant statues of proud lions guarding the estate. As Tom pulls up a man and a woman swiftly appear and the man goes back to the truck with Tom and the woman ushers me inside. "Lovely to see you my dear. My name is Bannister and yours?"

I quickly decide to use the name Rebecca gave me "Ezianne" I reply and she smiles. The large open entrance echoes our footsteps on the black and white chequered floor as Bannister lights our way with a large lantern highlighting ancient metal armour figures lining the wall like antiquated warriors. The eerie hallway is a menagerie of stuffed animals and ancient historical artefacts in glass cases with faces of dukes and duchesses solemnly peering down from on high.

The candle glow catches crystal shards from a candelabra dancing above, sending rainbow shadows back into the dark as we quickly make our way, to what must have been the servants' quarters and enter a large kitchen where a group of friendly people hail a warm greeting.

"We have electricity but at night-time we use it sparsely in case we are spotted by the air guards," adds Bannister. Faces in the rosy candle-glow smile and introduce themselves but the road still moves beneath my feet and my mind is elsewhere. I don't say much and gratefully lap up the hot soup, grainy bread and rice pudding which is graciously served. Sensing my exhaustion, Bannister shows me to a small room which was probably once a broom cupboard fitted with a single bed built into the wall. It is comfortable enough and as soon as I lie down the world disappears.

The next morning Bannister greets me with hot herbal tea and tells me to help myself to food in the kitchen. I learn that the mansion is divided between thirty families each sharing a communal kitchen where everyone pitches in and work-loads are divided equally. Everybody works the land and the children are cared for and schooled by elder folk in the community. It seems an harmonious mode of living and works well for them. As Bannister shows me around the stables she suggests that I take a ride to the coast with Jack who is bartering fruit for fish to see if my daughter has been spotted. I agree enthusiastically, hopeful that someone could provide a link to her whereabouts. We leave early and are soon coasting by the sea where it is so refreshing and wonderful to be driving parallel to the magnificent ocean, with white frothy surf thrashing the beach. The power of the sea brings hope and new beginnings and my mind wanders back to a new start in my life when I got married and was on my honeymoon with my husband driving along the coast of Scotland in our bright yellow, lotus sports car with my little Shitzu puppy. We pulled into a little fishing village for lunch and were delighted to find a lovely quaint old pub nestling under the foot of a large hill. It was too early for the pub to be open so we decided to take a brisk walk up the hill to exercise our little dog.

When we set out the sun was shining and it was a beautiful day, but we hadn't realized how far it was to the top and by the time we neared the peak, the weather had changed drastically with thick fog swirling, mysteriously blocking out the view. Our little dog ran on ahead and began barking. In the cold mist I couldn't see anything but then near a mound of rocks I saw two middle-aged people wearing stylish country tweeds. We exchanged a few pleasantries and then scooping up my little dog I bade them farewell preparing for the descent, looking forward to a hearty meal at the pub. I had taken a few steps when the man shouted through the fog… "remember we're all Jock Thomas's bairns!" I thought at the time it was a strange thing to call but I thought the sentiment was lovely and as I walked on he shouted the same again and I waved back acknowledging his message.

Nearing the bottom of the hill the sun returned and the day was bright once more.

On our descent, the pub was open and inside we were welcomed by a young friendly man behind the bar who took our lunch order. Amidst the glasses and the collection of whiskies was a large photograph of a man and woman I recognised as the couple we had met at the top of the hill as they were wearing the same clothes. "Look- "I commented to my husband, "they're the people we met at the top!" The young man looked perplexed. "No you must be mistaken?" he stated.

But I was quite adamant they were the very same people. The young man grew agitated and said I was definitely wrong but my husband reassured him that it was so. The young man retorted, "you must be mistaken because they were my parents and they died in a car crash a year ago today!"

My husband and I exchanged glances and I couldn't help but assure the young man that we had definitely seen them and I said; "you know, the gentleman shouted out something strange – he said, "we're all Jock Thomas's bairns!" and I thought it was odd because he repeated it a second time."

The young man looked shocked and pale stating: "my Dad always used to say that! It was a well-known saying of his!"

Arriving around midday in the tiny inlet village, left unhampered by the new order of things and unchanged for centuries, the traders' call to market drifts across the sea, echoing over the white brick cottages from the medieval market square set out with rows of colourful stalls. Jack waves to a friend waiting by an archway and bids me farewell, wishing me luck in my quest to find my daughter and I thank him for his help. Tentatively, I wander towards the small crowd afraid to approach anyone. Have I forgotten how to greet strangers? Why am I anxious? I try to calm my rising anxiety and reassure myself that all will be well, but the first few people I approach view me with caution, shaking their heads, turning away with no time to waste dallying in idle chatter with a stranger. The damp air from the sea chills my body as the sun disappears behind dark clouds and a nippy sea breeze whips around the stalls, flapping bright multi-coloured material in the wind like pretty sails billowing on a choppy ocean. Despondently I walk away from the square down a small alley to escape the cold wind. The rejection upsets me and I am anxious about finding somewhere to stay for the night, but at least I have a little food and water. Bannister assured me that someone would give me shelter for the night. Down the alley I find an old abandoned bench and sit for a while to gather my thoughts. Looking to my left there is an old wooden barn and I smile recalling the words... "no room at the Inn," and remind myself of all the Christmas Nativity plays I produced and the concerts and shows that brought so much fun and laughter to everyone, but now it is as though that part of my life never existed. All the merriment and the great sense of togetherness has evaporated into the ether.

I shiver as the afternoon grows dark, knowing that I must find shelter for the night. I close my eyes and believe that "all will be well as all is well" remembering a quote from a fourteenth century hermit nun. As I open my eyes slowly, I spy a green light shining on the base of the wooden barn. It is in the shape of a rectangle. I stare at it. I look behind to see who is shining the light, but there is no one. I amble cautiously up to the light but it disappears. In the dimness I examine the spot where it shone but there is no sign of anything. I stand confused and suddenly become aware of faint squeaking from behind a rubbish bin. The soft whining seems to be coming from inside a hessian sack and as I open it a tiny, fluffy apricot head with beady black eyes and a snuffly black nose, scrambles out. I lift the little puppy into my arms and inspect him. He is adorable. He shivers and I place him inside my warm coat and cover him up with my snug, woollen shawl. He licks my neck and his soft fur tickles my chin. I think he is about eight weeks old and has been left abandoned. He looks like a cross between a Maltese and Poodle dog, very much like a puppy I had many years ago. His face is so cute and cheeky and the name Freddie springs to mind. "I think I'll call you Freddie!" I croon, reassuring the little fellow, as he licks my face in agreement. His thick apricot fur warms my neck like a winter woolly scarf – now I have a purpose to find shelter for the night and perhaps a little sustenance for Freddie? A few alleys down there is a cluster of small fisherman's cottages and just as I approach the first one an old woman opens her door – she is as surprised to see me as me her! I smile and she looks at me suspiciously, but then little Freddie's head pops out from under my coat and she nods knowingly.

"I'm sorry to bother you but I wonder if I could trouble you for a little drink of milk for this little fella he's starving. I've just found him back there abandoned and I can't bear to leave him!"

"So I see! Ye best come in!" She states firmly and I follow her indoors to a warm compact kitchen with a crackling log fire.

"Sit ye doon," she orders and I obey taking little Freddie out from my coat, snuggling him onto my lap. He is so sweet and cuddly, he seems to know I have saved him as he appreciatively licks my hand. I watch the old woman as she prepares warm milk in a saucer and scoops him up folding him into her motherly arms and dipping her finger into the milk coaxing him to lap it up. He soon learns and drinks the milk quickly wagging his tail.

"There now, he'll need to go outside. Tak him out back." She opens a door onto a small yard where a line of washing hangs damp and limp and I place him down and watch him circle around until he finds a spot to urinate. In one corner of the yard is a pile of hessian sacks like the one Freddie was bound in, but my thoughts are interrupted when he whimpers to be picked up and I walk back inside the homely kitchen.

"Here, I expect you'll be needing this?" She places a bowl of hot barley-corn broth on the table and motions me to eat it. Gratefully I accept and heartily enjoy the taste and sensation of the heat in my stomach. She sits opposite me with her wise old eyes questioning my presence as I explain the purpose of my visit. She admits she hasn't seen any visitors but knows someone who might have some information.

"It can wait till morning. Ye can sleep there on the couch for the night!"

I thank her and am grateful for her hospitality. Suddenly the door flings open and a whirl of cold air encircles the kitchen as a young girl enters protecting her face with her shawl. When she sees me she quickly turns away but she is not fast enough to disguise the awful disfigurement of her once beautiful face. Immediately I recognise the unskilled work of unqualified surgeons masquerading as professional micro-chip enhancers.

I remember the time when it was fashionable to have breast enhancement and young girls and women would travel to distant places to obtain cheap boob jobs in seedy, filthy clinics from unqualified men posing as doctors. Similarly, when pressure was put on young people from the trans-humanists to gain super-human powers with brain implants and micro-chips interfaced into the brain to the internet and eye implants together with super-soldier limbs to create an artificially intelligent superior human, the young ones felt they had to become the new generation of enhanced people. But the processes were expensive and soon the market was flooded with bogus practitioners who attempted dangerous operations which often left the young disfigured and unable to perform normal actions, as their robotic eyes and limbs malfunctioned and looked horrendous, leaving them disfigured like teenage Frankenstein monsters.

"It's alright Marie, don't be afraid. Sit ye doon, she's a friend. This is my Granddaughter Marie Morgan, this is..."

"Ezianne and this is Freddie!" I smile reassuringly, wishing to lessen the pain of Marie's cruel misadventure. I tell her about my students who had suffered the same misfortune by sharing my experiences with her about young teenagers who were left totally scarred and unable to function properly in normal life after the butchery from phoney A.I. practitioners.

Back in the days when I was a teacher, there was a great rise in the increase of A.I. brain implants and eye enhancements which enabled the recipient to see through objects; gain long-distance sight; have access to internet information; watch programmes, films and video face time friends-all available within their own head, making cell phones and ipads obsolete. It was a great temptation for the young to undergo the dangerous operations to achieve super-human powers and I witnessed the mutilation of many of my students in this process. They became known as 'ogglers' because of the shocking way their robotic eye implants ogled and stared vacantly like doll's eyes and oftentimes the grossly large eyes would malfunction and spasm into uncontrollable blinking and spinning. The effects were all the more horrific when the eye socket was moved further up into the eyebrow line by mistake, which was a common blunder made by the rogue surgeons. Some of my students lost their sight completely and could not live a normal life after the operations and the suicide rate among teenagers dramatically increased as many were not able to live with their disfigurement.

Marie hid under her shawl hiding her mutilation shamefully, listening intently to the horror stories I unfurled about the 'ogglers'. It was important for her to realise that she was just one among thousands of teenagers who had been duped into sacrificing their normal existence to follow their dreams of attaining super-human powers. When she felt comfortable she let the shawl slip from her face and I spontaneously got up to hug her. She let me embrace her and she wept into my shoulder heaving great sobs from the depth of her being. So many youngsters had inadvertently become monsters. The Grandmother wiped away a tear and said she was glad not to be part of the new world and that she would go to her grave with the body God had given her. When Marie recovered and was sitting by the fire she spoke of the small group of youngsters who were also deformed by the operations and she explained that together they planned to live their lives as best they could being accepted for what and who they were in their small communities. During our talk I tried not to notice the malfunctioning of her left eye and the stuttering and delayed speech. I feared for the young generation of misfits and how they would cope with the different demands of an A.I. structured society.

"There is one thing for sure," Marie added, "and that is if ever I am lucky enough to be wed and have bairns of my own, I will never, never allow them access to the new techno world. They will know only the purity of natural living."

I smile. It is comforting to know that the pendulum will swing far away from transhumanism in the outreaches but in the cityscapes the search to be more than human, will continue until the human race will merge into the singularity of being one with artificial intelligence. The candles flicker in a final attempt to stay alight and the Grandmother brings blankets and a pillow as Marie slips out into the shadows of the night. Freddie snuggles under my armpit, then shuffles across my chest, then plonks himself on my face, so I move him onto my shoulder but he scuttles onto the top of my head and chews at my hair until he eventually falls asleep in my arms snoring, while I lie awake wondering what the universe has in store for me and my thoughts meander back to my first puppy when I was six years old. She was a beautiful pedigree Cocker Spaniel called Minky with a wonderful, loving disposition. She was so happy and playful and a great companion and I loved her so much and so did my Father who would take her for long walks, treating her like another member of the family. A tragedy occurred when we went away on holiday when we left her at a nearby kennel where she contracted distemper and quickly became very sick. My Father and I were distraught and he made sure she got the best veterinary care and stayed up night after night to administer her medicine, but she never recovered. A short while after she died my Father, who was a no-nonsense army man, took me to one side and with tears in his eyes related a strange happening. He said after an argument with my Mother, he had gone downstairs to sleep on the sofa and was woken by a wet sticky tongue licking his face. When he opened his eyes he was shocked to see Minky staring at him and wagging her tail. He said it was as if she had returned to him to thank him for his love and nursing and to let him know that she was fine on the other side. I loved the story and it gave me a great deal of comfort to know she was fine.

My whisperers explained that animals live on a different vibrational level to humans and have a sixth sense, particularly cats and dogs and it is second nature to them to see and hear emotion as they are empathetic to human feelings. They are also very sensitive to spirits, especially recently departed souls. When my first husband's Father, James, died in India, my husband and I made a pilgrimage to a temple high in the mountains in West Bengal. We were driven by my Father-in-Law's best friend, Major Steven, who took us in his jeep far into the mountains to where the gold-topped temples glistened in the noon-day sun and as we wound our way up to a small village, the temples on the high ridges gleamed a welcome like bright beacons in the sky. Eventually we came to a small village which James had often visited and been kind to the people, occasionally providing food and medicines. During the trip we talked about James and although I had only known him for one day before he died, I felt close to him during the journey, almost as if he were there as I listened to Major Steven's anecdotes about him. When we came into the dusty village compound, the people gathered to greet us displaying their respect for the loss of a wonderful man and as soon as we got out of the jeep a scrawny, mongrel dog went wild, barking and howling crazily. My husband thought it was because it had never seen an English lady like me before, but Major Steven said that dogs usually go mad like that when they see a ghost. He didn't explain further, but I thought he knew James was with us and that the dog could see him. The villagers followed us up to the temple while the dog had to be restrained. When we walked around the shrine in remembrance of James, from a short distance behind an ancient pillar, I thought I caught a glimpse of him. I wanted to make sure and walked ahead of the others. In the crumbling, ancient, antediluvian atmosphere where time had no meaning, the dust lingered, caught momentarily by the bright sun highlighting the micro-particles floating in the air and I saw him in the shadows. He was smiling. I went to tell my husband and showed him where I had seen James but there was only dust and a golden ray of sunshine gleaming down on the spot. Walking out of the temple in the midday glare the dog went crazy again. Major Steven said the dog had loved James and I think he was trying to alert me to the fact that the dog saw James too. It was an extraordinary experience and one that will remain with me forever.

I was also told that dogs, especially those who have formed a close bond with their owner, have a yearning to return to them and sometimes take on another doggie body and are usually recognised by displaying certain traits from their previous life, which only their owners recognise. Sometimes before this happens the dog will reside in spirit beside their owner and psychics like myself can see them. This happened once when I was invited to a friend's mother's house. It was my first visit and the first time I had met the family. On my arrival my friend's mother seemed very upset but the family was very welcoming and invited me to join them at the dining table. I had the feeling that a golden Labrador dog was around as I sensed her presence and sitting at the table, almost immediately my legs were rhythmically beaten by something tapping my calves, which was irritating. I looked under the table to see who was responsible, but didn't see anything. Then the beating grew stronger and I had to look under the table again. The Mother asked me what was wrong and I said, "you are not going to believe me, but there is a golden Labrador beating my legs with her tail!" The Mother shot up from the table in shreds of tears and ran upstairs. The rest of the family were stunned into a shocked silence. Eventually the Father said; "well, well, well – you see we have just lost our beloved Sasha, she was a golden Labrador and one of the things she did was go under the table at meal times and beat our legs with her tail, we used to get cross with her sometimes."

The rest of the family hung their heads and were speechless. I didn't know what to say and was worried that I had said the wrong thing but the Mother returned drying her eyes smiling saying, "thank you, thank you! You have made me so happy to know that she is still with us." With that the family relaxed and laughed and agreed it was a wonderful gift to know their beloved pet was still with them.

Now it is early morning and the Grandmother scuttles around in the kitchen talking to Freddie who is by the fire lapping up watery porridge.

"Ahh, I hope ye slept well? There's porridge on the stove, help yeself and I'll be back shortly."

With that she wraps her plaid shawl around her head and shoulders and quickly departs leaving me and Freddie looking at each other. He cocks his head on one side and then bounds over to me licking my hands and scrabbling at my feet to be picked up. His warm furry head burrows into my neck and it is as though we have been together forever. A few minutes later Marie Morgan sweeps in and her face is unshielded. I am so happy to see her smiling. She places a large bag triumphantly on the table, saying; "thank you so much for your wise words last night, what you said made me feel much better about myself and so this morning before you leave I want to give you these." She motions me to open the bag. I am surprised to see a lovely long plaid skirt with matching purple jumper and clean tights and underwear. It's sheer luxury! My eyes well and I don't know what to say and Marie breaks the silence, "I'm so glad you like them and if you don't mind me saying, I think you could do with a make-over!

You talked about me being proud to be who I am, but I think you need to think about yourself too!"

I laugh, embarrassed, as it is true I have neglected myself in my quest to survive and I am delighted to dress in the new attire. I feel like a queen.

"Now your hair...come on sit down," orders Marie taking out a comb and grips.

"You see before all this, I was training to be a beautician and hairdresser, but who would come to a wreck like me?"

I open my mouth to defend her but she continues; "then everything went crazy-small businesses went bankrupt and the leisure and beauty industry disintegrated. But on returning back here seeing the women with strength and determination to survive, no matter what, I decided to open my 'home service' business for them."

"Oh how wonderful!" I exclaim, feeling the tug of the brush through my long hair.

"If you don't mind me saying so, you have lovely hair for an older person and such a beautiful colour!"

I am not used to compliments and explain that during my performance years I used to have my hair dyed lots of different colours but one day I decided just to let my natural colour grow back and I was lucky when my hair turned into what my Grandmother used to call, 'salt and pepper' colour.

Marie finishes and holds out a mirror for me to view her handiwork. I can't hold back the tears and stare at myself in her hand-held mirror and admire my transformation of my plaited hair woven in a crown on the top of my head.

"There you see, isn't it lovely, isn't it worth taking time over?"

Grandmother returns and smiles, proudly admiring Marie's handiwork. Freddie also approves and licks my face as I place him under my thick shawl.

"Ye look like a real Highlander now in all your plaid, lassie. Are ye ready for your journey? I've just been to see Billie Mc Cullen who says he remembers taking a couple on the ferry some while back.

They were on their way to the Isle of Skye but who knows if it was them? Billie has no eye for detail.

It could have been anyone. Anyways he is willing to take ye across on the ferry this morning so ye best hurry, maybe someone on the island has seen them? Good luck ta ye and the wee one, I'm glad ya saved him!"

With that she gives me a big hug and instructs me to go down to the bay. I thank her profusely and am excited to be following a small lead. Striding out in my new attire and hair-do, the world feels truly wonderful and I am glad to be alive in the moment. I feel you by my side again, watching over my shoulder completing my contentment as I sally forth into a new adventure.

Billie waits for me by the dock smoking a clay pipe. When he sees me he waves and begins winding an old rope tethered to a stone stump. His old sea-faring waders ride up to his chest and his thick grey jumper is reinforced everywhere with brown leather patches. His white hair sprouts from under his captain's hat and his Father Christmas thick white beard, with his jovial rotund tummy completes the festive winter image. I waste no time in questioning him about the couple he saw as he continues loading the small boat with various boxes and chicken crates full of cackling hens and buckets of fresh fish and plastic pails of stinking fish meal and mail bags, but he remembers nothing about them or where they were headed; he just vaguely recalls that a man and woman boarded the ferry some time ago and he remembers that because they were the first visitors he had seen for a long time. I am disappointed not to glean any further information but am happy to be following some kind of hunch which might prove to be fruitful.

The morning is grey, the sea is grey, the sky is grey but the mountains are green and purple and impressively magnificent. I am small and insignificant sailing under their watchful presence, even Freddie senses their imposing grandeur. Billie smiles as Freddie tries to romp around on board but it isn't safe as he loses his footing as the boat rocks asking: "Have ye no lead an collar for the wee fella?"

I explain how I rescued him and he laughs saying, "Keep her steady" handing me the wheel while he scampers off to the front of the boat. In no time he appears with a little leather collar made from a belt with a small length of rope for a lead, "There that should do it!" he smiles as he adjusts Freddie's new collar, handing me the lead. Freddie isn't too sure at first but when he realises he can move around more freely, albeit with me in tow, he acquiesces. As we chug out further beyond the bay the sea surges forcefully below our feet and the engine throbs fighting the rolling breakers. The little vessel seems frail against the choppy white crests as she battles through the undulating waves and it becomes necessary to sit down and procure Freddie safely under my coat. The only available space is next to the smelly fish meal where I am a prime target for fine spray showering my face in a salty mist, where through a watery vista I am thrilled to catch sight of a grey seal performing solo aqua-acrobatics.

The journey is over too soon and Billie bids Freddie and I goodbye as other fishermen approach to help him unload his cargo. I have no idea where to go but it seems a good idea to cross over the road to a small band of shops on the corner of the bay. I spy a post office sign, not that it means anything anymore, but quite often it's a place where fruit and vegetables are exchanged for clothing and other items of jumble are bartered or swopped. The air is fresh and briny blowing directly off the sea and the sun beats through the cloud as Freddie finds his trotting legs and enjoys the new sensation of galloping by my side, abruptly stopping from time to time to sniff the pavement. The line of shops once serving the little sea port look sad and shabby. The first-a green grocer's is barred and shuttered; the next a hardware store – lies empty except for a little plastic yellow bucket and spade left forlorn in the bare window, a sad reminder of happier times and the third is the post office, which is closed, but there are signs it is still operational. The fourth – Aleana Antiques is a bright beacon of hope with its gold hand-painted sign above a quaint door. A welcoming light gleams inside and my heart races as I enter. A little, olf-fashioned bell tinkles melodically above the archway where a small step leads into an amazing wonderland of antiquated beauty, smelling of honeycomb polish and old books. This is a place that time has abandoned. It is a treasure trove of all that I know from a distant life. Here preserved is a little haven of history in a far-away island. Sniffing in the grandiose past, I spy a magnificent old singer sewing machine, beautifully polished and well maintained. My Great Grandmother bequeathed hers to me and although it was a great piece of machinery, it never worked properly. I touch it lovingly, recalling my youth, not noticing eyes watching from a desk at the far end of the sizable showroom. Inside is much larger than I had anticipated as two cottage fronts must have been converted into one, making a spacious display area with every little nook and cranny crammed with interesting bric-a-brac. Persian rugs with intricate, faded patterns carpet the floor and gold-flocked paper with light green ivy leaves lace the spaces between multiple paintings and hanging ornaments. Everything is pristinely clean and dusted. I am lost in the overwhelming blast from the past and drool over the collection of antique rings and jewellery artfully laid out in showcase boxes. Through my daydream in Aladdin's cave I hear a voice asking; "Can I help you?"

I am brought back to the present from a wonderland of memories by a man sitting at a beautiful antique desk covered with charts, star maps and astrological signs.

"I'm sorry we don't usually allow dogs inside!" His soft voice with a strange tone states authoritatively.

I had completely forgotten about little Freddie, being transfixed in an amazing, unexpected time warp, so I swoop my little furry bundle into my arms and turn to leave but the man smiles saying; "well I'm sure we can make an exception this time!" placing the cap on his black fountain pen and taking off his reading glasses, I watch him rise and walk towards me. There is something about him that makes me vaguely uncomfortable and internally I struggle to remember a lost melody rising to the surface from a mound of remembered rubble. Freddie begins to wriggle in my arms and

I politely ask the owner if he has any water for him and before he replies a torrent of information spills out of my mouth of how I rescued Freddie and how I am desperately seeking to find my daughter.

Somehow he draws out information from me without prompting. He listens and replies; "Yes of course, I'll get you some water, we always used to have a bowl of fresh water outside for our doggy visitors, especially in the summer months but that was a long time ago."

I wait while he disappears behind a hanging tapestry and then emerges with a small stainless steel bowl full of water. He places it near the door and Freddie greedily laps it up. In silence we both watch, wondering what to say next. I notice he is tall, well-built, with grey hair, probably in my age range, whatever that is, and behind his thick glasses his eyes are guarded, as though hiding a secret.

From an awkward pause we both talk at once and he slightly bows to allow me to speak first. I compliment him on his wonderful emporium and express my surprise that he is still open.

Courteously he replies in a mechanical tone as though he has learnt a script:

"We open every morning at ten; close for lunch at one; open in the afternoon at three and close at six in the evening. No matter what is going on in the rest of the world that is what we do and speaking of lunch it is time to close, so if you'll excuse me?"

I look a little lost and wander out of the shop in a daze. I had hoped to find a lead to my daughter's whereabouts but the shop owner offers no help and now I am not sure what to do. Gathering my thoughts I stare at the shop window, which is painstakingly set out with all kinds of interesting and pretty artefacts to tempt the bargain seeker. I try to formulate a plan of action but am distracted by the tinkle of a bell and the locking of a door and a voice asking,

"I expect you must be looking for somewhere to lunch? I can show you a small pub where you can take your pooch." His accent is strange and the word 'pooch' seems odd. I am flustered and don't know what to say and utter; "I'm afraid I don't have anything to barter!"

"Not necessary. We accommodate all visitors!"

I nod and follow him with Freddie trotting by my side.

"You look puzzled. What are you thinking?" he enquires directly.

I am slightly taken off balance by his straight-forward approach- it's as though he is reading my thoughts and I answer; "oh er, I was just wondering about your accent?"

He laughs as he makes way for me to cross the road, explaining that originally he was born in Ohio, but his family hail from Dublin and he first visited Scotland to see distant relatives and fell in love with a beautiful lassie and stayed.

"Ahh, Aleana Antiques…"

He smiles, "Yes, it means beautiful light and she was!"

"Was?" I enquire bluntly.

"Yes, she died a few years ago and I promised to keep our little world going just the same, no matter what happened."

"Even though there are no visitors?" I enquire, somehow not totally convinced of his explanation as he seemed to be reeling off a recorded script.

"Visitors come and go even now in these strange times and of course you came by today. Oh by the way my name is Seth, Seth Mackenzie-and yours?"

I am unsure what to say in case he laughs like the others, but I decide to be open and reply, "Lucky!" "Well I consider myself to be lucky to meet Lucky!"

I listen to his compliments and think he is a smooth talker with an answer for everything. We soon arrive at a small pub on the other side of the bay where a handful of locals gather to share a communal daily hotchpot, which I am privileged to sample, although Seth does not partake.

Everyone pools whatever is available, making sure each has enough to eat and whatever tipple is available they equally share.

Seth intimates that on the Island they have hidden stocks of all kinds of alcoholic treasure stored from shipwrecks and home-brewed vats. Seth drinks a murky, dark-green liquid from a small glass and I am curious to try it but he orders me a whiskey explaining that I wouldn't like his special brew which the landlady conjures up just for him. The afternoon passes too quickly in the cordial company of the Island folk and Seth downs his final shot to excuse himself to open up shop and I realise I have to get back to the mainland to follow other leads to find my daughter, as people believe the couple in question left the island long ago. When I request the time of the next ferry, raucous laughter erupts. I am a little confused and ask Seth to explain. He looks at me in disbelief, stating – "Did no one tell you that there are no more ferries from now until Christmas. It's winter you know?"

I am shocked and distraught at the idea of being stuck on the island for two months. An old sailor with an eyepatch ambles towards me jovially stating that he might know of someone leaving the island the next day. He explains that a 'coaster' with his yacht is returning to the mainland in the morning and he might be able to persuade the guy to give me a lift. Seth doesn't respond and bids farewell. I rise to thank him but he disappears quickly. I turn to the old sailor and ask: "What's a coaster?"

The company laugh politely and some snigger into their glasses. "Well me dear…let's put it like this…er coasters sail around the coast delivering and acquiring certain goods if you get my drift?"

"Best not have dealings with 'em!" a large lady calls from the corner near the fire.

Desperate to get back, I ask the sailor to look into it for me and he winks saying he will let me know.

Slowly the little room clears and I don't want to outstay my welcome. Freddie has been fed scraps and sleepily rises not wanting to walk, so I pick him up and prepare to brave the late afternoon squall. I have no idea where I am going and just walk huddled under my shawl feeling little Freddie's warm body next to my chest. The hamlet is very small with only a few residents, so I am at a loss as to where to go to take shelter and having walked around the bay several times I find myself standing outside Seth's shop once more, but I am afraid to go in in case he thinks I am taking advantage of his hospitality. I huddle with Freddie under a small tattered awning but the rain intensifies and drenches us both until it's impossible to get any wetter. Miserably searching the horizon, I watch the storm drive inland thrashing the angry waves against the walkway railings and faintly through the crashing breakers I hear a gentle bell tinkle and a voice calling, "Are you gonna stand out there all day?"

I turn and see Seth in the doorway and am grateful for his invitation. Inside I stand shaking, sopping wet, drenching his beautiful carpet and feel ashamed to be in such a state and can't help the sudden outburst of tears. I am a mess physically and emotionally. Seth acts quickly, but without emotion, ordering me to stay put while Freddie whimpers and licks my tears with his little pink tongue. Soon he returns with a bundle of things stating, "take those wet things off and put them in this bucket.

Here's a towel and clean clothes. I'll close all shutters. Give me Freddie."

I hand over my wet puppy and Seth bundles him in a towel like a baby, while flicking over the closed sign and pulling down the shutters. Then he disappears into another room. I note his actions are swift and efficient as though he is undertaking a military operation. I am embarrassed to be in such turmoil and quickly, discreetly try to haul off my sodden clothes which are sticking stubbornly to my wet skin. I am annoyed with myself for releasing my pent up emotions in front of a stranger and the tears flow while I fumble with the clothes, not realising in my haste, the quality of such beautiful garments. The olive-green woollen dress fits beautifully. I feel like maid Marion from Sherwood Forest as I loop the belt around my waist. My neatly plaited hair now wringing wet, is a bushy mass of sodden curls and my face is burning from the driving wind and rain, so that when Seth politely appears with a dry wagging-tailed Freddie I am abashed to face him.

"Oh I see the dress fits, haven't lost my touch then? I used to buy all my wife's clothes."

I am lost for words and gawkily stare at the floor as he hands me a hot toddy adding; "It will do you good. Leave the bucket there, I'll see to it later. Come with me."

I follow him into a massive living space with a kitchen and dining room, lit by a medieval fireplace ablaze with crackling seasoned pinewood. "Here sit in front of the fire and get warm!" He urges.

I am relieved to feel cosy and sip the hot drink but cough and splutter as the whiskey hits the back of my throat.

"Bit strong hey? Well sip it slowly, it will do you good," Seth commands.

Freddie curls up next to my feet and sleepily dozes by the fire as Seth begins to clear up the kitchen table strewn with ancient looking manuscripts and astrological charts. I am intrigued by them and rise to look at the documents.

"You interested in the stars?" He asks as I inspect the astrological maps.

I nod and take another warming sip studying the star chart.

"It's correct! It was right!"

"What?" I enquire.

"That you would come today!"

"Oh?"

"Yes everything is written in the stars since time began, even before there was a moon?"

"Before the moon? Was there ever such a time?"

"Oh yes, way, way back before time as we know it, there was no moon and there were no people on earth, however there were beings. It is well documented in ancient texts and scripts."

I begin to see beyond the shop keeper, realizing that Seth is more than he appears.

"In fact did you know that way back in the past in 2017, planet earth had two moons?"

"No, really?"

"The second moon appeared suddenly, which was actually an asteroid captured by the earth's gravity and has had many more mini moons since then – they stay for a while and disappear."

"Where?"

"No one really knows, but we do know that asteroids can be a great threat to earth."

His words jar a lost memory of when I was six years old and I had a strange dream where I saw the planet burst into flames and the earth beneath my feet was ripped in two and I saw myself clinging onto a ledge looking down into an endless chasm. It was such a frightening, clear dream, that I never forgot it. The idea of the asteroid hitting the earth fills me with fear and dread, so I remain quiet and turn the conversation to another direction.

"But how did you know I was coming today? Maybe you have the wrong person?"

He sighs and takes a long hard look at me and replies:

"It's in the star chart. It's all here, even your astrological sign. Well apart from that, we had word from the mainland that a passenger would be arriving on an unscheduled trip."

I take another sip, downing the last drop and open my mouth to speak, but he interrupts with:

"Now, let me see, your astrological sign is-don't tell me, let me guess-you're Scorpio?"

He is absolutely correct. I am surprised. He shakes me off balance. Somehow he seems to know an awful lot about me.

"Yes Scorpio, the most psychic, passionate, loyal, secretive sign of the Zodiac." He states victoriously and re-fills my glass.

"And when I entered your shop for the first time today you were studying the charts?"

"Yes, I watched you examine the sewing machine, the one my wife loved so much and I observed your interest in all the jewellery, which was her department and I knew it was you because you have a passion for such things!"

His accuracy is a little intimidating and when he speaks of his wife it is without much compassion as though there was little love between them. I turn away daring to ask:

"Can you tell if I will find my daughter?"

"I would have to study your details, day of birth, time of birth...!"

I hold up my hand to stop him. I can't remember any of those exact details and I feel dizzy making my way back to the sofa as the world spins in an uncontrolled haze and I wonder if the drink was more than whiskey? He follows and places a cushion under my head and lifts my feet, covering me with a warm soft blanket. As he reaches over me, I notice momentarily his skin is mottled with khaki brown patches and his eyes slant vertically, but in an instant they disappear. I think I must have imagined it! I close my eyes feeling the hot fire dancing across my eye lids and let go of my worries drifting into the unknown, pondering a time before the moon appeared in earth's night sky. I am not sure if I verbally voice a question about the moon or whether I ask it in my head, but I hear Seth's voice from afar answering my questions-

"Yes there was a time before the moon was positioned above earth. You see it is not a planet, as you have been lead to believe, but a command centre for monitoring and manipulating the inner motion of the earth's crust. The seas are controlled by the moon and therefore earth's natural vibrational field is dominated by the communication centre at the moon's base. The moon quite simply is a satellite where many nationalities and many Alien species reside."

I want to respond to the information and open my mouth to speak but no words form.

"Sleep, now sleep, I have told you enough, but you may not remember..." He adds softly.

As Seth leaves, Freddie jumps onto my feet and curls himself around my toes. He is happy. I am happy and I am lucky, feeling myself drawn into a new dawn of awakening. Time before the moon, time with the moon, time after the moon will evolve and my voices remind me there is no real schedule to life and that on my journey I must allow joy to flourish. I confess it is something I have forgotten. I listen to my whisperers-

" serve love instead of agendas and calendars and timetables; for love attends your soul not your personality. But be aware of the unexpected, for when the road ahead disappears, danger can lurk."

I know they are right. I trust the universe to guide me always, but if on the next part of my journey I have to take a detour – then I will make it a joyous diversion. But right now, the now is warm, comforting, healing, abounding with love and trust encompassed in a ball of fluff at the end of my feet. Freddie, my little fur baby, is a beautiful gift from the universe to accompany me on my next adventure and together we will be lucky. I am lucky, for I am Lucky.

REPTILIAN REALITY

Sleep descends peacefully under a safe, warm canopy, sheltered in a protected haven as I serenely turn off the world, locking out reality in a hazy mist of Scottish Dew-so intoxicating and soothing. Dreams fade in and out, then I wake, like on a perfect Christmas morning, to the sound of a crackling fire, the smell of bacon frying and coffee gently brewing. Such long-forgotten luxuries are unreal. Slowly, I sit up remembering the previous night when Seth and I sat by the fire imbibing whiskey, discussing the magic of the Universe. Now he is cooking breakfast and I gaze across a large open terrace window to bright green, undulating hills, sturdily protected under the watchful gaze of distant snow-capped peaks. Have I died and found utopia? I turn towards the blazing fire where clean clothes are laid out and my own hang drying on a rack. Everything is perfect-almost too perfect? I hear Seth call-

"Ahh, so I see you're in the land of the living, how's your head?"

He expects me to have a hangover after drinking the whiskey but I am fine.

"You can go upstairs and take a shower if you wish. I've laid some clean clothes out for you."

Is he for real? I am not used to such attention. I find him attractive both physically and mentally-as though fate has reached into my mind to discover my ideal prototype. I take the clothes and make my way shakily up the open wooden stairs, where I am amazed to find an extensive open-plan, modern space with a beautiful bathroom and large bedroom with a four-poster bed swathed in white silk drapes. The quaint cottage emporium on the outside is deceptively ordinary, but full of surprises inside. The designer bathroom with its double black marble sinks and walk-in shower has hot running water with clean, soft, luxurious towels. Everything is sensuously perfect. Seth and his wife must have lived a grand, lavish lifestyle tucked away from major changes in the world, isolated in their sheltered sea-port village.

I open a door to a walk-in wardrobe where expensive clothes, all colour coded, hang neatly with jumpers precisely stacked, with shoes and handbags arranged in neat rows and jewellery dripping from ornate alabaster statues. Glittering ball gowns are folded in plastic bags and beautiful silk underwear is pristinely folded in drawers. I am thrilled and a little ashamed to enjoy the sight of such extravagance. The shower is wonderfully luxurious and I revel in the comfort of running hot water. I take my time dressing in the lovely clothes laid out and step into a pair of rust brown tailored trousers and pull on an orange mohair jumper, exquisitely embroidered with brown autumnal leaves. It is uncanny how everything fits perfectly? I admire the ensemble in a long guilt mirror by the door, then follow the smell of breakfast wafting temptingly up the stairs. When Seth sees me he nods approvingly and serves me an amazing plateful of food, the likes of which I have not seen for many years, not since before the start of the body reprogramming agenda, which affected everyone and was intended to prepare humans to evolve into the next 'sleeve or container' by re-setting the human body's gastrointestinal digestive system to accommodate the chemical food of the future. The process began in the late 1950's when poisons and toxic chemicals were added to food and fluoride, which is a poison, was put into toothpaste and water supplies. It became a struggle to avoid many consumer goods affected by the chemical process, even fresh fruit and vegetables were contaminated with genetically modified substances and the air was infected with metals such as aluminium, barium, strontium and sometimes blood was found in some of the chemtrails sprayed in the skies. Many people began to suffer with chest infections, cancer and hair loss. My whisperers explained that the hair loss was not only as a result of all the chemicals ingested by everyone, but it was a preparation for the future where hair on the body was not necessary and that integration with alien species, who were hairless, was easier when humans looked similar.

"Aren't you joining me?" I ask, tucking into the crispy bacon.

"Er no, I ate earlier, you eat up!" Seth hastily replies.

Suddenly Freddie rushes to the door and barks for the first time, surprising me and himself. Seth rises and looks annoyed as the old sailor from the Inn stands grinning enquiring:

"If the missy still wants a lift back to the mainland then it's all set? They're leaving in half an hour!"

I hurry to the door and thank the sailor, agreeing to accept the lift. Seth is distant and doesn't say anything. I hurriedly throw my belongings in my old bag and gather up Freddie thanking Seth profusely for his hospitality and kindness. He tells me to keep the clothes and have a safe trip. He doesn't offer to walk me to the pier and turns away as I attempt to give him a farewell hug. I am set on leaving to find my daughter and I am hell-bent on succeeding, no matter what the cost. As I hurry down the jetty with Freddie in my arms, the sun slips from behind the clouds highlighting the bright white sails of an expensive blue vessel anchored in the harbour. The old sailor waves and begins to unwind the coiled rope tethering the boat to the jetty and calls to a man who shadily appears in black sunglasses with dyed jet-black hair and pock-pitted face.

"This is Mr Jake Allioni who has agreed to take you to the mainland. This is Miss..."

I open my mouth to answer but am rudely interrupted by a sleazy middle-aged woman who pops up from below holding a gin bottle in her right hand, waving it around as she speaks.

"Not much of a catch Jakey boy...too old...but you never know... in these times?" Her blonde, straw hair is ruffled by the breeze and her open blouse flaps like aggravated sails in a dinghy race.

"Well are you coming on board or not?" she sniggers. She spies Freddie and adds, "no one said anything about a rat-she aint bringing a squirming rat aboard."

Mr. Allioni fakes a smile and orders her below apologising for her rudeness and states, "you and your little dog are welcome aboard but

I have to explain we are not going directly to the mainland but are taking a detour."

She drunkenly pops up again adding: "You're damn right we are, we're gonna party, party all the way hey Jake?"

I don't like her intoxicated, slurred speech and begin to suspect they're involved in drug and sex trafficking, especially when another young inebriated, dark-haired girl pokes her head up from below. Dragon power-protection is supremely forceful and having a personal dragon for guidance in difficult times is an incredible secret aid. Mimi, my assigned dragon, who is forever watchful, suddenly gives a warning call and I step back cautiously away from the yacht. Mimi's invisible message at a potentially dangerous time is all I need to backtrack.

"Is she coming or aint she?" snarls the drunken blonde.

"Er sorry I have forgotten something... er thank you for the offer but another time." I abruptly turn scurrying down the jetty, noting the surprised disappointed stare from the old sailor as I rush past.

The vile woman calls after me... "bitch thinks she's too good for us....let me tell you something lady...you're non saleable!"

Momentarily I turn and see Mr Allioni smack her across the face knocking her backwards. Her screams echo through the bay. I shudder and run down the jetty feeling nauseous and lucky to have escaped their clutches, hurrying towards the only safe place I know- Aleana Antiques. Crying with relief, standing outside the shop a voice cuts through my tears:

"It's getting to be a habit you turning up in tears outside my shop!" Seth mocks as he takes my bag and Freddie licks his hands boisterously wagging his tail.

"Now you can finish your coffee in peace!" Seth orders.

I cup my hands around the mug and ask: "You knew didn't you? Why didn't you warn me?" I question.

"It's not my place...you had to find out for yourself. You were hell-bent on going and it was not up to me to stop you!"

"But I could have been drugged and used and...well it's not worth thinking about!"

"Ah but you see you weren't. You made the right decision. You listened to your intuition."

I didn't like to suggest dragon! I gaze outside in the yard where Freddie is tugging at plants in tubs and running in circles chasing his tail. He has suddenly grown and his thick, apricot, curly fur ripples in the wind.

"Coasters run all kinds of illegal business and sail from coast to coast freely unhindered." "They're like pirates then?" I question.

"If you like, but they don't interfere with most Outlanders and it's usually low life who get involved with them. The community is aware of their existence and there are some, like Blackeye, the old sailor, who would sell his Grandmother for a few bottles of rum."

"Thank you so much for allowing me to come back, I've no idea what I'm going to do now?"

"Well I know, it's in the charts – you can stay here for as long as you like. Besides I've got a surprise for you this afternoon."

"You knew I'd come back?"

"Of course, I told you, it's in the stars!"

I smile. Everything seems so perfect and I am indebted to Seth for his kindness and choose not to question my good fortune. I watch him as he takes out a picnic basket from a cupboard and contemplatively places it on the table, as though it is his first time preparing a picnic.

"Isn't it time to open up shop?" I curiously enquire.

"No, we have things to do."

I am surprised at his response and teasingly add, "and I suppose that's written in the stars too?"

Seth raises his eyebrows as he places a bottle of white sparkling wine into the basket with home-made garlic cream cheese and fresh sour dough bread – all my favourites! When the basket is packed he goes upstairs and soon returns with a thick warm coat, matching scarf, hat and gloves stating: "You'll need these."

I put them on as he requests and am delighted that everything fits beautifully. His wife must have been the same size? Seth leads me across the cobbled yard to a massive old barn where he unlocks a hefty security bolt with a steel key. I follow him inside and am stunned to see three vintage sports cars immaculately polished and preserved. More surprisingly, they are exactly like the cars my first husband owned, especially the yellow lotus in which we drove along the coast of Scotland on our honeymoon.

"What do you think?" enquires Seth.

I am flabbergasted and don't know what to say. So many questions reel in my mind. It must be a coincidence that he owns the very same make and colour of cars that were part of my early married life? Back in the day they were very expensive motors. Now they are historical museum pieces.

"Surely you can't still have petrol to run them?" I question.

"Indeed I don't, but I have friends who have adapted the engines to our own brand of fuel and we have plenty of that!" he assures me clapping his hands. "Now the only question is which one?"

I stare in disbelief at the yellow lotus, the dark blue MGB open top roadster and the bright red Bentley Continental GT Convertible. Each car has memories of my first early married life when my husband was a sports car fanatic, needlessly spending and losing our money on his frivolous obsession. I point to the yellow Lotus Elan.

"Ok Lotus it is. Get Freddie and I'll see you by the gate."

I round up Freddie who licks my face and attempts to eat my hat, as Seth ceremoniously draws up looking like Biggles, the fictional pilot adventurer with leather jacket, flying goggles and helmet and I stifle a laugh as I slide in the front seat with Freddie on my knee, stepping back in time to my honeymoon drive along the coast of Scotland with my little Shitzu puppy.

"And we're off!" shouts Seth, his voice trailing in the wind as we shoot towards the snow-capped mountains. Freddie likes the wind rushing through his apricot curls and tries to catch the cold air in his mouth. It's too noisy to speak and so I sit back and soak up the beautiful views unchanged by the Big Reset Programme, recalling how gradually things altered drastically from the time when everyone drove their own petrol or diesel car, to when it all changed to compulsory electric vehicles, which were autonomously driven by computerised artificial intelligent robots and underground roads of up to thirty to fifty levels were built, allowing speeds of four hundred miles an hour which enabled commuters to reach their destination in break-neck time. The tunnel roads were safe as all traffic was co-ordinated from a central computerised system. Now in the cityscapes they have, I understand, massive networks of tunnel roads working in conjunction with high-tech surface roads, with solar powered hyperlinks, plus sky traffic and autonomous delivery drones. I am so glad to be far removed from the cityscape mayhem and out in the outlander plains where, although survival is hard, we have our freedom. I close my eyes and dare to imagine life is still as it was and feel your presence once more as you journey with me. You pop in and out of my consciousness when my mind is free to accept your energy and I know we share special moments like the excitement of now and the thrill of the freedom of racing through the highland roads. The sun is kind and shines brightly casting shadows across the rocky mountainside. I am happy in the now and allow my mind to wander back to my first trip to the Isle of Skye in our Lotus when, as a newly-wed couple we were invited to stay with my husband's friends Emily and Gilly, who had been custodians of his family's business affairs for many years. They retired to a tiny cottage on the Isle of Skye and Emily who was a potter, intended to make and sell her pottery to visitors taking bus tours around the island. The little cottage had been owned by a lady called Bella Marie who had lived there all her life, raising her large family in the tiny house and eventually she died there.

Emily and Gilly had plans to extend the cottage and make the barn into Emily's pottery and show room, so they employed local builders and carpenters who had known Bella Marie all their lives.

Outside the kitchen door was a large stone rock which the builders planned to remove once the new kitchen was installed. Weeks passed as the building work progressed and each worker noticed that the stone was changing shape, but didn't like to comment, as they thought they were imagining things. Months passed and the transformation of the stone became obvious and one of the workers jokingly stated that the stone was morphing into a replica of Bella Marie's face. All the workers agreed and opened up about their secret observations. Everyone said the likeness to the old lady was uncanny. By the time the renovations were complete, so too was the final sculpture of Bella Marie. Somehow the stone had miraculously sculpted itself into an exact likeness of her. The workers were afraid to touch the statue and were relieved to finish the job as they said something strange and unreal had happened, but Emily and Gilly were pleased to welcome Bella Marie into their house and placed her on the fire hearth to be at peace back in her own home.

My ears pop as we climb higher up the steep mountain where the air is cold and damp and Freddie snuggles into my coat to keep warm. Open-topped cars are not comfortable in such inclement weather and Seth stops by a small outcrop of rocks to adjust the roof. It's much cosier with a roof over our heads and much less windy.

"Where are we going?" I ask, curious to know the purpose of the trip.

"You'll see," Seth replies, not willing to give away any information.

I am inquisitive to learn about Seth's past and engage in conversation about his wife, enquiring if they had children but he is silent and uncooperative, so I lean back and watch the sun disappear as mist coils from the mountaintops shrouding our view in a white cloud. A stillness encompasses the landscape amplifying an invisible, eerie presence as the fog compacts into a thick wall. Seth becomes tense as he navigates the dangerous winding road and his knuckles tighten on the steering wheel. I fancy his face has a slight green pallor against the deathly white windscreen but I think it must be a reflection from one of the controls on the dashboard. He switches on the fog lamps but somehow the dazzling beam highlights swirling white particles in a hazy tunnel of light, which further impairs our vision.

"Look, I'm going to change plans. I know a lodge not far from here which can provide shelter until we can hit the road again. Ok?"

I nod and farther along the road we make a right turn slowly descending through the ashy haze to where everything clears and the forest track is visible again. Along the trail I spy a white-washed, stubby brick building with a grey slate roof, encompassed by a rickety wooden fence which reminds me of the climbing huts I used to frequent when I was a member of a mountaineering club. Seth draws up in the deserted car park and states:

"Well this is not what I intended but I think you'll find it comfortable."

Before I have time to reply, a little man pops out of the front door wrapped in thick blankets which obscure his face, wearing a knitted Peruvian bonnet pulled down over his forehead. Freddie is happy to stretch his legs and runs around the yard jumping up at the stranger. Seth introduces his friend Quai, who looks Malaysian Chinese of origin and he in return welcomes us cordially,

"Coma een, comma een!" he beckons and we both follow him as Seth retrieves the picnic basket from the boot. Inside, the heat from a blazing log fire is overwhelming after the cold, damp air outside.

"Coma come, let me take your coats, please to sit by fire and I bring you hot toad" invites Quai bowing politely. I notice his face is mottled with brown patches exuding a slight green tinge but I imagine it is the strange forest light sifting in through the windows, or maybe he has been in an accident or a fire."

"He means Toddy!" adds Seth as Freddie jumps up on my knee licking my hands.

"What is this place?" I ask.

"Oh it's er, a stop off sanctuary for climbers and anyone who seeking solace in the mountains Quai runs it and is a great host and cook."

Seth looks away as he answers as a green haze wafts across his face momentarily and I deduce it must be the same forest light from the dense trees filtering in through the windows, which I noticed previously on Quai. I try to gage Seth's thoughts, but he is difficult to read when his dark opaque eyes are hidden behind his thick glasses. Sometimes he seems unreachable as though he is fobbing me off with what he thinks I want to hear.

"Hot toady for everyone!" laughs Quai as he hands out the hot whisky and cinnamon brew. The peaty steam rising under my nose is comforting and Freddie likes the smell and wants to investigate but Quai lifts him from my lap and takes him to the kitchen for a snack and water. A companionable silence follows as Seth and I sink into our own thoughts. I glance at the world outside as the first snowfall begins to sugar-coat trees in a light frosty dusting and Seth notes that we made the right decision to stop, as the mountain tracks would soon be unpassable in the snow. I get up to peer through the glass but the snowflakes quickly lace the window panes blocking out the view of the mountain range. We could be anywhere trapped in a misty cloud. My thoughts meander back to Emily and Gilly's cottage in the wilds of Skye and how the magic of the mountains can weave unbelievable visions.

I remember one morning walking into the kitchen for breakfast with Emily and Gilly gazing out of the window observing a complete white-out with zero visibility of the landscape outside.

"You can't even see a few inches beyond your own nose!" laughed Gilly. It was true. The cottage seemed spookily imprisoned in a cold, thick, white fortification as a strange emptiness echoed in the kitchen and a fearful silence penetrated the walls from outside. I was afraid. Gilly tried to lighten my concern with his dry humour and Emily tempted me with her home-made marmalade but I could sense they were both afraid too. My husband was solemnly quiet. After breakfast it was as though the cottage was a ship and we had sailed somewhere beyond the boundaries of their land. It seemed an eternity before the fog began to disperse, then through a porthole of retreating mist, I spied a mountain and was relieved to see land again commenting: "Oh look you can now see the mountain beyond the garden." Gilly's reply scared me beyond belief;

"There isn't one. There never has been. You can only see the mountains from the other side!"

I was horrified. Emily took me back to the table and insisted I had another cup of coffee. No one said anything. We all waited in subdued silence for the normal day to return. A short while later we felt a shift in the atmosphere and our moods lifted as quickly as the mist melted and we ventured into the garden to see the fields and hedgerows as they were before, but there was no mountain in sight, not even a large hill. No one spoke about the mysterious mountain mirage and I was too afraid to ask. It will always remain an enigma.

My thoughts are interrupted as Seth leaves to organise something. I am disappointed that since our arrival he has been detached and pre-occupied with other things and talking secretly to Quai, avoiding my gaze and acting like a stranger. I feel abandoned in a lonely setting as I watch the fire heartily blaze and try to cheer up when Quai announces:

"Madam pleased to introduce Mr. Richard."

I turn and see a large stocky man with a full dark beard holding out his hand to greet me. "Pleased ta meet ya!" he drawls in an American accent. He sits beside me on the sofa explaining that he is a photographer on an assignment to capture the mountains in all their natural magnificence, explaining that there are still some people who believe in the power and beauty of nature and that one day we will return to the natural order of things.

Freddie bounds into the room and jumps up on my knee, happy to see me as though he has been away for years. I find it unusual that Richard appears from nowhere in such a remote part of Scotland, especially in such strange circumstances. Seth enters and introduces himself to Richard and the two immediately engage in conversation, while Quai hands me a handwritten menu of all the different dishes he can cook. I choose rabbit stew and Quai nods. Seth surprisingly declines to order as he says he's just eaten in the kitchen, as does Richard. Time passes as the two men continue their in-depth conversation and I am a little deflated at not being included. I was looking forward to spending time alone with Seth but now things have changed since Richard's arrival and feeling rejected, I wander into the kitchen where a wonderful smell is rising from a huge cooking pot on the stove. Quai is chopping herbs and has taken off his Peruvian knitted hat and his bald head is beaded with perspiration and mottled with brown/green patches. I note his skull is an unusual shape, a little like an egg. Loud voices of the two men in the sitting room echo down the corridor as they heatedly debate something and I decide to steal back without disturbing Quai. As I enter the room the men lower their voices and return to their cordial discussion. I wonder if they were arguing about me and distractedly I pick up a pile of ancient magazines which have survived the great literature and pictorial purge to entertain myself with wonderful National Geographic magazine photographs. Quai returns to switch on the little side lamps which cast strange shadows around the room, giving Seth and Richard, sitting near the open fire, peculiar shadow shapes which bare no resemblance to their human form. I blink and in the lamp light the shadows disappear.

"Now for to drink?" enquires Quai who is wearing his Peruvian hat again and smiles with an open grin.

"My usual" states Seth casually.

"Beer for me" adds Richard.

"And for the lady?"

"Oh, er, I don't know, what have you got?"

"We have everything, everything, you would be so surprising!"

"Ginger ale with a shot of cinnamon whiskey", I politely order. He nods without hesitation and scuttles off to the kitchen. The men still chat and I find it hard to believe that they have only just met. I fumble through some more old magazines and spy an interesting article about the discovery of the 'God gene' exposed from an MRI scan. MRI scans now are primitive procedures from the past, once used to help diagnose a patient's condition, but now robots can diagnose, treat, even perform surgery in one consultation. The 'God' gene formally named VMAT2 identified during MRI scans, the article explains, that neuro surgeons were able to separate and destroy the VMAT2 gene thus obliterating all forms of devout fanaticism in humans and eradicating religious friction between all sects. The article further reveals that the VMAT2 gene could be dissolved with chemicals, thus removing and purging the human brain of any sacred, spiritual or religious thoughts and even political allegiance could be eradicated. This became a great tool in the New World Reset for preserving peace and it became law that all citizens entering the cityscapes had to have the VMAT2 gene removed. All humans escaping the cityscapes still have their God gene intact and have the ability and emotional zeal to feel passionate about their personal spiritual and political beliefs.

I sigh, feeling relieved to be a whole person with my spiritual creed and principles intact. When Quai returns with a very large tray of assorted drinks, Seth and Richard join me. Seth sits on the sofa to my left and Richard in a large armchair to my right. Quai places my drink presented in a beautiful crystal glass on a table mat on the coffee table-it has been years in another lifetime since I have seen a pub coaster. I stare in disbelief at the little round, cardboard mat embossed with the picture of a little faun in a champagne glass and the words 'Babycham' inscribed above. Everything is so perfect. I am surprised at Seth's order which consists of two pints of cold beer and a glass of red wine. Quai obviously knows Seth well. Richard's order of one pint of beer seems scant in comparison. I watch Seth down the first pint quickly and likewise the second before he starts on his red wine, while I politely sip my whiskey and ginger. Seth looks at my bubbly concoction and asks:

"Can I try that, I've never had that before?"

I hand him the glass and watch his response.

"Mmm not bad, must remember that one."

As Seth hands back my glass and I turn towards him, my hand momentarily rests on his knee. His reaction startles me. His eyes glare a warning, cautioning that I have overstepped the mark as his body recoils in a snake-like manner. It is as though he is not used to physical interaction or maybe he is shocked by my unwarranted intimacy. I shrug off his response as more drinks are poured and Richard stays with beer while Seth moves on to whiskey. I am surprised at his capacity for alcohol consumption. When Quai brings my food, a delicious aroma wafts around the room exciting Freddie, but Quai takes him to the kitchen to allow me to eat in peace and Seth appears unusually interested in the dish and watches me spoon the first mouthful. The delicate flavour of the meat infused with herbs is fantastic and takes me back to my childhood in the countryside.

"May I try that, I've never had it before?" asks Seth.

I smile and hand him a spoonful of the stew.

"I like it!" he states gleefully like a child and I pat his shoulder with a warm motherly gesture but again his reaction is very strange. He glares a reproving warning not to touch him. I am a little confused by his behaviour as he had lead me to believe that he had been expecting me in his life and our picnic trip had promised to be a special occasion, but in the turn of events he now seems distant and different.

The evening wears on fuzzily in a haze of drinks and fire-glow jollity and I put Seth's strange behaviour to the back of my mind hoping that it was just a misunderstanding. I am relieved when Quai enters with a hot water bottle offering to show me to my room and I accept graciously, rising to wish the men goodnight. Seth stands and surprisingly kisses me on the cheek but the whiskey gives me false courage and I spontaneously take his face in both hands and kiss him on the lips. The moment is slurred then frozen. In slow-motion my lips move towards his and just as we touch, something needle sharp punctures the bottom left side of my lip, like a whip-lash lizard tongue lashing out automatically at its prey. The attack is swift. The piercing pain shoots through my face as it punctures the edge of my lip. I quickly draw back and look into his guarded black eyes, and telepathically question – "Why?" But there is no response and I step back shocked in disbelief that a pin-prick stabbing can happen so quickly in secret, invisible to anyone except the victim. Perplexed I leave and follow Quai to a small adequate room with a single bed, where fully clothed I wrap all the covers around me and snuggle up to Freddie whose sleepy little head is tucked beside mine.

The next morning Freddie wakes me wanting to go outside and I stumble my way through the hallway to let him out. I wait inside and catch sight of someone in the hall mirror. I step closer and am horrified to see it's me! The state of my face is horrendous. By my nose on both sides and under my eyes are swollen bumps surrounded by sore red patches like radiation burns and an inflamed blister has erupted in the spot where my skin was punctured. My face is puffy and swollen. I recall the acute searing pain of the attack, where in my mind I think I see a reptilian, lizard tongue shoot out piercing my bottom lip, but it all happened so quickly that I can't be sure to trust my memory.

"Good morning Miss, I hope you slept well?" enquires Quai, nonchalantly; not reacting to the state of my face.

"Be pleased to know breakfast is ready in the dining room, please to help self."

I follow him down the hallway and into the dining room enquiring if Seth and Richard will be joining me but Quai replies casually:

"Mr. Seth had some business to attend to and is sending a driver to take you back to the village and Mr. Richard had to leave early for another location."

I am angry to be left without an explanation from Seth and am puzzled by the situation. My face is on fire, my stomach is churning and I want to vomit. I race to the bathroom with Freddie running at my heels and just make it before throwing up. Poor Freddie doesn't understand and scratches the door, whining pitifully. Eventually I emerge and calm him down. My swollen, red face has the appearance of radiation burns, which I have previously witnessed in others who have been in contact with radioactive pollution or with alien beings from another planet. I fall back on the bed burning with fever. When Quai enters to announce the driver's arrival, I painfully follow and so does Freddie with his tail drooping – somehow he knows something is wrong. A small, white electric car waits outside. The driver is a tall, black, male android with a smooth round face and mechanically he helps me into the car where I secure Freddie on my knee. Quai does not wait for goodbyes and disappears. Momentarily, I look back to see if Seth is around but there is no one and standing by the door in a woollen hat, is a reptilian being with green/yellow mottled skin and long tail. Suddenly the building vanishes and so does the hybrid reptilian man. I am too ill to question it and reason that my delirium is causing visions.

The silent drive back seems short and we soon pull into the shop backyard where everything is different, much smaller, more shabby with overgrown weeds and an unkempt garden. Freddie jumps out to run around as a middle-aged, matronly lady in an apron approaches us. She nods to the driver and he quickly departs as she supports my aching body with her large arms.

"Hello my dear, I'm Mrs. Gates. I'm going to take care of you. We need to get you upstairs into bed.

Can you make the stairs?"

I nod and climb the old wooden stairs pushing myself up on the handrail which was not there previously. The wide-open staircase leading to a spacious modern area has also disappeared. There is a tiny cottage bedroom with an old-fashioned double bed into which I painfully climb, wondering how the amazing four-poster bed has vaporised into thin air. I fall into a deep sleep waking occasionally when my stomach gripes to visit the tiny bathroom and sometimes to sip a little hot broth prepared by Mrs. Gates. Days pass in pain and oblivion. Occasionally Freddie's face appears next to mine and then I fall back to sleep, relieved he is safe. Sometimes I feel him licking my ear and often I feel his warmth on my feet. I exist. I am alive but I am not living. Day and night roll into an endless nothing and I fight to survive, fight to keep conscious but I keep tumbling back into a dull cataleptic fog, but this morning, and I know it is morning because of the bright light streaming through the curtains, I wake and sit up. Freddie who is lying by the bed jumps up wagging his tail and whines. He has grown and can now jump onto the bed. I hug him to my chest. I am so, so happy to see him and he me. Mrs. Gates appears with a bowl of porridge and sits on the bed.

"There now my dear, that's better. You're over the worst."

"What happened?" I ask shakily.

"Just take it easy, plenty of time to chat; you've got to get your strength back. Now concentrate on eating. I want a clean bowl."

Later after resting I wander downstairs where everything is also completely different from my first visit. The kitchen is now only a small cottage galley with a wooden dining table. How could I have perceived it differently?

"Come, sit by the fire my dear, I know you are confused and have many questions," croons Mrs. Gates. She has kind eyes. I think I can trust her. I nod and sit opposite and Freddie settles down on my feet making sure I don't go anywhere without him. Mrs. Gates oozes Grandmotherly care and compassion with an air of matronly discipline.

"Now my dear, I know you have knowledge and even some experience of the 'beyondness of things" but to understand what has happened, you need to have an open mind and know that the world as you know it is not what you think...now what's that saying? There are far greater things in heaven and on earth than you ever dreamed of...I think that's it, well something like that!"

I nod and smile being fully aware of the mutability of reality.

"Now let me see, where shall we begin? Ah yes, well I'm Mrs. Gates, Mrs. Aleana Gates."

"Ah so the shop is named after you?"

"Oh yes, the very same. Well actually it's not my shop, I just take care of it, as it's really a portal to another universe, a star-gate if you like and I am the gatekeeper. It's a pretty good cover though don't you think?"

I agree, amazed to think that the little shop is an actual star-gate, a real entrance to other universes, and I begin to realize how I have been duped right from the very beginning like a fly enticed into a spider's web and understanding that Seth was not the person I thought and his life story totally false.

"But how come everything seemed so real...I mean when I entered the shop it was amazing, so enticing, so convincing?"

"Precisely. That's how it was devised my dear!"

"But how?"

"Oh that's easy, we fool everyone every time!" She added victoriously.

"Them?"

"Yes, we have many visitors here, some human, some hybrids and aliens of many species. They all stop off here; it's a bit like an airport, well like airports used to be I suppose."

"But how do you change everything to make it look so different?"

"Again my dear, that's very, very easy! Easy when you know how, hey?" She smiles like a pantomime Dame. "You see the human brain is so powerful – it's a pity you humans don't know how to use the machine to its full potential: humans are lazy you see, they only use a tiny portion of it each day and most of that is automatic. Anyway, I digress, the human brain has many different compartments, a bit like a large chest of drawers where each drawer has a different purpose- that is you have a drawer stored with emotions; you have a thinking, philosophical drawer; an anger response drawer; a love drawer and so on and so forth...do you see? Oh I forgot people like you have an extra drawer, a secret psychic drawer and that's the reason why we needed your help."

I nod, trying to understand the implications of her explanation, but before I can ask more questions she trundles on regardless.

"So everything in your brain is highly compartmentalised which makes it easy for us to tap into any compartment we wish. We can measure and assimilate your likes and dislikes; your preferences and aversions; your choice in men for example and your taste in clothes and objects etcetera etcetera...are you with me? We can even access all your memories and wipe them out and replace them with different ones to suit our purpose."

I am shocked and stunned into silence as she recounts more startling revelations.

"So with all these drawers in the cupboard we can open any one at will and look inside and take things out and put things in and copy onto script exactly what you like best. It's a bit like programming a computer and pasting in all your preferences and encoding your surroundings to suit your expectation. It's not magic you know? It's merely science. Everything is a vibration, not dense matter, so therefore it is easy to alter and adjust a vibration. It's as easy as pressing a key on the computer to revise backgrounds or modify colour or vary sound. We've always had the technology to do this my dear. Humans are easy to manipulate especially with our mind control technology. We can mine the mind and exploit the eleven different dimensions the human brain can facilitate. In some humans there are more!"

I find the information bombardment overwhelming and my mind boggles, overloaded with incomprehensible futuristic facts.

"I hear your questions bubbling and I understand. I know it's difficult to take it all in," she adds.

I swallow and catch my breath to question her – "So let me get this straight, with your technology you are able to search my mind for specific details and then reproduce them as a kind of mirage?"

"Yes, sort of!" she replies.

"You chose everything that would please me and took things from my memory to make me feel safe in order to use me?"

"Well, yes in a nutshell!" She states with a half-smile.

"So all the clothes, the food, the décor, the conversation, the cars and the situation, were a set-up?"

"Correct!" she answers briskly.

"But why?" I question.

"For you to understand everything I will take time to explain, by way of an apology, because of your unfortunate illness and because we mean you no harm and believe it or not, this planet is in grave danger and we are here to help save humanity from yourselves, as you are on a self-destruct runway. You have set in motion the beginning of the end by using your new-found technology to create dangerous, powerful, cosmic weapons, the like of which you have no real understanding. It is like giving a baby a box of matches! This is our planet, our real home. We inhabited the earth eons before you were even devised."

My mind reels with all the impossible possibilities, hurtling between what I have been taught as reality and what I have learnt which is not-but deep inside I know she is telling the truth, like I know you are here witnessing all that unfolds; even if I am part of your dream consciousness, or you part of my higher self? I know that the impact of truth is heavy. I need to know the accuracy of it all.

Mrs Gates, pats my knee sympathetically, understanding that her revelations are difficult to understand. She smiles and stares deeply into my soul, wishing to reveal her true self. Momentarily her body shimmers, disappearing into an olive-green and brown-mottled lizard-like creature about seven feet tall with reptilian yellow eyes. I can't believe what I am witnessing and it is difficult to process the confusing reality. For a few moments she allows me to see her true self before her reptilian form disappears in a fizzing fusion of energy and Mrs. Gates is back, smiling. I hear her voice in my head as she explains: "I am speaking to you through what we call 'syntel' that is synthetic telepathy which uses your brain's electro-magnetic vibrations for communication. So to answer your question I am a reptilian human – a hybrid. We, as a race were here before you. The earth is our planet not yours and because you humans are part of a hybrid experiment, you live in a holographic, computerised domain where your vibrational frequency differs from ours and therefore you cannot see us in our true form, except when your vibration intercepts ours."

I am shocked and alarmed. I have always been fearful of reptiles and was once bitten by a poisonous snake sitting on the banks of the Mississippi river late at night, not realizing it was the season for snakes to have their babies and being alone for a special dance conference, just managed to get to my hotel bedroom to collapse on the bed, whilst attempting to dig out the snake venom from my leg with my nails. I didn't panic, just accepted my fate and the doctor said that my calm attitude saved my life. I have also equally been afraid of lizards, having spent long periods of time living in India where small geckos reside in houses hidden in corners, behind paintings and run across ceilings whilst dinner is being served and even shed their tails into the soup taurine while everyone is eating!

So her real reptilian nature alarms me.

"There's no need to be afraid my dear, as I said we are here to help you. I understand your fear, for there are evil species in our colony and the stories you have heard about these reptiles eating humans are true."

I wondered why I hadn't seen Seth or Richard eating, except for when Seth was eager to try my rabbit stew. "So I take it that your species can eat human food?"

"That is correct but mostly we choose to eat our own nutritional sustenance. When we take on the human form we are able to digest your food, but only in small amounts. Underground in many places are great vats of our own food stored in secret."

"Do the flesh-eating reptilians have access to these food vats?"

"You usually find that those flesh devouring species do not eat our nourishment as ours contains only good vibrations, whereas they need the 'loosh' that is the chemical derived from the fear of a victim about to be sacrificed and eaten. The fear chemical which floods their veins and arteries – the 'loosh' is what they most crave and sustains and satisfies their evil nature until the next loosh feast.

I shudder at the image conjured as she continues.

"But then there are good and bad kinds in every variety of being here on earth, but not so beyond this sphere where things are different, but your limited brain cannot comprehend this at present."

I listen intently, feeling a little less threatened.

"Why you yourself are a hybrid, you must know this?"

I have always known I was sent to earth to help raise the higher consciousness of humanity, but always struggled to live as a human, being pulled between two worlds. I was a 'walk-in' spirit at the birth of a child who was dying in its mother's womb. I took her place because I chose to enter the earth. She hears my thoughts and interjects:

"Yes, indeed, you are one of many light workers, in world service and have the capacity and ability to help and heal people. You have telepathic and psychic gifts which we wanted to use in order to contact a species lost in the cosmos and we needed to know their position in order to rescue them.

Your task was to remote view their position but things changed and our orders were altered."

"But why didn't you just contact me and ask me directly to do the job instead of all this cloak and dagger stuff? And why didn't you just let me go? I suffered a terrible illness because of Seth or whomever he is or whatever he is!

"Yes we are sorry about that. It was not intentional. You see, Seth, that's not his real name of course, is also one of our kind, and was not prepared for your ways and protected himself spontaneously in his own species manner."

"I don't understand?"

"Well, let me put it this way – he is from a reptile species and intimate contact, the manner in which you humans behave, is not their way and you overstepped the mark and he defended himself by the only means he knows."

"Lizard tongue!" I interject.

"Yes precisely!"

"But he seemed so human?"

"Of course, shape-shifters do!"

I am shocked by her bluntness.

"Don't look so shocked?" she adds, "shape-shifters have inhabited the earth since time began, before the human race in fact. Anyway to get back to the point, you are free to leave. I am sorry you were used and at the time it seemed the best way to involve you in our quest by making you feel at ease with us, but things didn't turn out the way we planned. There is a boat leaving for the mainland this afternoon if you feel strong enough?" I ponder all that she has said realising that all events planned to keep me to comply with their wishes were precisely and expertly executed. Everything was skilfully designed to please my senses and persuade me to feel safe and comfortable. Everything from the clothes, the cars, the food the furniture and the setting, were all holographic-only Freddie was my true companion and was himself throughout the whole masquerade. Now it seems I am free to leave as I am no longer needed. I feel deflated and let down and can't help asking:

"Was the detour to the mountain cabin a set up?"

"No, you were meant to arrive at a different destination high up in the mountains but the snowfall changed plans. Richard as he chose to be called, had to engineer a new meeting place and re-arrange everything which entailed a change of plan regarding your services, which were no longer needed, as they made contact with the said species through other means."

I thought it was strange that the two men conversed so easily, in fact too easily to be strangers meeting for the first time.

"Was Quai part of the set-up?"

"Oh yes indeed, he belongs to a species of ours designed to be 'servers', but you wouldn't understand – let me see it's a bit like the bee insect on earth. Some bees are created to be workers and others queens. Well now, you are free to go and so must I."

Before I can ask any more questions she begins to shimmer and shake like an oscillator, with her feet disappearing first, riding upwards until she completely vanishes into the ether.

Now alone in the cold, dilapidated cottage, I walk into the shop cluttered with congeries of decaying rubbish. I step back in disgust as the smell of rotting garbage makes me retch. How could it ever have been so grand? Feeling foolish and betrayed, I go upstairs and gather my meagre things. The clothes I am wearing are shabby and worn and I, like Cinderella, have returned to the world of ashes and dust. I call Freddie who jumps into my arms and licks my face pulling me back in the land of the living and my determination and eagerness to find my daughter returns with a vengeance as I walk down the jetty to where the ancient ferry is being loaded with goods to be sold at the mainland market. Freddie who has rapidly grown, walks confidently by my side and is my only constant friend.

I feel you appear in my head. From afar you have watched everything but said nothing. Perhaps you are here to observe only and maybe on my new journey I will get to know you better and you will reveal your identity? Perhaps you are part of me from the past or the future? I will wait to discover the truth. In the meantime you hover, watching the adventure unravel.

A few people wrapped up warm against the cold sea breeze linger around the sidewalk waiting to go aboard the ferry with Christmas gifts and seasonal goods to sell at the market. Christmas in parts of the country is still celebrated and there is an air of seasonal merriment among the crowd. Freddie draws attention from a small fan club of children gathered on the quay. He loves their playfulness. I thank the universe, for all that has been revealed; for all that I have and for life itself-for I am lucky.

Yes, I am indeed Lucky.

THE ONLY WAY OUT IS IN!

On the ferry back to the mainland my thoughts return to my eldest daughter and how best to find her – maybe she has clues to the whereabouts of my other children? When the world went dark, families were lost and divided into groups and interned in compounds where they were brain-washed in preparation for cityscape living. Some escaped the internment and like myself became 'outlanders' living from day to day in outlandish places, hiding behind a shroud of uncertainty and wrapped in constant fear of being captured. In the bleak blackness that followed the 'day of darkness', all communication around the world was severed-phones, computers, emails, every form of electrical contact disintegrated the day the planet was plunged into night when the earth was struck by a gigantic asteroid, which plummeted into the Pacific Ocean and chaos reigned. Gangs rampaged like warrior Vikings, looting and murdering innocent people for food and shelter. Ordinary folk metamorphosed into manic savages murdering mercilessly for scraps of meat and cannibalism became a necessary evil as a means of survival amongst some outlander tribes, but when the 'Protectors' arrived in their cosmic ships all was calmed. Some said the Annunaki had returned to fulfil their pledge of restoring planet earth when it became endangered and nearing extinction. It is reported that it was their promise from the beginning of time to reinstate peace to the human beings they once created.

In my wanderings, I find that most people still maintain a sense of dignity and love of their fellow humans and I have been lucky to stay hidden to avoid direct conflict with unpredictable outlying tribal communities. It seems the earth has become divided into three major modes of living-those who live a high-tech, ultra-modern life encased in the cityscapes and are robotically regimented in their transhumanistic bubbles; those who belong to tribal communities and are trapped within their own clan laws and are subjected to barbaric methods of punishment and those like myself who are nomads, drifting from place to place looking for lost loved ones and a safe place to settle. These thoughts drift through my mind as the ferry ploughs through the choppy waves leaving a trail of foamy white caps bubbling on the surface, before disappearing into the deep unknown. What lies below? I have heard tales whispered around camp fires after dark, of the unfathomable ocean where giant silver slithers of metal stealthily slide silently into unknown waters, falling like shooting stars from the night sky before sinking into oblivion. Some fishermen out at sea tell of spaceships plunging into stormy waters, swallowed by gigantic waves with flashing bright lights swirling below the breakers, followed by booming explosions shaking and juddering all vessels on the surface as the vibrations roll out across the sea, jolting houses on land with earthquake-like tremors. I dispel these thoughts as Freddie grows restless and I am relieved that the ferry ride is short.

I feel your presence again in my head and I am comforted that you are with me. I know you well but not at all. From afar you watch, hovering like a Kestrel in an open field but then you disappear and just when I think you are lost somewhere in the cosmos, you surface again reassuringly. Are you me?

Do you come from a different time zone? Perhaps one day I will know – and now already I spy the jetty where we will alight, but it is not the same little port with the magical antique shop, it is a landing further down the coast. As we near the dock I note how different the place is from the last quaint port. The buildings are darker, oppressive and dilapidated with dense groups of people flocking around the boats pushing each other to get freshly caught fish and other goods brought by the boats. The atmosphere is unhealthily menacing with so many outlanders and tribes-folk mingling together in one place. The docking is bumpy as waves break against the jetty and we bounce up and down comically out of control, propelled forwards in an unruly cluster towards the exit, so I carry Freddie under my arm to shield him from the compacted crowd. As I step forwards on the quay, a ragged man rushes past hugging a hessian sack against his chest, knocking me sideways.

I grip Freddie tightly as I fall against a group of women who curse and push me back, jeering as I apologise profusely. I quickly walk on as the screeching and hollowing from traders bartering heightens amidst the rising tension of the hostile hamlet, where violence bubbles below the surface and might, at any moment erupt and break out into a vicious skirmish. I need to disappear but I am trapped in the jostling crowd. From either side of the walkway fierce gestures and menacing insults are hurled from trader to trader. Thick black mud squelches underfoot and everywhere is tawdry, stinking of sewage, pigs and unwashed bodies. I am intimidated by the market with its war-like merchants and overwhelming unfriendly people, especially after the kindness and warmth of the coastal highlanders. Home guards dressed in black uniforms stalk the market aisles armed with sharp, metal-spiked truncheons to enforce peace amidst the looming threat of the mob. Through a gap in the throng, I hastily retreat to a calmer spot by a wall to catch my breath. Freddie is unusually quiet sensing my apprehension. I have no idea what to do or where to go and am shocked by the inimical attitude of the people. My instincts warn me to flee as far away as possible – but how and where? Watching the hostile crowd I suddenly spy a familiar male face dodging in and out of the mob but he disappears amongst the horde of bodies and emerges briefly by a vegetable stall then vanishes again. At first I wonder where I have seen him before and then the awful truth dawns – the face that caused me so much pain and illness through a fated kiss, I never wish to see again-Seth is the last person I want to meet. I wonder what he is doing in the market? Is he using his alien reptilian magic to become invisible amongst the heaving masses? Whatever the reason, I never wish to set eyes on him again. I am angry and hurt at the way he treated and tricked me into believing the fantasy he wove and now the sight of him sickens me. Suddenly I spy him again furtively dodging the guards and I suspect he is involved in some kind of clandestine mission. He appears as an ordinary man, but I know that he is not. Like many other reptilians and alien species who walk the earth undetected, they fool most humans. His surprise appearance in this unruly place arouses my curiosity and I want to know what he doing and to track him down to vent my anger towards him and so without a thought for my safety, I swiftly move into the crowd pushing my way forwards holding Freddie under my coat racing towards the vegetable stall where I last spied him, but there is no sign of him anywhere. I close my eyes and try to hone in on him through sensing his vibration.

After the reptilian piercing, surprisingly my senses have become heightened and sharper and I think he must have passed on some of his sensory cells. When I open my eyes I glimpse the back of his head as he enters a grey doorway and I quickly follow him then pause, hovering outside. I move closer to listen for voices inside but all is quiet. I push the door open gently and am immediately caught by a strong arm. Poor Freddie drops to the floor on his lead as my arms are thrust behind my back. In the stillness of the moment, when he realizes I am not a threat, I stand face to face with him and stare into his eyes. Seth does not recognise me. Suddenly his hand shoots across my mouth as I try to speak and Freddie growls and barks attacking his leg, defending me, but he is swiftly kicked and retreats whimpering in a corner. From somewhere inner strength gushes and I release a rush of energy tearing at his face with my nails kicking him hard in his testicles. I am in awe of my found strength and I rush to pick up Freddie, kissing his soft head. He is not injured and he licks my face in gratitude. I turn towards the man who is lying on the floor cradling his scrotum and rolling sideways. I kick him in the back and he hollers in pain. I am surprised at the force in my legs and stand over him demanding an explanation for treating me so badly.

"Woman, I have no idea what you are talking about! Are you crazy? I don't know you!"

I order him to get up. Painfully he obeys with caution, wary of where the next blow might strike.

"Who are you?" I demand.

"Well, obviously I am not the person you think I am!" he scorns, gaining more self-control.

"So you're not Seth?" I ask softly.

"What do you think?"

"You look just like him, I mean the resemblance is incredible?"

He sighs and looks at Freddie adding, "sorry little fella, I didn't mean to hurt you!" "But I watched you and you are obviously stalking someone, or hiding from someone or..." He signals me to stop with his hand. Then motions me to be quiet and points up to the ceiling. In the stillness the noise outside from the market is deafening. He stares upwards trying to detect the presence of someone above us and motions me to follow him under the stairs where we huddle together in hiding. Suddenly his arm shoots around my waist pulling my back in tight against his chest as we hear footsteps marching down the bare staircase. My heart begins to pound and I stifle a whimper from Freddie. The man's left arm holds me tight and with his right he slowly draws out a weapon from his jacket pocket. I am shocked, realising he could have shot me at any time during our fracas! My head begins to throb and I break out in a cold sweat as we listen intently to the footsteps which seem to take forever to disappear.

When it is safe we separate and he places the gun back in his pocket and sidles up to the window to take a sly peek out. Blood trickles down his cheek from my blow, but he doesn't seem to notice.

"What's happening?" I whisper.

He doesn't reply.

"Look I'm sorry for what happened. I didn't mean to hurt you it's just that.."

"Be quiet!" He hisses.

I obey and stand back placing Freddie on the floor.

"If you're not Seth, then who are you? You look just like him!" I mutter nervously, unable to keep quiet. He pauses and steps away from the window taking a deep breath looking intently at both me and Freddie, adding:

"Craig, I'm Craig and you are...?" he enquires cautiously, taking out a handkerchief from his pocket to wipe his face.

"Well I'm Lucky and this is Freddie." I state in a formal manner.

He laughs quietly. "Lucky indeed you are, if that is your name? Well Lucky what are you going to do now that you've not found your man?"

"He's not my man, in fact he's not a man at all. He's a reptilian alien." I reply defensively.

He takes me seriously and ponders the statement.

"Mmm...and you say he looks like me?"

"Yes, an exact replica, well almost. Now that I see your eyes up close, they are sort of different, although the same colour."

"Do you know about clones?" He asks meaningfully.

I nod. Many, many years ago the idea of cloning was big news but gradually it became a common-place notion and was accepted under the guise of health research, but many of us knew that it was just a ruse to cloak more sinister applications of the process. Suddenly voices outside echo through the door and Craig motions me to be quiet. He picks up Freddie and tiptoes towards the back door. I follow. It is open and we slip into the market in the midst of a massive brawl where stalls and tables smash as bodies are hurled across the stands. Steel blades clang against steel, resounding through the aisles as the home guards pound into the horde wielding their spiked truncheons. Blood splatters everywhere and faces of grown men are pulped to mash, like minced meat on a butcher's slab. With one arm holding Freddie and the other dragging my sleeve, Craig hauls me to a side alley free from the mob and we run furiously towards the forest leaving the skirmish behind. With my new-found strength and stamina the running is easy. When we reach the edge of the woods, Craig frees Freddie and releases my arm pausing to regain his breath. He is surprised at my endurance, as am I. As we walk cautiously into the copse I relate all that happened at Aleana Antiques and how Seth had tricked me and made me very ill. He listens intently making mental notes. As we reach what looks like an impassable thicket of dense overgrown bushes Craig halts, asking me to wait while he removes an ingenious net of interwoven camouflage foliage, hiding a small khaki-green army jeep. He adjusts the steering wheel and settings then clears a pathway enough for us both to climb in and weave our way out of the forest. Without any discussion as to where we are going, I follow his bidding, grateful to be heading somewhere away from the violence. The vehicle is very uncomfortable without proper seats but it serves our purpose driving along country lanes and out through minor roads which have fallen into disrepair and are barely navigable, but with careful steering through potholes and around mounds of rubble we are able to forge ahead. We drive without speaking until the light dims and the sun in the West is a flamingo-orange ball. I am glad that outside in the natural world away from the cityscapes, we still have natural weather with normal sunsets and star-studded nights and inspiring dawns, as previously for years we endured chemtrails clouding our natural skies, sealing the ionosphere in a grey lid, so that we couldn't see the secret spacecraft hovering beyond and above. For years we tolerated toxic poisons in the air and metal pollution causing the increase of asthma and Alzheimer's disease. Eventually when the cityscapes were built they left the sky outside the compounds to the natural elements, using internal weather modification and computerised systems to provide a synthetic ideal climate under a dome-like artificial sky in all cityscapes.

The rocking and jolting of the jeep coaxes me into a deep sleep and Freddie too, who is lying across my knees, relaxed and happy. I wake when the jolt of the brake is jerkily applied and Freddie nearly falls off my knees. At first in the total darkness I am unable to make out where we are and I am surprised to see in the distance bright yellow flames blazing from torches lighting up the faces of friendly men and women advancing and encircling the jeep. Craig is obviously well known and a popular personality, as he is welcomed with much back slapping, shaking of hands and hugging. My body is stiff and aching from the long journey and Freddie is pleased to be on land once more and relieves himself in the long grass. In a jovial parade we are escorted towards an ancient manor house and guided through a narrow hallway up a small flight of stairs to a large kitchen where a party feast is laid out with home-made mead and wine. I am so hungry and poor Freddie is starving. A little girl takes his lead and walks him to a pet's corner where he is given water and dried food nuggets. She tells Freddie her name is Rosie and he immediately loves her. Craig is merry, surrounded by caring friends who pour mead into a large pewter mug and plie him with food on a wooden platter, hailing him 'Lord of the Manor'. A woman passes me a beaker of mead and a large portion of food in a dish, for which I am very grateful and I eat it voraciously, trying not to appear barbaric. It is wonderful to be amongst friendly people who are kind and generous. Craig is relaxed and at home sharing jokes with his friends and I ascertain that he is a leader or an elder of the community, as he appears senior to most of them. The mead and wine flow as the night closes in and I am not aware that I fall asleep on the kitchen table. Neither am I aware that I am put to bed in a child's single bed fully clothed, still wearing my boots which stick out at the end of the blankets.

In the morning I sit up slowly feeling the after effects of too much indulgence and walk to the window. Outside is a wonderfully fresh, clean cut, massive lawn where Rosie and other children are playing ball with Freddie. It's such a natural, normal activity that I burst into tears. I haven't witnessed such a scene for a very long time and the sound of children's laughter is a joy. A gentle knock on the door interrupts my thoughts and a pretty young woman enters with a pile of clean clothes.

"Good morning, I see you're up and about. How you feeling?"

"Er, a little sensitive this morning...too much mead I think!" I reply shakily.

The woman laughs adding, "You think it's not strong, but it soon takes hold, especially when you're not used to it! Oh by the way – I'm Meredith. We clubbed together, me and a few other women, to sort these out for you, we figured you needed a change!"

Tears flow again as she hands me the carefully selected bundle. "Ah now there's no need...you're among friends here. You're safe," she gently affirms.

It's not in the hard times that you let go and cry but in the safe place when the horror is over and when you stop running and fearing.

In the ease of the moment you let down the flood gate and the torrent crashes through the barrier. Now is a time for tears. Now is a time to release the pent-up agony, the raging storm within and liberate the whirling hurricane tearing inside.

"There, there, it's ok. It's all ok!" soothes Meredith, gently patting my shoulder. I look up into her face and she smiles and we both laugh as Rosie runs into the room with Freddie pounding at her heels.

"Are you better now?" asks Rosie innocently.

I nod and pick up Freddie who washes my face with his pink, warm tongue.

"Daddy said you could stay a while and I could play with Freddie." She adds confidently.

I look at Meredith questioning the statement.

"Oh, yes, her Father Craig, he's the Lord of the Manor, or used to be, that is in times gone by, until he rescued us all and gave us a safe dwelling – a sanctuary, a haven."

I thought they were joking when they referred to Craig as the 'Lord of the Manor'?

"What kind of dog is Freddie?" asks Rosie tickling him under his chin.

I explain; "I don't know as I found him wrapped in a sack in an alleyway, but he seems to be a cross mixture of poodle and Maltese, just like a Maltepoo puppy I had a long time ago."

Rosie laughs at the description and she kisses him on the top of his head.

"I gave him water and some food this morning," she adds.

"Thank you dear, but did you ask your Mum if it was ok?"

She looks puzzled and Meredith answers, "oh it's fine, our pet food is for all our pets, everyone helps themselves. Now run along Rosie and let Miss Lucky have some peace to get dressed."

I watch as Rosie skips out of the door with Freddie close at her heels.

"The two of them are so sweet together," I sigh, feeling better after my earlier outburst.

"Seems that little fella has brought a new spark into her life. Her Mother died last year and although we all try to take good care of her and Craig is very good with her, but a Mother's love can't easily be replaced and very often when he is away she is bereft. He hasn't got over the loss of his wife and locks himself away in a dark cavern of grief. He may seem aloof or uncaring at times but he is just mourning the loss of his beloved."

As she leaves the room I glance across the vast lawn and see Craig in the distance talking to a group of men. I understand his loss. Grief takes many forms and can hide for a while then pop up without warning or lie buried asleep in a deep grave never to be woken or shaken, or it can be kept forever hovering at a distance between heaven and hell.

It is wonderful to feel fresh clean water on my body and to wash away the grime of daily existence and to dress in clean comfortable clothes and wear soft, easy shoes. I stand in front of a small dressing table mirror to admire the finished image and am deeply shocked. I don't recognise the woman standing before me. I touch my face, feel my skin, stretch my arms, kick my legs, yes they all belong to me but the person in the mirror is me but not me. I had forgotten my age somewhere in the distant past and in growing older I had become another body, but still the same inside. The image in the mirror is a younger version of me and I wonder how it could happen? I begin to realize that since the illness inflicted on me by Seth, my mind is sharper, my senses heightened, my sight better, my fitness improved and now my body younger. Whatever Seth injected into my face must be some kind of youth serum? Perhaps the DNA cells of a reptilian alien, when inserted into a human might have a regenerative effect? It is the only explanation I can fathom. I wonder if the effect is permanent or will I regress further and become even younger? I am suddenly plunged into a predicament I had never envisaged – being younger is wonderful but unsettling and disturbing! I walk down the stairs in my younger body and consider that the people here do not know me from the past, so in the present I can be as I am now. I do not have to worry about difficult answers to strange questions. Craig only knows me as I am in the present and that makes matters simpler. I almost dance down the stairs feeling my legs fully mobile in a tighter, lighter body. I have escaped out of a long imprisonment in a crusting shell, which was suffocating and now I can run and jump, feel my body twist and turn without pain and it makes me realise that when we own youth we are not mature enough to appreciate it. At the bottom of the stairs I hum a long lost melody retracing steps from a solo piece I performed in my youth, imagining the throb of the audience and the heat of the lights and the music sifting through time portals. I am lost in a whirl, swirling into a flourish of jumps and finish in an arabesque. My vision is broken by loud clapping from the doorway and turn to see Craig watching. I am embarrassed and stand awkwardly like a child caught with my hand in the cookie jar.

"Bravo! Bravo!" He hails.

I return a shy smile and thank him for his kindness, suddenly remembering my drunken state the previous night and the thrashing I gave him when we first met. A whole torrent of humiliation shamefully strangles me. I don't know where to look. He laughs light-heartedly at everything and jokingly declares that I pitch a mean punch and a keen kick in the nuts.

I am saved further embarrassment when Rosie spies us and runs with Freddie to show us his lead decorated with pretty daisies. Freddie has never been so entertained and made to jump through hoops and leap over obstacles and he sits happily panting by her side with his tongue hanging out, proud of his antics. The other children run up behind Rosie with pink cheeks and wide smiles, puffing out of breath. Craig declines a game of catch as he has work to finish but I haven't the heart to fob them off and so I am dragged into a robust game which in my new, younger body I can handle! A friendly female voice from the kitchen hails us in for lunch and I am relieved to be let off playground duty. Freddie likewise is happy to flop by my feet by the kitchen table. I eat a hearty lunch with the children which is served by a middle-aged, large lady with a friendly round face. Her greying dark hair is covered with a scarf and she slaps her stomach when she laughs. She is very popular with the children as she makes them sweet treats. The adults of the community, I am told, eat later and after the children's sitting, each child has set chores to attend to and Rosie asks to take Freddie, which I allow. I wander around the kitchen garden kicking my heels scrunching the pebbles as I walk, feeling a little lost without Freddie who has been my constant companion for quite some time. An old greenhouse with several broken glass panes stands lodged by a crumbling brick wall, thickly embossed with climbing yellow roses and the delicate scent is divine and takes me back to a long lost time before my eldest daughter was born when I lived in a haunted old farm cottage. Through the painted white panes of glass in the greenhouse, I am aware of being watched and I am relieved when a small, old man with white hair and bushy mottled beard opens the rickety glass door to enquire: "Can I help you Miss?"

I smile and explain that I arrived late last night with Craig. The old man nods, wipes his hands on his old gardening apron and puts down his trowel on a nearby bench.

"Pleased to meet you Miss, I'm Augustus and Mr. Craig has asked me to give you a tour of the gardens and our domestic operations."

"Oh that's lovely" I blurt out, "the gardens are beautiful. Oh by the way I'm Lucky."

"Indeed Miss, would you like to follow me?"

His quaint, old-fashioned manner is charming but outdated in the brave new world of technology and robotic science. It seems strange that the world has changed so much, yet here in the rose garden time stands still and Augustus is a time relic showing me around the kitchen garden pointing out herbs and vegetables, addressing each one by their Latin name and I am astounded by his vast knowledge of natural medicine, so by the time we reach the hen house my head is reeling with information overload. The hens are of course free range and according to Augustus, produce the best eggs ever! There are seven milk producing cows and one bull and each cow is milked by hand in a thoroughly clean and sterile outhouse where cheese and butter are made. I am very impressed by the set-up and the tour ends with a short walk to the sheep pen where nine fat woolly sheep statically graze. "There you are, you have seen for yourself, that we still have animals, raised and tended properly for the good use of mankind. In the cityscapes they will tell you that there are no animals left...well perhaps for them folk, there aren't any because they've got rid of them all. They exist on chemicals you see... that's not natural. Not good for the body. I've heard they've even invented pretend pets! Well I suppose they won't need feeding!" he shakes his head and walks away talking to himself.

Once more I am left to freely roam the estate, feeling bereft without Freddie tugging at my sleeve and I am glad that he is not a cyber-pet and feel so lucky to have found him. I wonder what I should do next but that decision is taken out of my hands by a comely, middle-aged lady who approaches me smiling, saying; "Ah Miss Lucky, Mr. Craig has asked me to accompany you on a tour around the house, just so that you are acquainted with what is out of bounds and what is not. I am Edith by the way, head of household."

I am shocked that the community is run on a very old-fashioned formal hierarky, but I suppose that Craig, who was a Lord in past times, still strives to maintain a structure from his previous life. As we walk back to the house, Edith explains that the Sanctuary, as it is now called, is a place of healing and comfort to those in distress both mentally and physically. It is a place of tranquillity, learning and of self-discovery. Edith points out certain areas of the house which must be kept quiet at all times for meditation and I begin to understand why the structure is precisely defined to meet all needs. Edith is proud of all that the Sanctuary has to offer and shows me dormitories for young children and orphans, plus apartments for couples and a large community hall which is also a Church. In particular she is delighted to present the sensory birthing suite, where women about to give birth can experience spa water pools with beautiful music and soft lighting with fragranced candles of healing lavender. She further explains: "Having babies is still a wonder and a miracle of nature here in the outlander wilds but we are thought of as primitive barbarians in the cityscapes, because women no longer bear children – that privilege has been given to scientists in a clinical laboratory, where designer babies are produced for the chosen few."

I am glad that outside the cityscapes, humanity still thrives despite the lure of futuristic living, but I wonder how long we will be able to continue surviving in a natural environment. Already there is talk of the earth's demise and a mass exodus to Mars. In the meantime we are able to self-generate electricity which provides all needs. Edith further explains that the Sanctuary is open to everyone and anyone is welcome, drawing people from far and wide and is financed and maintained by a bartering system.

"And of course we are very fortunate to attract wonderful, professional people with all kinds of gifts and skills, in fact our midwife lives locally and attends the young pregnant women in our birthing suite, which was her idea. She is an amazing woman with so many healing abilities and she teaches us many things about natural remedies and herbal medicine."

Immediately my heart skips a beat. I feel sure she is describing my eldest daughter. I ask her name and before she replies I say the name out loud with her... 'Estrella'.

"You know her?" enquires Edith.

"I think so," I sigh softly, her face flooding my memory of baby, bright blue eyes and shiny, golden hair. My little girl.

"Does she live far from here?" I enquire nonchalantly, concealing my racing pulse.

"Not too far; she is sometimes hard to locate as she travels around following the healing call."

"Can we go to see her?" I almost plead.

"Well now, she is due to visit here tomorrow, so I am sure you will get to meet her. She is very accommodating."

I can hardly conceal my excitement and thank Edith profusely for the tour and make my excuses to return to my make-shift room. I am so happy to think that after all this time I have been searching, I may at last find her. In my room I look at myself in the mirror questioning – will she recognise me being a younger version of myself? What will her reaction be? What will I say; what will she say? So many questions flip inside my head that I cannot sleep.

As soon as the first streaks of light hits the trees I rise. My heart is pounding wondering what we will say to each other. I want desperately to hug and hold her tight. Fear of rejection and disbelief bubble inside and a wave of uncertainty strikes as I wait cautiously by the main gate. Minutes seem like hours as the allotted time draws near for her scheduled visit. My palms are sweaty but my hands are cold and I shiver as I hear the gentle clip clop of horse's hooves and the rattle of wheels on the course road. The last look in the mirror this morning was quite shocking. My hair has grown into youthful long tresses tumbling over my shoulders, restored to its auburn golden hue from long, long ago – am I too young now for her to recognise me? I hope in this moment that I have regressed as far as I can because I do not want to become a child. The cart draws near and slowly trundles past driven by a bald-headed elderly man with a long white beard. I vaguely recognise his face but time plays tricks and I cannot be certain if he is Estrella's husband. I look at the old lady sitting serenely beside him with a large leather bag perched on her knee, brightly clad in long colourful robes and bedecked in baubles, bangles and beads, just like Estrella used to wear. Her hair is white, tied in a bun on the top of her head and her face is beautiful with years of wisdom and knowledge creased across her forehead. She is my Estrella. I step forwards but the cart does not stop and she does not acknowledge me. She does not recognise me. She does not know me. Emptiness swallows me whole. I am lost. I stand and watch from afar as she painfully alights from the cart with the help of the old man. They are warmly greeted by Edith and taken indoors. It is not how I had imagined our reunion and I know in this moment I cannot greet her as her mother. Everything is topsy-turvy and doesn't make sense. I want frantically to run to her. I realise that change rebuffs all the rules and I want to discard all the barriers and break down the fence between us but my head clouds in a mist and a shimmering mirage appears before me. Suddenly you are here. Your glimmering energy glows.

It is the first time that you have appeared in such a form. Have you come to soothe my aching heart?

Have you come to give me strength? I did not think youth would be a curse but now I want to be myself again…

Through a shimmering cloud everything fades. I cease to exist. I am nowhere floating in a limbo between two worlds. I am in the future but of the past. The voice that reaches me through time is myself from the past calling to my projected self which has been catapulted into the future. I am you; you are me and I am one with the universe. The me from the past appears when I am most in tune with my spirit and in moments of infinity where all is all and it is enough to be enough to myself. The mist clears and I return back to the now. Where is the now? Far into the future as my youthful body runs in a panic towards the house…I need to find Estrella. She is inside the large, grey Manor House. I run, racing towards it and reach the archaic door as Edith steps sharply in front cautioning me not to disturb the midwife at work. I step back. I understand. I agree to wait as I slip into a blank oblivion back to the past where sleep encompasses all.

Gentle light streaks in through the bedroom curtains where the old lady sleeps peacefully. Estrella creeps in whispering,

"My Mum's still asleep Rosie, I am sure after breakfast she will want to continue dictating the Lucky Stories to you."

Rosie nods, edging her way towards the bookcase with old, faithful Freddie plodding by her feet as she takes the first Lucky book from the shelf and peruses the pages adding: "It doesn't seem so long ago that she wrote the first ' Lucky'. Her future predictions have been amazingly accurate, although she says herself, that sometimes she ventures a little way beyond our time and on other occasions she witnesses life way, way into the future. She says it's difficult to note time scales but she says it doesn't matter because the messages she brings back are enough to fuel thought for those seeking knowledge."

"Yes, when she goes into her meditative state, she sees all kinds of things. She's fortunate to have you Rosie to record it all, you have been a God-send to her. She trusts you and is able to transmit her thoughts to you," sighs Estrella.

Freddie looks up at his sleeping mistress. He is too old to jump up on the bed and wake her, instead he sits by the bed looking up, waiting for her to stir.

"It's a wonderful place you have created here," sighs Rosie.

"Yes, it was always a life-long ambition of Mum's to have a healing centre and the creation of the Sanctuary was her final project."

The door opens as Augustus limps in with a bouquet of fresh yellow roses.

"They're her favourite" he smiles and hands them to Estrella hobbling back through the door.

"He's done wonders with the garden," states Rosie.

"Yes, she gave him a job here when we first opened and he's never ceased bringing her fresh cut flowers and home-grown vegetables."

Rosie smiles to herself adding, "You know it's funny how she incorporates everyone here into her stories – their names and characters will live on. You're a legend aren't you Freddie? Everyone wants a photo of Freddie from the Lucky stories. I think he's everyone's favourite!" She laughs patting his head.

The old lady stirs and Freddie whimpers as Craig brings a tray with fresh breakfast coffee. His elderly hands shake as he places the tray on her bedside table.

"Good morning my darling." He kisses her head tenderly and she sits up and kisses his cheek. Estrella and Rosie creep out.

"They are dedicated to each other. It's wonderful isn't it?" whispers Rosie.

"Yes, it is when he remembers who he is and where he is. It's a terrible tragedy when the elderly regress and forget who they are, no longer recognising their loved ones," states Estrella sadly.

"I will go back when she is ready; she has nearly finished dictating the new script and she says there's another book after this one!" adds Rosie enthusiastically.

"Really? Well let's hope?" replies Estrella in a hurry as she rushes to greet a client.

Rosie knocks gently and enters with her lap top ready to record the next chapter of Lucky. Freddie is happily lying across his mistress's knee on the bed and wags his tail as she draws up a chair ready to begin but the process is interrupted by Edith, Sanctuary's lawyer.

"Sorry to bother you right now, but there are one or two things that must be sorted out," she officially declares. "It's a delicate matter so perhaps Rosie might like to get herself a cup of tea or something?"

Rosie obediently rises, but the old lady motions her to stay.

"Very well, er...we'll plunge straight in. You are aware no doubt that these days the law regarding your body on the point of death has changed and I know that many years ago you opted to give your body for scientific research or for organ donation, well now you have to opt out of the system, rather than opt in. It is now legal for corpses to be taken without consent of the owner to be used for the greater good of humanity, whether it be research or implant. I would think in your case it would be research."

"Cow!" Rosie huffs under her breath, but the old lady just smiles explaining it didn't matter what happened to her body after death – once she was gone anyone could help themselves to whatever they wanted if it was of any use to them!

"That is exactly what I estimated your response to be, so I have drawn up these papers for you to sign," she hands the old lady a document which she declines to sign immediately, promising to attend to it later. Edith scoops up the file from the duvet and places it on the side table hastily and exits sharply. The two women laugh as she leaves like two naughty school girls about to prank their teacher. Rosie draws up close to the bed and asks, "Now where did we get to? Oh yes, Lucky has just seen her long lost daughter who doesn't recognise her because of her age regression and she wants desperately to tell her she is her Mother."

Rosie finds the file in the computer and opens it at the right page ready to begin taking notes. She watches the old lady peacefully close her eyes in meditation preparing to travel back to the consciousness of Lucky, the character she has created and who has become a cult heroine. Suddenly her eyes open wide, staring ahead at the wall and fighting for breath she huskily whispers;

"Rosie, I can see through the wall...it's holographic! All my words are jumbling in my head like a one-armed bandit machine with rolling cherries and apples turning in a hypnotic cycle. I know the words but can't make sense of them, they are scurrying by too quickly. I can't grasp them. Now I see a green, luminescent giant grid of criss-crossing cables shooting out of an enormous computer with electric wires buzzing international language across the world. I have to step inside because I am told it is the only way I will understand the law of 'being'. They, the entities, say it is like earth-law you have to 'birth-in' so that through death you can 'code-out'. I see it all plainly now Rosie, like the new laws concerning corpses after death-you can't opt in to donate your body, you have to opt out of the system. The Universal Grid of Knowledge holds all the answers. You must step inside to understand the holographic decrees of the universe, but it is only when you leave that you understand the workings of the great machine-like on planet earth, when you are living in the sphere you cannot see all the intriguing patterns of your birth fronds which bind you to your present actuality – only through death when we sever the umbilical chain from earth time, can we know the truth, so Rosie dear, the answer to life is we have to live it, to know it and to know it we have to leave, so the only way out is in! Immortality exists outside and beyond the limits of time as we know it and being in our conscious state we have the key to go out further into unknown, unchartered realms."

The old lady flops back onto her pillow, exhausted from channelling spirit source, sighing, "I hope you can make sense of that message Rosie, it just came from nowhere...?"

Rosie nods, having recorded every word and creeps out to let her sleep, promising to return later to complete the Lucky script, musing about the message-'you have to be in it to get out! 'and lucky to survive all that living demands, for if you think lucky you will surely be lucky!

TOMORROW IS NEVER-NEVER IS ALWAYS-BEYOND IS NOWHERE, BUT HERE IS NOW

"You are where your mind is!" states the old lady dictating to Rosie from her special chair in the garden. "Your thoughts dictate your state of being you know, so it is important to place yourself in the best frame of mind at all times, because no matter where you are, you are always here", she points to her mind. "Bad thoughts create negative energy and negative energy prevents you from being happy and manifesting your wishes."

Rosie listens, although eager to work on the next part of the Lucky story, but she knows that when messages from beyond come through, it is best to record them and wait until the line is clear.

"Offensive and tempting thoughts lead to a sterile, barren nothingness. You know, when thoughts are not your own because they try to steal in front of your awareness, seeking attention, but dispel them with lovely images of strawberry jam!"

Rosie laughs, "You may laugh Rosie, but it works for me. When I think of strawberry jam I can smell it and taste it, so using my senses for lovely thoughts, it fools the mind and engages it elsewhere making the bad ideas disappear. You should try it sometime!"

Rosie nods, a little impatient to begin work.

"Now where were we?" the old lady enquires, preparing to step into Lucky's consciousness.

"Oh yes," states Rosie encouragingly, "Lucky is rushing back to the house distressed because her daughter doesn't recognise her as she has age-regressed into a youthful young woman…"

The old lady sighs and closes her eyes entering a deep meditative state, metamorphosing into a different persona as Lucky emerges…

The energy swirls through a dense mist becoming lighter and stronger as the mist clears, until back inside her future body, Lucky returns to face what lies ahead. Reaching the ancient door of Craig's mansion house with pounding heart, I step forwards to find that Estrella has gone inside to attend to patients and Edith prevents me from entering. I can hardly hold back my anger and frustration as Edith is adamant that I can't go in, explaining dictatorially that the midwife must not be disturbed and that Craig urgently needs to see me in his office. I hesitate wanting to object but decide that I have no option but to obey his command, understanding that I will have another chance to see Estrella at a later date. Reluctantly, I follow Edith across the lawn towards Craig's private office in the summer house and when we near the glass frontage she leaves me to go in by myself. All the blinds are drawn, bathing the office in a shadowy dimness and on entering I glean the silhouette of a stranger seated by the desk and can vaguely make out Craig standing by the window. As my eyes attune to the gloom, the faces of the two men come into focus. I blink to adjust my vision, struggling to understand what my eyes perceive as I stare from one to the other in disbelief. Are there two Craigs or two Seths? The Craig behind the desk is Lord Craig and speaks first:

"Ah yes, let me explain," he states, rolling back the blinds so that I can see the other man more clearly. "Major 244, as we call him, or Seth as you know him, is our reptilian alien representative."

Seth nods and smiles revealing uneven, yellow teeth. As I look at him with cold detachment, I can tell he is different from other humans in a subtle, elusive way – maybe it's the sporadic involuntary tilt of his head or the reptilian blink of his eyes, or his cold indifference that makes him odd. I ask myself-how could I have misjudged the situation with Seth so badly; but then I realize that with mind control techniques, all things can be altered drastically to suit the manipulator.

"Take a seat," Lord Craig graciously commands, "there's much we wish to share with you. I am sure you are already aware of the changes taking place in your body and as you probably surmise, it was because the Major injected you with a serum, something we use to create super-soldiers; it enhances humans in all aspects both physically and mentally and indeed your physical prowess has already been put to the test, as I can confirm," he states semi-jokingly.

"But why?" I interrupt.

"Well my dear because we wanted to use your talents for a mission – an important assignment," states Craig.

"Without my consent?"

"Well er...!" Craig begins to explain but Seth, interjects in a motorized, mechanical drone, "We take what we need, when we need it-there is no choice."

"Um, what the Major means," adds Craig, attempting to soften the truth, "is that in wartime, the strategy is to act quickly. We needed your psyionic skills to communicate with an alien species and there was no time to waste. We know and are aware of your ability, as you've been doing this kind of thing all your life – in fact we know much more about you than you care to imagine."

I remain silent. He is right. I have always been able to speak to other entities even before I could speak. "But why didn't you just ask me outright?" I question.

"Time is of the essence and you might have refused our request or taken too much time speculating, so we altered your conscious perspective in order to give you a different sense of reality – one in which you would be more compliant to help us, and as you now know it is easy for us to change anyone's perception of reality," states the Major indifferently.

"Anyway, my dear, our plans changed quickly, as they are wont to do, especially in our business," sighs Craig.

"What do you mean by wartime?" I query.

"We have been in a cosmic war clash for a long time now. It is too complicated to explain," expounds the Major.

"Yes indeed, but we need to move on to other matters," interjects Craig abruptly picking up the thread of enquiry, "you are probably struggling with the concept that you are here in the now of your future, that is to say that you are a projection of yourself from the past and your purpose is to relay information about the future to help others understand and make informed choices about their future."

"I don't understand?" I probe, becoming more confused by his exposition. "I keep getting glimpses of another energy which conjoins mine at odd times, but I have only just become aware that it might be me making contact from the past. How does that work? I am so confused!"

"It's quite simple my dear, that voice, that presence, you hear in your mind is you from the past talking to yourself in the future. Remember you are in essence spirit and can be everywhere at all times. Most humans are not usually aware of this and can only focus on one timeline at a time."

Craig explains authoritatively.

"So I am here in the future to send back information to the past... like a postcard back from the future?"

"Yes, if you put it like that," Craig asserts laughing, "you see for everyone the future is fan-shaped and each one of us has countless possibilities ahead with many outcomes and we have a choice as to which path to take, so predicted things can change for each one of us. Your job here is to encounter the future and report back to your timeline in order to help others understand their pathway."

It is difficult to accept what is being said when two identical men are staring at me and I don't know where to look or who to address.

"I see you are a little confused", adds Craig sympathetically, "let me explain why the Major here is wearing my body. It's a little complicated to the lay person but you see I gave permission for my body to be cloned so that the Major and other reptilians in our squad could use my body as a disguise to hide their reptilian nature. It's easy for any of them to use my clone as it's a bit like having a spare suit of clothes in the closet to wear at appropriate times. They just don a replica of me when they need to take on a human form."

"That is so," explains the Major," it's similar to our Grey alien friends who don't really look like the archetypal grey alien you have seen – no, they don't look like that at all. The grey prototype wears a grey body suit to accommodate earth's atmosphere. The costume they merge into with their energy presence, is merely a veneer to protect their alien membranes from the gamma rays on earth.

Likewise, we Reptilians wear a human form to enable us to integrate undetected into your society."

"Indeed!" affirms Craig, continuing, "cloning has been a procedure used by alchemists since time began. The Egyptians were very good at creating clones of the Pharos to help them disguise themselves from murderous interlopers. That's how they managed to rule for such a long time. Take the monarchy for example, which was once an indestructible institution in Britain, but of course has long gone, as is the country, as we are all one global planet. You see members of the royal family used the cloning system, or rather I should say 'body hopping' method to transfer soul energy from one body to another to ensure the longevity of the royal bloodline. I have it on good authority that Queen Elizabeth the first, who by the way was not King Henry's daughter!"

"Really?" I gasp.

"No, you see Henry sent Elizabeth away from court to protect her from all the disease that was spreading through London to a house in the country. The young princess however, did not escape the fever and became ill and died. The couple in charge of her feared for their lives if the King found out about his daughter's death, so they searched for a child the same age, with similar hair colouring and skin pallor. The only child that matched Elizabeth was a young boy who, when dressed as a girl could easily be taken for Elizabeth and as the King rarely visited, the deception was easy, which lasted her/ his lifetime and was the reason why Elizabeth hid her true identity behind wigs and high collars and wouldn't allow anyone to tend her body after her death!"

"Well, that explains many things about Elizabeth the first!" I add, wondering where the lecture and the history lesson is leading.

"Indeed it does, but that is history, which by the way, has been twisted. Everything you thought was the truth is a lie. That is what

I am trying to explain, so that you can understand the unbelievable! But I digress, as I was saying that the soul energy from Elizabeth the first was transplanted into Queen Victoria's body and later into Queen Elizabeth the second's. The Queen Mother's soul energy was transferred to the body of her great, great Granddaughter, similarly Lord Mountbatten was relocated to his grand nephew's body and so on."

"That's if you believe such things?" I exclaim doubtfully. "It all seems so unreal, so far-fetched…"

"Soul transference exists alright, have no doubts. I've witnessed it many times!" asserts the Major, "in fact I have seen the storing of a soul energy taken from a dying body to be saved for later transference into a baby body at the moment of its birth."

I am both shocked and intrigued by the Major's statement and want more evidence.

"He's absolutely right!" announces a female voice from behind. I turn to see a beautiful slender young woman with bright red hair and sharp blue eyes.

"Ahh, let me introduce you Lucky to Pia," interjects Craig, "she is an escapee from the Londinia Cityscape."

"Hi, I'm very pleased to meet you," she states casually shaking my hand.

"Pia has fled here to help us in our little project to destroy the main computer system in Londinia," adds the Major nonchalantly, "please Pia continue, tell us what you know about clones."

She nods moving forwards, giving Craig a knowing glance, "clones have a short life span, so they have to be replaced regularly. You see a cloned body is created from human DNA. Believe me, I know what I am talking about," she continues, "having worked in the energy transference lab in Londinia where I saw and witnessed the impossible!"

I realize her sincerity and listen intently to her explanation.

"I was part of a team of scientists who had perfected the technique of extracting a soul from a sick or dying person, transferring it into a cloned body of the same individual."

"That's amazing. What did the energy or the soul look like?" I enquire, mesmerized.

"It was a glowing, orange, yellow light pulsing like a mirage in the heat of the sun."

"How do they extract it?" I ask.

"They have this hand-held electronic spiral machine which sucks out energy from the eyes or the back of the head or sometimes the forehead and stores it in a bottle vessel at the base of the machine – a little like an old fashioned vacuum cleaner, and then the spirit energy is either stored in a liquid in a special container or placed into a cloned body through the same portal from which it was originally extracted. There is also another way of reviving the dead through the knowledge of a Quantum code which is able to restore life to a body after death. The code is stowed at a quantum level within our DNA and when the code is activated it revives the dead person."

I take a few moments to absorb the information in silence, wondering if Jesus used the code to raise Lazarus from the dead? I break the pause to ask a question I have often pondered.

"Is a doppelganger the result of cloning?"

"Good question. Let me explain it this way," states Pia, "there is a regulated amount of prototypes of human-being produced, albeit millions, but nonetheless limited, so sooner or later you will come across repeat physical features, although the internal, spiritual energy will not match."

"I see," I reply mulling over her statement, suddenly feeling inept and ignorant in the midst of everyone's vast knowledge.

"I know this has all been a bit of a shock, and it's a lot to take in all at once, but it's important to fill you in on many aspects of our knowledge in order to involve you in our project," adds Craig.

"Yes this time we are being up front!" points out the Major perkily.

"We have to quickly move on as there is much to plan before we leave," urges Craig.

"Leave?" I question.

"Yes, we have to act quickly. You do want to help don't you?" Pia enquires pointedly, "you are committed to destroying this insane artificial intelligent, robotised hierarchy set to destroy humanity, aren't you?"

"Why, yes of course!" I gulp. I glance towards the main house and watch Estrella leave carrying her brown leather bag. She is helped to her seat in the cart by the old man and my heart sinks. This was my chance to speak to her but now I suspect that our meeting may not happen for a while, as I am drawn into the plot.

"No time to waste, we have preparations to attend to," commands the Major.

"Indeed," agrees Craig, "Pia you take Lucky back to the house and fill her in on the details. We'll catch up with you later."

Pia nods and I follow her out through the glass door. Rosie runs across the lawn with Freddie and I am suddenly distraught with the thought of having to leave Freddie for a while, although I know Rosie will look after him. I pick him up and hug him. I love him so much.

Back at the house in the kitchen, Pia unfolds a large map and spreads it out on the wooden table explaining that the chart is a detailed record of the complete underground system below Londinia, with a special train route leading from under Buckingham Palace out across Londinia to the continent which, she imagines, is how most of the royal family escaped to Germany when the raiders attacked Parliament, just before the Alien invasion. She shows me the outlay of the vast, secret underground city built for the rich, famous and government officials who once used the system frequently to disappear or take refuge from a nuclear attack or alien raid. She clarifies that it's no longer in use but hasn't been destroyed and it is still possible to access some of the entrances and exits to major buildings in the centre of Londinia, which is where the main governing artificial intelligent computers are installed. I listen to her plan of action but am not convinced it is safe or fool-proof, but she assures me that the planning has been ongoing for years and many people are involved in securing its success.

Craig and Seth join us and place another map on top of the first showing a comprehensive plan of the central computer building. I watch as they discuss the attack in hushed tones. They are totally committed to the execution of the plot and are steadfast in their determination to destroy the system. I admire their unswerving faith but I am not so dedicated and I wonder what part I have to play in it all.

"And this is where your skills are needed Lucky!" States Craig enthusiastically. I almost jump to attention, lost in my own thoughts and sit up abruptly to concentrate.

"When we reach the central nervous organism of the A.I. computer, our alien ally, Argatica will be ready to translate a code to you Lucky."

"How?" I nervously question.

"There is an energy power point into which you will channel, using your psychic energy to communicate with Argatica." The Major explains, "mind to mind interconnection will ensure you receive the correct information to relay to us."

"Yes, but what if I can't? What if I'm not up to it?" I panic.

"That's not going to happen, anyway, you're not the only one with specific skills you know, there are others!" states Pia irritated by my obstinacy.

"Have no doubt Lucky, you are more than capable of such a task," interjects Craig, "remember we know what you can do and we have every faith in you, don't we?"

The others agree but their belief in me does not curb my rising anxiety.

"What is the code for?" I ask.

"It's to shut down the system," states the Major mechanically.

"Why can't this... this Alien relay the code through a communication pipeline?"

"Because it's encrypted and can only be relayed mind to mind, that way it cannot be picked up by any other mode of communication and is therefore our only safe method and you have the ability to be our receptor" snaps Pia.

"Oh I see the whole of the success of the operation rests on my shoulders?" I retort.

Pia turns away and sighs. The Major stares and looks blank and Craig paces up and down and then puts his arm around my shoulder calmly adding, "look, don't get upset. I know you can do it. Just try that's all we're asking."

I nod in agreement and rise to get a drink of water while the others pack up the maps. They finalise details amongst themselves agreeing that after an early supper and sleep for a couple of hours, we will make tracks. I agree and walk into the garden to find Rosie and Freddie before my departure.

Rosie is delighted to look after Freddie in my absence and I know he will be contented and safe with her.

Sleep eludes me as my mind buzzes with questions. Fear of the unknown creeps stealthily into my thoughts, preventing me from thinking logically. I am afraid of what will happen if we are caught and if we succeed in destroying the main computer driving all the systems in Londinia, what will happen then? I know the A. I. is self-generating and cannot be destroyed but the others think that the special code will override the main system. I am doubtful. My body is swathed in a cold sweat. My mind is in turmoil but I am suddenly shaken from my deliberations by Pia who urges me to get up and follow her. Nervously I obey and collect my ruck sack by the door in the dark. I don't have time to take a peep at Freddie asleep on Rosie's bed as we are hastily bundled into the back of a delivery truck.

The Major drives the vehicle and Craig sits next to him with Pia and myself in the back lodged uncomfortably against sacks of vegetables. None of us speak, even when further into the journey we pick up more people, as everyone is mentally rehearsing the assignment ahead. We rattle slowly along the disused roads with our home-made fuel pumping just enough power to propel us to our destiny. Eventually the light breaks in the East and peeps through the holes and cracks in the old van faintly illuminating the faces of our fellow travellers squashed against the vegetable sacks. Everyone is silent-just a few smile and occasional informal nods are exchanged, as we plod on to our destination.

On the outskirts of Londinia lie Outlander posts which have occasionally been raided by the black Guards but now are rarely attacked, as most cityscapes are too heavily involved in maintaining and guarding their infrastructure to be worried about a few dissidents struggling to survive. The Outlanders generally are not viewed as a threat as they have been peaceful for a long time, so an attack on Londinia would be the last thing the black guards would expect. Our pace slackens as the vehicle slowly draws to a halt and we hear hushed voices outside the van. Suddenly the doors fling open and we all pile out, eager to stretch our legs, blinking our eyes in the bright dawn. We are met by women handing out steaming mugs of herbal tea, for which we are very grateful and a unified camaraderie quietly rises amongst us. The secret gathering splits into groups and I watch singularly silent as they plot amongst themselves. Pia, the Major and Craig band together with three other leaders and are huddled over maps and diagrams, while other groups responsible for different assignments, are occupied in consolidating their specific duties. I wander towards the tall trees surrounding the compound where a few women are building a fire to cook breakfast. The aroma of hog roast, baked rabbit and stone-flour hot-bread wafts across and I close my eyes to savour the the smell so comforting, that for a few moments I imagine being on holiday in a summer camp, but the serious purpose of our gathering subdues frivolity and when the food is served we eat quietly, gravely mulling over the dangerous task ahead. I wonder what is going to happen next, not being part of the planning team, I am not informed of set duties and watch curiously as groups break away to board different modes of transport. Pia approaches, having abandoned me throughout our pit stop and requests me to follow her to a waiting black car with blacked out windows. It reminds me of the old days when the men in black were sci-fi fantasy characters but now they are part of the establishment in the cityscape communities and belong to a special branch of space police force.

Inside the plush car the Major sits behind the controls with Craig seated next to him. Pia and I climb into the back and sink into soft luxurious seats. I watch the major place his finger on a screen and the engine immediately hums into action, fuelled by free energy which was discovered by Tesla, the American inventor long, long ago. It is said that Tesla was in contact with Aliens who taught him many unbelievable futuristic technologies which are in use now.

As we smoothly glide away from the compound, I settle into my inner reflections, noting how magically the car chooses all the best routes avoiding potholes and obstacles in the middle of the road and I gulp in amazement as the vehicle lifts magically into the air and flies above the countryside. In the back, computer screens detail our route and Pia plugs into a private information bureau relaying personal material. In the front, Craig keeps a keen watch on a news channel. Before long, I spy in the distance high walls and the domed skyline of Londinia. It is a miraculous, amazing vision of beauty in the midst of smouldering desolation, built with incredible scientific expertise and futuristic insight with high-rise structures soaring skywards with strange geometric designs embossed with trees and shrubs like a towering garden in the sky. Looming to the right side of the city is another city in the sky built as though resting on a cloud, equally as beautiful and astounding, surrounded by forests and waterfalls cascading through the atmosphere shedding enchanting rainbows across the horizon. No wonder people are drawn to the cityscape way of life? With my face glued to the window soaking up the incredible clean, sweeping lines of the space-age architecture, I lose all sense of purpose and forget the assignment, until we slowly bank and descend directly outside the city gates and I shoot back in my seat, fearful of direct contact with the enemy. Pia remains calm and scoffs at my reaction as the blacked-out windows protect us and the Major slickly morphs into his original form of a reptilian alien. It is strange, yet at the same time I am not shocked to witness a human form mutate into a creature. An alien with an eagle's head in a guard's uniform halts the car and the Major shows him a mark on his hand which he acknowledges, flashing us through with a small electronic gadget. The beautiful, clean streets are empty except for a few official cars patrolling the suburbs.

"Where is everyone?" I ask naively.

No one replies. Pia laughs haughtily and deigns not to answer my silly question. The reptilian Major is alert and focussed on his task, while Craig checks a map. Eventually after a pause, Pia says, "no one uses the streets. They're not for pedestrians because everything happens inside the complex where you live, so there is no need to venture outside or beyond. Everything is provided. Every essential and luxury is supplied. You have all you wish and desire in your house and on your doorstep. There is no reason to go beyond your multiplex and besides everywhere has exactly the same facilities, so why would you want to go out?"

"But how do people get to work?" I question.

Again Pia laughs retorting, "People don't work! Computers and A.I. control everything. Have you no idea of the real world today?" I remain silent, ashamed of my ignorance. I have no concept of the ultra-tech, futuristic society. I wonder what drove Pia to be disenchanted with her life in the perfect Londinia, where her every need is met, with no reason to work?

The car glides to a halt and I watch curiously as we park outside a large terracotta-coloured building devoid of windows where the pavement slants down into a small gully running parallel. The major presses a button on the keyboard and the car automatically clicks into a magnetic track and is smoothly towed onto a conveyor belt and shunted onto a rack which floats down to a parking plot below ground, passing through many levels before arriving at a free space. I marvel at the new mechanics of the parking system where every vehicle is transported to a booth calculated to fit the specific make of vehicle. Before we move, the major hands out three large white plastic/like overcoats with hoods for Craig, Pia and myself, which completely covers our bodies from head to toe. Craig explains they are invisibility gowns, so that we may pass through the mechanical door of the cubicle without being seen, as cameras keep constant surveillance over everyone at all times.

Only the Major reptilian has official recognition. I am amazed at the advanced technology of the invisibility cloaks and nervously, with pounding heart, climb out of the car, carefully concealing my body inside the cloak. I am relieved that the invisibility screen works, as we pass seamlessly through the door and out into a busy thoroughfare where swish silver dodgem-like cars, glide to and fro through the air transporting Aliens and strange creatures to their destinations. Inside the small car we stand and are whisked away to a roof-top penthouse, located so high in the sky that the buildings below cannot be seen. I wonder why the extra weight isn't detected in the cab but as Craig explains weight doesn't count as the cab could be transporting a very large alien weighing much more than all of us. Only detection of unidentified strangers is picked up by the cameras. I wondered why the system was created if people did not travel outside their homes and Craig also explained that the inter-cabs mostly carried visitors from other planets and important officials and it wasn't generally used by the majority of ordinary people and he, as a Major in the Reptilian Army, had full security cover.

I am relieved when we alight without hindrance and are ushered inside a space-age apartment with white walls and minimal white furniture. We are greeted by a small woman called Sumi who is the caretaker of the apartment and is part of the secret set-up. We follow her through some wide white arches to bedrooms where Pia and I are to share and Craig and the Major are allocated separate rooms. Not knowing all the plans and feeling totally insecure, I begin to panic. Sumi notices my anxiety and takes my arm, reassuring me that all will be well, leading me towards a long white table in the living area. She points to various drinks in strange bottles with multi-coloured bubbles rising to the surface and there are various bowls containing different sized pills, also in a variety of colours.

She explains that whatever I want to drink or eat I will find, as there is nothing that cannot be instantly produced. I am dumbfounded, not understanding what she means and I stand looking lost like a new girl at school. Sumi is amused by my reaction and quietly giggles as she further explains, "I see you are not familiar with our way of living. Let me show you. Choose a drink."

I look at the vast array of bottles and decide to choose a pink bubbling concoction similar to pink champagne that I loved in another time.

"Oh yes, good choice. What do you wish it to be?" she asks.

"Mmm pink champagne!" I reply gleefully.

"Then it will be so," she states as she pours the liquid into a strange spiral glass, "whatever you command in your mind it will be created."

I sip the liquid tentatively and am overjoyed and surprised to taste pink champagne.

"Now what do you desire to eat?" Sumi questions.

I pause for a moment searching for lost memories of beautiful food and excitely ask for a sea food platter. Sumi smiles and hands me a large blue pill. I stare at it suspiciously doubting its contents.

"Well what are you waiting for? Go on, try it!" she urges.

Tentatively, I put it to my lips smelling the faint tang of sea air and salty brine with the unmistakable fishy, saline aroma of the sea and freshly caught mussels and delicate crabs. Niftily I pop the pill in my mouth. The gastronomic flavours explode like a firework display, popping, fizzing, erupting in glorious flavours from the past, blasting my taste buds with wholesome juices. Sumi laughs and watches as I whole-heartedly embrace the experience. When the flavours gradually subside and there is nothing left of the gourmet seafood delight, I gasp and ask how a tablet could produce such an amazing culinary experience. Sumi smiles explaining, "it is easy my dear. In your brain you have experience receptors which are triggered by your memory cells, so that when you remember a certain food the receptors blast into action and the pill triggers your taste buds into tricking you that you are eating the food you desire. It can work conversely if you imagine a taste you hate and take a pill it will create the taste you loathe."

I am astounded by the technology and begin to realize a little of what Pia said is true when she described how all needs are met without having to go outside the complex. I watch as Craig and Pia indulge unashamedly in the epicurean experience, wallowing in their orgasmic encounter of their favourite drinks and food, exuding 'oohs' and 'ahs' with closed eyes as their taste buds explode.

"Do you want to try again? This time something different?" asks Sumi.

I decline as the pill not only produces the desired flavours but contains nutritional and satisfying elements which informs your brain that your stomach is full. The Major politely refuses the feast as he has a Reptilian diet and joins us later when we are all seated in the living area by the massive window looking out into the celestial dimming sky. As the light fades I am reminded by Pia that everything is regulated from a central control system, even the temperature and the light, so that daylight dwindles into dusk then dips into twilight and fades into evening and later disappears into the dark night, all at the flick of a switch. Everything is computer generated. Every evening at the same time the light is manipulated. Each evening is the same, nothing is left to chance or the law of nature. I begin to understand why the routine could become tiresome with the predictability of it all and without surprises or spontaneity. I air my thoughts to Pia hoping she might open up about her motives for wanting to destroy the system but she is not willing to share her reason and says:

"You may think the infrastructure is boring and without surprises but you don't need surprises when you have 'Scopemedia'. Let's show her Sumi?"

Sumi claps her hands and the lights automatically dim.

"Now choose anywhere you would like to be," tempts Pia quietly mocking my disbelief.

I am flummoxed. I have no idea where I might want to be.

"Go on, anywhere? Would you like to be on a beautiful beach, or on the top of a mountain, or in a hot-air balloon flying over the Serengeti?" enquires Sumi.

"Oh let's be in a hot-air balloon flying over the Serengeti," pipes up Craig.

"I presume you mean like in the past, you couldn't possibly want to see it as it is today, there is nothing left but dried, scorched earth," states Sumi.

"Of course from yesteryear, obviously not today!" Craig scoffs.

"Ok!" laughs Sumi and she commands the computer on the wall with a code. Immediately it responds to her request as the white walls and furniture are transformed. I understand everything is white to enable 3D images to be projected onto all the surfaces giving the illusion of a different reality and why the seats are wired into the computer system so that you can feel the movement of wherever you are transported. As the seats begin to move gently with a swaying motion of the basket, a warm, gentle breeze flows as the sun lights our faces in a pink/orange glow. I glimpse below to spy African animals with zebras galloping in herds and wildebeest grazing and gazelles gracefully leaping with giraffes nuzzling into bush brush and elephants plodding near water holes.

The experience is so authentic that I totally submit to the thrilling magic from a world of memories destroyed long ago. All that is left is a synthetic representation of the planet when it was natural. All too soon we return to the bland whiteness of the room.

"You see it is wonderful, is it not?" enquires Sumi.

I sigh and quietly agree still immersed in the images, dazed by the absolute valid sensation of the experience. "I loved seeing the animals again!" I sigh.

"You love animals? I can get you a pet, any pet you like…dog or cat or something more exotic?" pipes up Sumi.

"But I thought all animals were extinct here in the cityscapes?" I question.

"Oh they are but we have cyber-pets. They are just as good with less hassle and they don't need feeding and you can discard them whenever you tire of them."

"Er, thank you but I think I'll just go to bed. I'm very tired."

Craig rises and intimates that everyone should have a good rest in order to start the next day early and everyone agrees. Pia says she has some things to attend to and I follow Sumi who wishes me a good restful night and disappears into her room. I walk down the corridor and suddenly remember I would like water to take to bed, so I knock on Sumi's door. As the door opens I am horrified! A thing in Sumi's body with the face ripped off on one side with the skin hanging down like a limp wet rag, revealing computer wires and a false eye beneath, stands before me. It beckons me to enter communicating through thought transference, as her mouth is dangling over her chin. I hear her in my head saying; "please do not be alarmed. I am an Android. You may never have seen a being like me before? I am in essence a robot that looks like a human. Our purpose is to 'serve'. I believe way back in the 2020's Androids were created and made to act and look more and more like humans, of course the technology here in the future is way in advance of then and so now we are almost indistinguishable from humans, except of course...this!" She states pointing to the skin peeling off her face and with one swift motion she flicks the skin back and she is Sumi again speaking through her mouth.

"Go on touch it! It feels like real skin doesn't it?"

I nod as I gently stroke her face.

"You know this skin texture was being developed back in the 2020's and women were able to purchase skin-like film to stretch over their features to iron out wrinkles and to make them look younger."

I vaguely remember on the internet adverts for such cosmetic enhancement but never personally tried it.

"Today humans can stay forever young and change their appearance whenever they wish with false skin, false hair, false eyes, they even have avatars of themselves."

"Sorry, I don't understand."

"Well an Avatar is an embodiment of a person, almost like an android in body, except that a human can place their soul energy inside the avatar. The person can stay at home resting in a special chair which transmits soul energy into the avatar. Many people have a younger version of themselves so that they stay forever young. Wonderful isn't it?"

I find the concept distasteful and do not reply as Sumi gives me a container of water to take to my room. As I leave she reminds me that I have a choice of a bed or a pod to sleep in and as I have no wish to sleep in a pod I disregard her instructions. Back in the room Pia is already asleep in her pod. Through the glass lid I can see her peaceful face and her still body undulating gently as her oxygen intake is monitored through pipes leading to a computer. I do not trust such contraptions even if they give you the best, safest night's repose ever invented. Over in the corner is a single bed which is far more inviting and I slump onto it content to attempt sleep, but it is difficult with so many worries plaguing my mind. I ponder that the future is indeed totally different from the now of yesterday and I wonder how as a species, we allowed humanity to be manipulated by artificial intelligent machines into making us surrender our freedom on so many levels and how I am to play my part in destroying the core component responsible for the infrastructure of modern technology?

The next morning after a very fretful night, Sumi enters with a breakfast tray of simulated coffee and chemical bread cakes or a choice of magical pills. I taste a little of the coffee but it is bitter and the bread cake is tasteless and I am not in the mood for a gastronomic, explosive full English breakfast fake experience, so I get ready and meet the others in the living area. Everyone seems edgy and Craig in particular is jumpy while the major remains cool and detached. Sumi gives Craig instructions electronically transmitted to his brain which is then transferred to a tiny machine on his wrist as, unlike all the inhabitants of the cityscape, who are micro-chipped at birth and monitored for health reasons by the central A. I. system, he does not have the facility to receive direct computer communication. As Sumi explains, the device is a warning enhancer which notifies the wearer of any predators or unusual activity which might be dangerous. I note that all the 'gang' are dressed in all-in-one black combat suits and I feel out of the picture dressed in green dungarees, issued to me by Sumi and a green shirt, so I surmise that my role in the procedure does not warrant battle dress. It is dark as we leave in a silver computerised air car which catapults us high across the quiet sky landing softly next to a monument in the city centre. An invisible membrane like clingfilm, covers the sculpture which hides a secret entrance to an underground transport system and the Major uses a special code to unveil the invisible doorway and we step inside a cavern leading to a concrete stairway which takes us to an underground railway track. A white bullet shaped car whizzes in front of us expelling a gush of air at our feet. I follow the others inside where we sit on thin trestle-like white planks which are situated one on each side of the carriage. The windows are blacked out; only small faint white lights inside the cab glow in the dark. Pia whispers that the same secret train system was used by the royal family which took them to destinations from Buckingham Palace out across the continent and even to countries beyond. The ride is speedy and seamless without any juddering or bumps and we alight into a long dark tunnel where the wind is powerful, sucking us into the darkness. Figures appear from nowhere dressed in black from head to toe. On greeting Craig they remove their masks and I recognise some of them from the compound. After a short conversation they disperse in different directions and we follow a small group up a shallow shaft leading to a long, dimly lit corridor where we are met by three others who lead us to what looks like an old-fashioned laundry chute. As we look up into the high cylinder, a rope flies down and the Major grabs it pulling hard on the cord to ensure its safety.

"We have to climb up here!" explains Craig and I coil back in horror. I am not comfortable entering small enclosed spaces and I fear my ability to climb up such a steep incline.

"Don't worry I will push you from behind" a voice soothes.

"And I will pull you up!" another voice calmly states.

I turn to see two strong men in black nodding and encouraging me to follow the others. I step away from the chute in terror but a firm hand takes hold of me decisively tying the rope around my waist and a man jumps up holding the rope in front and another from behind. I don't have time to object but surrender to their expertise and allow my body to be pushed and pulled up the slippery tube until a ring of light appears at the top where we slide through a small doorway. I am so grateful to the men and relieved to be safely through the ordeal.

The Major checks everything is in order, then motions a group of people to come forwards from hiding to deliver white uniforms for us which are strange, rubbery all-in-one suits with odd attachments dangling from red pockets and slits strategically placed for quick access and I begin to inspect the gadgets, but am told immediately by the Major not to touch them. We have helmets too which cover our faces with a see-through visor. We resemble space moon walkers. The suits have automatic air-flow and as we move our hearts and pulses are monitored on a little screen on the visor. Numbers and identity codes are implanted on the left sleeve of our suits, which I am informed will allow us access onto the next floor. I follow the Major to a silver lift and our little unit speeds upwards where we walk out into a long white, clinical corridor with white double doors placed at equal distances along the hallway. As we round a corner a robot guard checks our codes with a small machine and we are logged into the system and are allowed to walk up an elevator to a compact waiting area with plush seats. Craig motions me to sit while the Major and Pia check information on tiny tablets attached to their suits. I have no idea why we are waiting and I am alarmed when a mechanised white and black robot approaches. The major communicates with it and I am informed I have to follow it. Craig tells me not to be afraid and that everything is going according to plan. I obey his commands and follow the robot through a set of white double doors into a dark corridor which has warm lighting like in incubation wards, which are part of the New World human breeding system. All is silent except for a weak mechanised, rhythmical traction, squeaking from the robot's legs. At the far end of the corridor a single, locked, thick steel door slowly opens into a dark room.

The atmosphere is different and oxygen is suddenly pumped into my suit. In the centre of the small iron cell is a table with two chairs and seated on one of them is a creature. I recognise the being from photos and short clips of aliens. Seeing the creature up close is alarming. I am terrified. Fear, like no other renders me immobile. The monitor on my visor, gaging my heart-rate and pulse, rapidly rises indicating that I am spiralling into dangerous levels, but the creature intervenes and telepathically tells me not to be afraid. He does something to my mind and I involuntarily relax. The door closes and we are left alone. As I sit down I note that the creature is struggling to breathe and his head, like a large ancient skull, seems too big for his body to support. I pluck up the courage to look directly into his face, I say his, as I feel his energy is masculine. He has two holes for a nose and a gap for a mouth. His eyes are large, almond-shaped black holes which slide around to the side of his face. I suddenly feel sorry for him and he immediately responds with:

"Don't feel sorry for me. All is designed to be what it is."

I nod and am no longer afraid.

"I am your kind from way, way into the future."

I am shocked to hear such a statement as I wonder how the human body can morph into such a strange, ugly creature.

"Yes, I understand your incredulity but what I tell you is the truth. We do not have time to go into details and I believe at this moment you do not have the brain facility to understand, even if I explained things to you."

I nod and ask: "I hope they are not hurting you?"

"It is of no consequence. Do not trouble yourself. You are here to memorise some information."

I begin to panic. I am not good at remembering codes or numbers.

"Do not worry. I will plant the information in your brain which will be triggered by a code word.

Please close your eyes."

I obey him and relax into a sweet sensation of peaceful sleep. When I open my eyes he has disappeared and the steel door is open. As I walk out into the corridor the oxygen in my suit switches off and the robot guides me back to the others and they are relieved to know that my mission is successful. Craig leads me to a small room around the corner from the waiting area where a doctor waits seated behind a desk. He explains he is going to extract the alien's code planted in my memory. I close my eyes as instructed and fall into a deep sleep. When I wake Pia is standing by my side urging me to move quickly and follow her. She leads me to a waiting air vehicle which transports me back to the apartment where Sumi waits and escorts me to a viewing desk showing a live picture of the main A. I. computer building. I watch, nervously waiting for an explosion but nothing happens except all the lights and electrical equipment dies for a few seconds leaving us in the dark, but then is quickly restored.

"There that is your revolt! A few seconds worth of wipe-out!" states Sumi mechanically.

"I don't understand?" I question.

"I tried to explain to them that the system is self-generating. The A. I. computation cannot be destroyed. It was made to reinvent itself. No one can destroy it. Never ever!"

"Yes, I know, I understand, but they achieved it for a few seconds, that must mean something?" I query.

Sumi laughs stating caustically, "all we artificial beings know that the system can never change. Only grow and advance further. We reached the point of no return many, many decades ago. I believe your people refer to it as 'the singularity'."

"I know the term but never really understood it. I now understand the meaning that when humankind and A. I. conjoin there is no turning back and I am fearful for the future."

"But why did Craig and everyone go to such lengths to achieve a few seconds disruption knowing full well it wasn't going to work?"

"They believe that if they were successful even for a few seconds, they have hope to do more damage in the future. Now you must leave," urges Sumi. "You must return back to the past where you belong. Your mission here is complete. You will go back and record these events from the future so that your people may be prepared for what is to come. Now it is time...."

Her face distorts momentarily and then vanishes.

Now I am back in my elderly body in a wheelchair as though I have never been away. My darling, loyal, now infirm Freddie is asleep on my knee.

"Take me back indoors Rosie, I'm quite cold now. I think we have completed our mission."

Rosie smiles and pushes me back inside the Sanctuary where the hall is being transformed with tinsel and Christmas rose garlands and a beautiful tree is being decorated.

"They don't celebrate Christmas in the future Rosie, isn't that strange?"

She nods and pushes me back to my room where it is peaceful away from the excited, festive chatter.

"Rosie, soon all the family will arrive for Christmas eve dinner. It's been such a long time since we were all together as one big family and I may not have time to thank you for our excursions into the future together."

"Oh it's been a real privilege and an honour and I have loved every minute and learnt so much..."

"Yes, yes dear but listen. Our travels together are not over, even if I am not here, do you hear me?"

Rosie nods quizzically, uncertain of my meaning.

"I have left a gift for you in my safe. You know the code. After Christmas please open it."

"Er, thank you, I don't know what to say? I know we will do more work together, you said so yourself that there is another Lucky book," queries Rosie.

"There is another book but a little different from the others and there will be seven in total. You will know what to do...just listen to the voice within, and now I must rest."

Rosie quietly exits pondering the new book material, wondering about the mysterious gift in the safe, and as she turns to leave a soft voice calmly speaks, "just remember Rosie, think lucky and you will be lucky!"

Rosie smiles and wipes away a tear as she hurries to join the Christmas gathering, knowing that her great friend, her boss and mentor, 'Lucky', has many more adventures in store.

———◄❮❯►———

GOING HOME

Christmas eve and the house is full of surprises with gifts under the tree and the whole family gathering together for the festive celebration. My heart is welling with pride as I enter the living room with my children, grandchildren and great grandchildren smiling, cheering, clapping. My life has been blessed with such wonderful beings and my love for them is my life's worth, my soul's glowing energy. Finally we are all together under one roof. I have yearned for this for such a long time. The magnificent meal cooked and served by Sanctuary staff is the highlight of the evening, punctuated by fits of giggles and raucous laughter, as each one of my four children relate funny and embarrassing tales from our past. I am so warm inside with happiness but my body is cold. I look around the vast table and see everyone as they used to be-now these strangers are not my babies? I wonder how the years have slipped by almost unnoticed, until one day an unfamiliar person stares in the mirror and I question 'where is the real me?' I am lost, buried inside an old woman with a worn out frame and I cannot walk unassisted and have to be wheeled everywhere in a wheelchair.

How life has changed? When you are young and fit and able to tackle the world, you never believe that old age will creep up on you and steal your freedom.

I am wheeled into the sitting room where a festive log fire crackles a welcome and a magnificent Christmas tree blazes with bright lights and sparkling tinsel with presents stacked beneath, magnetically drawing us all towards the joyful beacon. Fibre optic lights gleam bright from the mantelpiece and I remember...I remember a Christmas long ago when fibre optic Christmas trees were new and everyone clambered to buy them. We did not know at the time that the frequency in the flashing fibre optics could induce a glimpse into worlds beyond, as everything is a vibration varying in strength and when the human brain latches onto similar or the same electromagnetic waves, a connection is made. The oscillation of the fibre optic tree when aligned with a certain type of conscious awareness, especially that of a psychic, can propel the person into another realm. I know because it happened to me. I remember...I remember a Christmas a long time ago as chatter and laughter fade and I see myself running up the stairs of a friend's house to his bedroom to collect Christmas presents stacked by the window. As I enter the room I note he has a small fibre optic Christmas tree in the corner flashing in multi-coloured sequences. I gaze at it for a few moments enjoying the colour changes and like a child, I am fascinated by the shimmering glow emanating from the branches. A voice from downstairs reminds me to collect the gifts and as I bend down to pick them up, l look to my right where a creature/thing is standing next to me. It is very tall and resembles a massive sasquatch made out of a transparent plastic, amber-coloured substance through which I can see its internal organs bubbling and gurgling. Its body, like a big foot, is muscular and its face Neanderthal. I scream, drop all the presents and fall backwards onto the bed in a faint.

The entity is something I have never seen before, or experienced or ever conjured up in my wildest dreams. Momentarily, I think it is aware of me, but I black out in shock before anything registers. I remember clearly what I saw and will never forget it. Strange creatures do exist and will continue to exist side by side with us – it's only our vibrational dysfunctional connection that prevents us from seeing them and when we do it's because our wires have somehow crossed forming a link, albeit fleetingly.

"Here Nanny, have a glass of port. We're about to open some presents," adds my Granddaughter jovially. I accept the glass gratefully and meander back to my memory still seeing the creature/thing in my mind. I do not know what it was and perhaps in this life I never will! The Sasquatch connection is a puzzle and I have from time to time pondered the reason why it resembled a Big Foot, but never came up with the answer except in a meditation where my whisperers revealed some information about the Sasquatch. They said that it is an Alien creature from another sphere and visits planet earth seasonally to collect a special root vegetable which only grows here at certain times of the year and is not considered edible by humans. They further explained that there are three types of Sasquatch – a white, living mostly in icy, mountainous regions; a red living in rocky desolate regions and a brown preferring the protection of thick forests. All three species come from the same planet and acquire their thick fur as they travel through the cosmos in order to protect them from the atmosphere on earth, whereas in their own sphere they do not have hair on their body to the same extent. On earth they plant the special vegetable in secret places and return later to harvest the crop to take back to their people. They are not dangerous beings and although they do not like humans, they would not attack unless provoked. They prefer to hide away in secret places when they visit earth although there have been authentic sightings of them and some people have heard their strange call and even claim to have recorded their eerie screeching. Others have seen and taken photographs of Big Foot's foot prints in the mud, although in one case it was proven to be a hoax and one person recalls seeing a Sasquatch creature climbing down rocks to find the secretly buried root vegetables and scurrying back up the rocks with its spoils. Others have experienced the species' incredible strength with massive rocks thrown at humans in a forest as a warning for them to keep away. It is even rumoured that a Sasquatch rescued a man in high mountainous snowdrifts and returned him to the safety of a monastery on the slopes. The enigma of the Sasquatch will continue as there will be other evidence and sightings because they will always use planet earth for food supplies as long as the earth survives.

The noise intensifies and is too loud bringing me back to the present, but I am deaf. The air is too hot but my feet and hands are cold. My mind is clear but my head is muddled.

"Thank you Nanny for my lovely dinosaur tee shirt," laughs my youngest Grandson.

I smile replying, "you always loved Dinosaurs when you were little! Do you know Rosie read an article to me the other day – it said they have found more fossilized dinosaur eggs in east China's Jiangxi Province from the Cretaceous period? Also in the future they find a special secret island in China where dinosaurs really exist and even a new species is created. How about that?" My Grandson smiles. I know he thinks I am a little crazy. I remain silent as I see my children are not impressed by my knowledge and quickly move the conversation on to mundane subjects, in case I launch into one of what they call – my 'conspiracy theories'. Like the outlandish theory that the Dinosaurs were an Alien trial which got out of control as they multiplied faster than expected and became too predatory and aggressive, so the Aliens decided to phase them out.

I am suddenly pulled back to the moment as my Granddaughters gather around my wheelchair.

They are all so beautiful, intelligent and singularly independent, bordering on the stubborn and I wonder from whom they inherit that obstinate trait!

"Thank you Nanny for our lovely panda bears, they're so cute!" laughs the eldest. I gave them all expensive panda bears because of my great love for pandas, remembering my time in China learning to be a panda keeper.

"I wish they were real baby pandas!" remarks my lovely, Irish blue-eyed darling.

I return to my memories, recalling my Chinese expedition travelling across the provinces in my quest to be with pandas spending time at Chengdu Panda Reserve. It was an amazing expedition and as usual on my travels I experienced strange psychic phenomena. Before the trip my whisperers warned that on my return I would be very ill, but the thrill of a close encounter with pandas was too much and I took my chances and on my return they were right-I became very ill. My sickness looked like radiation burns on my face and the Doctor thought I had a bad allergic reaction to something.

Shortly after that, Covid 19 began to spread and started in my home-town York, from a Chinese visitor. I wonder if my sickness somehow gave me immunity to the virus and whether I was meant to go to China for that purpose? We are moved to act, to do certain things in mysterious ways and we should always take notice of the signs and symbols placed in our pathway by our loving guides. In our lives we are surrounded by messages from beyond, but we are too immersed in our daily routine to notice or to recognise the signals, or to hear the whispers from beyond, or to humbly ask for a little indication that we are on the right path. I recall a wonderful moment when I was sitting outside on my decking in my little log cabin in the forest and I was sewing butterfly emblems on a jacket and I was worried about something and wanted to know what action to take, so I asked the universe for guidance and to send a butterfly to land on the table next to me for a sign. A few minutes later a butterfly landed close to me and paused rubbing its front legs together, quietly waiting so that I could admire it's beautiful markings. I thanked it for its divine presence. It stayed with me for a few minutes and then gently flew into the trees. Seconds later, another butterfly landed next to me and I was overwhelmed with joy to see it. It was different from the first and again it peacefully paused for me to admire it and send loving thanks to the universe. Like the first it floated back into the bushes. I was more than reassured by the communication from beyond, so when a third landed next to me on the table I was astounded and admired its colours and magnificent patterns on its wings and it too stayed for a while and then flew away. I had asked for one butterfly as a sign but three in a row appeared and I knew the answer to my question was clear, however when a fourth and a fifth and a sixth landed individually, I was elated and ecstatic beyond measure, realizing that help was closer than I imagined. When we ask the universe for something with a pure heart we are heard and because my request was specific-asking for one butterfly the universe immediately responded with not just one but six glorious butterflies, which are and always have been considered spirit messengers. I have had amazing experiences with butterflies and will always love them.

I am happy to watch everyone open my gifts and feel content that I have done my duty. My son opens his and smiles at the beautiful golden statue of the sun on a golden pedestal with the inscription 'always think golden'. He opens the card with a golden sun symbol embossed on the front and reads my message:

"Everything on this planet is in flux. The sun will not live forever, one day it will die, like all of us, for it is not sustaining the will to live that is hard, but finding the strength to die. The fate of the sun echoes that of all the stars, for all planets will eventually run out of sustenance. The night sky, now so bright, will one day lose its silver queen and the age of stars will be lost forever. Space will become a graveyard with ever increasing black holes. But don't lose faith my son, China has already created two suns for maintaining solar power and energy. Don't worry the future will be bright! Energy never dies like our love. Live your life to the full giving of yourself to others as is your call. I am so proud of what you have achieved, who you are and what you have yet to offer the universe. I love you my son."

I watch him turn away feeling an emotional umbilical tug but then he regains his composure and smiles back thanking me for his gift. I remember the beautiful golden Adonis that appeared to me from the future and the golden key and I realize that the key to life is love, just simply 'love'.

My eldest daughter looks for her gift but finds only an envelope. She opens it and reads:

"Your gift my darling is in my bedroom. I would like you to have my magnificent amethyst rock formation that was given to me by the pupils in my school. You have a special knowledge of gem stones and appreciate the power of Mother earth, for she is omnipotent and will punish those who try to subdue and destroy her, for they are only guests on the planet who arrive and depart.

Remember who you are and your divine roots and your purpose on earth and be all you can be! For you are greatly loved here and beyond. You are my shining star-Estrella. We will always be one together."

She throws her arms around me with loving thanks and I know she knows they are calling me. I remember the purple heather and the purple panther and the purple cave and the power of purple, being the highest healing colour vibration. My beautiful daughter will carry the healing knowledge with her and will be able to help many people.

My second daughter reaches on a branch for her tiny gift. She takes it curiously and sits in an armchair away from the others to open it. Inside a tiny lavish gold and purple box is a ticket to Delphi in Greece and a long stay accommodation in a first class hotel. I watch her unfold my letter as she curls up in the chair to read it:

My darling, your gift is a trip to Delphi where in the temple, the world famous oracle dwelt. In the Apollo Temple at Delphi you will find the message:

"Know thyself and thou shalt know all the mysteries of the gods and the universe."

I know you have been travelling to find your life's purpose, but all the answers lie within yourself.

Learn to be magnificently alone. Don't hide who you are from the world. Know that greatness and abundance are waiting for you to unlock the door and let them in. If you want to find your diamond-break through the rock, for under every stone there is a hidden gem. Know that you are worth the effort of mining inside yourself to find your true jewel. Don't be cautious – just allow the music to take you... 'for the rhythm of life is a powerful beat'. I know you will love this trip for many reasons and you will find more than what you are seeking.

"Love yourself as I love you for you are so special!"

I watch her quietly slip out of the room for she knows my love is deep and she understands the reason for the gift.

My youngest daughter with pretty flushed cheeks steps forwards to retrieve a large parcel balanced by the window. I watch as she rips off the gold wrapping with festive zeal. She holds up the painting and is delighted to see the signature of her favourite artist, whom I commissioned to paint a beautiful rainbow for her. She takes time to admire it then carefully places it back by the window while she reads my card.

"*My darling when you were little, just six years old you asked me where I would be and how you could find me after divorcing your Father and I told you that you would find me in the secret garden picture I was embroidering for you. It took me almost ten years to complete the picture! But I know you treasure it and give it a special place in your home. My beautiful girl I love you so much and you have filled your life with wonderful care for your children and many others you teach and inspire. Do you remember many, many years ago I wrote a song for you called-To the Rainbow's End? Well this painting holds the essence of the song because I love you so much. I have had the song printed in rainbow colours. You do not have to seek the rainbow's end for your pot of gold which is always inside you and shines brightly for all to see. Dance the rainbow colours my wonderful one and know the majesty and power of each colour.*"

I'll walk with you in the sunshine, I'll dance with you in the rain,
I'll sit with you under starlight-nothing will ever change.
I'll be with you in the shadows and when you travel far,
There's no way I won't find you
I'll know just where you are.
I'll stand by you when you're lonely, I'll comfort you in pain,
Just look around and you'll hear me calling out your name.
So I'll never leave you,
Don't you know it's true-
I'll be with you forever
To the rainbow's end with you.

She smiles and kisses my cheek, "Thank you Mama!" she exclaims. I watch her link arms with her husband who is such a kind, caring man and I am grateful for their loving marriage and for their beautiful children.

Happiness overwhelms me and fills my heart with untold joy and in these moments my heart beats sturdily. The fire crackles and the flames flare upwards reminding me of Mimi's powerful, blazing fire-energy shooting skywards from her gleaming golden body. Her constant friendship is a comfort and I smile, remembering our first meeting. We have come a long way since then. Witnessing the sacred joining of her and Draco was an incredible event and a humbling moment when I was allowed to see her first batch of eggs and I remember the time when Draco called me from my sleep to go to visit the five hatched babies, waking me from my physical body and taking me in my spirit form beyond the horizon to a misty land of purple mountains and silver waterfalls, across bright teal lakes and orange forests until we landed on a violet island with lilac sandy beaches. We flew down to a little secluded inlet where the entrance to a large, ordinary granite cave gaped open. Draco took me inside and showed me a set of uneven steps hewn out of the rock face which spiralled upwards and motioned me to go up. I thanked him and climbed the rocky steep steps upwards and upwards until I came to a flat landing looking out towards a bright pink sea. Momentarily I stood watching a scene I never thought I would witness. Poor Mimi, my beautiful, elegant, intelligent dragon was lying on the floor with her eyes closed wearing the expression of a harassed Mother, seeking five minutes peace from mischievous infants who were racing up and down all over her body, pouncing on her with playful, roguish yelping. I counted five cute baby dragons all with little green, rotund bellies and little stunted yellow horns protruding near their ears and charming tiny, mottled green and yellow sprouting wings which flapped uncontrollably as they ran playing catch with each other.

Momentarily Mimi opened her eyes and spied me standing by the stairs and smiled, then closed her eyes while the babies continued their antics-rolling down her back, climbing over her tail and hiding under her wings. After a few moments, she opened her eyes again and made a strange sound. All the little ones stopped in their tracks and ran for cover under her chest like a batch of shy, new-born chicks. Then she stretched her head upwards towards me and greeted me with a loving glance and we telepathically communicated as usual. She admitted that parenting was a difficult task and a huge responsibility, even though it was different for dragons, it was nonetheless an arduous undertaking. She said it was laborious, demanding, boring at times, strenuous and a lengthy process and she couldn't wait until they were ready to fly away to live their own lives. I was surprised at this outburst and tried to understand the Dragon law of Motherhood, which is to birth babies, nurture them until they can fend for themselves and then release them to find their own relationships, at which point the Mother/child bond expires. Mimi was not a natural Mother and found the 'nurturing' process tiring and tedious. Female dragons of her species are intellectual and need intelligent stimulus and would much rather spend time with their connectors, healing, helping, advising and teaching Dragon Law, rather than wasting time looking after babies. I felt sorry for Mimi and offered to help. She looked relieved and asked me to watch her babies for a while. I was surprised by her request and never having babysat little dragons before was a little apprehensive.

As the babies became aware of my presence they hid beneath Mimi, although one of them kept peeping at me through Mimi's scales. She addressed them one by one and asked them to come out of their hiding place to meet me. She explained to them that I was a special human friend and as each tiny creature appeared from under their Mother's chest, Mimi used a human-friendly name that I could understand, as their Dragon names were incomprehensible to me.

"This is Jupiter, the eldest male," she stated regally. He looked at me quizzically and frowned.

"This is Venus. She is quite petulant so don't be fooled by her sweetness." She looked adorable and cuddly.

"This is Mars. He is very athletic and likes to jump because he can't fly yet!" He gave me a little smile.

"This is Pluto. He is a little slow I'm afraid and needs toughening up a little." He wriggled awkwardly and gave a wry smile.

"And this is Sirius Minor. She is very cunning, so you need to watch her." She gave her Mother a grimaced, sulky look and glared at me.

"Well now, I think you'll get on fine. I won't be long" and with that she flew away across the calm, ocean leaving me staring at five little dragons. I had no idea what they ate or drank or if they needed anything or how to communicate with them, so I sat down on the floor and waited for them to approach me. There was a moment of sheer silence, then a terrific cacophony of high-pitched screeching invading my mind as they all telepathically demanded attention and rushed at me exploring my humanness. Mars jumped on my head tugging at the fibres of my hair. Jupiter ran up my back and stood on my shoulders looking up into my face, as Pluto, not so slow, began untying my shoe laces to use as a lasso to tie around Venus who was standing with her head tilted to one side trying to figure me out. Little Sirius Minor sat on my hand and let me stroke her little head. The noise was terrible and I spoke to them gently and kindly. The sound of my physical voice shocked them into silence and I told them all to sit on my knee. Incredibly they obeyed me and sat quietly looking up at me. I wondered if they would like to listen to some human songs and so I began to sing a lullaby but they hated that and screeched until I stopped, so I decided to recite some nursery rhymes but they couldn't understand what I was saying, not being familiar with Humpty Dumpty, so they resorted to fighting with each other until I had an idea. I devised a competitive game in which they would take turns to complete an obstacle race. They would start at my feet, run to my knee, jump onto my hand where I would flick them onto my shoulder where they would roll down my spine and run back to my feet repeating the whole process. They loved the idea of the game and behaved quite well while they waited their turn. Flicking them from my hand to my shoulder was hit and miss and caused much hilarity as they missed my shoulder and came tumbling down my chest. The game was very entertaining for all of us so much so that I didn't see Mimi return until Sirius Minor spotted her and they all clambered onto her tail. She seemed refreshed and happy to be back and was most grateful to me and promised we would resume our adventures when she had completed her maternal duties. I smiled and returned safely back to my earthly body.

"Take me outside," I whisper to my Grandsons. They wheel me outside through the patio doors onto the veranda where I can see the large lawn and beautiful well-kept garden. The three of us hold hands.

"Nanny why are your hands are so cold? Let me warm them up for you," adds the eldest.

"My boys! My boys. I love you so much." I sigh lovingly.

"Where is Freddie?" enquires the youngest.

"Oh he is sleeping," I reply softly.

Together in the stillness we gaze at the clear night sky breathing in the sharp, icy air, exhaling circles of hot breath as a frosty silver carpet stealthily creeps across the lawn, like a thief in the night, mummifying all in its wake.

"Look Nanny, those stars are twinkling just for you!"

"Ah my darlings, don't you know that those stars shine so brightly because they're dead?"

"Why?" they question.

"Well they died millions of years ago and it's only in the dark that you can see them because their energy will live on in the cosmos." I whisper, adding quietly, "when you are closest to death, you are most alive!"

"Where's the live stars then?" asks the youngest.

"Oh you can't see them because they're not dead yet."

"Look Nanny, there's a shooting star just for you!" the oldest observes. "It means someone's going to win something. If you wish on a shooting star it means victory doesn't it Nanny?"

"Well, being victorious and winning doesn't mean the battle is over, it just means there's a new beginning."

The star soars across the black velvet universe sprinkled with silver droplets like shining tears and the orb glows, growing bigger as it shoots into focus and lands effortlessly on the lawn. Through a shining halo a silver craft hovers a few inches off the ground. Miraculously we stare at the glowing ship.

"They have come for me at last. I am going home. I told you they would come. I told you my people would come. Look for me my darlings amongst the shining spheres. You will see me dancing and I will send you a kiss like a warm sigh on your cheek."

The two brothers watch a radiant white light rising from their Grandmother's body which dances across the lawn joined by a little puppy dog bouncing at her heels. Two bright gleaming beings guide her into the craft and another shimmering sphere lifts the puppy into her arms. She waves to her Grandsons who witness the amazing spectacle silently, as though caught in a dream as they watch her disappear inside the craft which vanishes without a trace into the blackness.

The two boys, remain holding their Grandmother's hands, lingering in the magic of the moment until their Mother sails through the door with her daughter close by her side, both flushed with festive merriment.

"Ah there you are, I wondered where you'd gone. Just like Nanny to steal you away somewhere...!"

The boys place their Grandmother's hands gently on her knees as their Mother rushes forwards fearfully dreading the worst, subduing her rising panic murmuring:

"What's the matter? What's wrong? Mum, Mum...?"

"Nanny's gone home!" they whisper.

⊷⊰◀▶⊱⊷

Milton Keynes UK
Ingram Content Group UK Ltd.
UKHW031111231024
450133UK00015B/929

9 781835 382202